LEGEND OF THE SNOW QUEEN

MANJIRI PRABHU

Readomania
An imprint of Kurious Kind Media Private Limited
readomania.com
Email: contact@readomania.com
Facebook: facebook.com/iamreadomania
Twitter: twitter.com/iamreadomania
Instagram: iamreadomania

First Published in 2022 by Readomania

© Copyright Manjiri Prabhu

Manjiri Prabhu asserts the moral right to be identified as
the author of this book.

This book is a work of fiction. Any resemblance to real
persons, living or dead, or actual events or locations, is purely
coincidental.

The views, opinions, and experiences expressed in this book are
entirely the author's own and her imagination. The publisher is
not responsible for the views expressed in the book.

All rights reserved.

No part of this publication may be reproduced, transmitted
(including but not limited to photocopying, scanning,
cyclostating) or stored (including but not limited to computers,
external memory devices, e-readers, websites etc.) in any kind
of retrieval system without the prior written permission of
the publisher.

Edited by Indrani Ganguly (Managing Editor, Readomania)

ISBN: 978-93-91800-35-2

Typeset in Palatino Linotype by Shine Graphics
Printed in Delhi

Map by Manoj Salunke

Dedicated

to

Shailaja Chaugule, my mother-in-law, for always appreciating my endeavours and for her invaluable encouragement to my writing

Map of Feldafing / Lake Starnberg

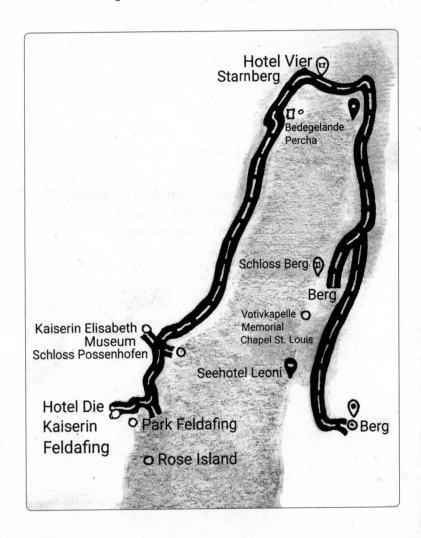

Author's Note

Legend of the Snow Queen is a contemporary destination thriller which takes place around Lake Starnberg, around 25 km from Munich, Germany. It has Re Parkar in the lead character and the plot unfolds in 2017, in modern Germany. But it borrows heavily from the history of German Europe, especially the Royalty of Austria and Germany.

Two colourful, fascinating and legendary personalities of German and Austrian history, King Ludwig II and Elisabeth the Empress of Austria, also known as Sisi, form a major part of the central backdrop of this novel.

King Ludwig II was born on August 25, 1845 and ruled as King of Bavaria from 1864, when he was an 18-year-old Duke. He was known as the 'mad king' because of his obsession for building opulent, magnificent palaces and castles like the Neuschwanstein Castle, Linderhof Castle and many more. In the process, he almost emptied the Government coffers and was declared mentally unstable and was under house arrest in Berg Castle, at Lake Starnberg. It was in this lake that he was found dead on June 13, 1886.

He was very close to his cousin Sisi, the Empress of Austria.

Born to Duke Maximilian and Duchess Ludovika, on Christmas Eve 1837, Sisi spent her summers in Possenhof Palace at Lake Starnberg, Bavaria. She loved the outdoors and was a carefree child.

When she was 15, Elisabeth's sister Helene was chosen to wed their cousin and young Emperor Franz Joseph.

But when Elisabeth accompanied her sister to Bad Ischl for the ceremony, Franz Joseph fell in love with the beautiful Elisabeth instead. Elisabeth too fell in love with the handsome Franz Joseph. Two days later they were engaged and were married on April 24, 1854. Romantic at heart, pining for love and freedom, Sisi soon realised that life as an Empress was lonely and depressing. The early years of marriage were difficult. After having three children and losing one of them at the age of 22, she began travelling extensively. She became close to her cousin King Ludwig II, and they shared a love for art and poetry and a special bond.

Sisi visited Starnberg every summer for 24 years. During this time, she would stay at the old hotel in Feldafing, later named as Kaiserin Elisabeth Hotel. Hotel Die Kaiserin is inspired by this hotel. She would visit her family home Possenhof as well as Ludwig II, who would be at Berg Castle or at Rose Island, the beautiful private island of the King in Lake Starnberg. They were such good friends, that after Ludwig II died tragically, Sisi was so shaken that she stopped visiting Starnberg.

The places and cities Sisi visited now form Sisi's route or 'Sisi weg' and is a popular tourist attraction.

Legend of the Snow Queen uses these two grand figures and their enigmatic auras, as a take-off to weave a fictitious story of thrill and conspiracy. The book and the events that take place in the hotel and in and around Lake Starnberg are purely a work of fiction for entertainment and I sincerely do not intend to hurt any sentiments or tamper with history.

Manjiri Prabhu
Pune, 2022

Prologue

"It's past seven, Vanessa. You may go home, I shall lock up and leave soon too," Dr Gordon suggested.

"Are you sure? I can stay a while longer," Vanessa remarked, eyeing the fat notebook on the table that the doctor was scribbling into.

He appeared a little tired. He shoved his glasses back in place, as they slid down his nose every few seconds and his long white beard brushed the top of the notebook he was scribbling in with marked concentration. When he was in this mood, she knew that his 'soon' implied at least an hour more. But she didn't like to leave him alone, in the clinic, after closing hours. For all his busy and long hours. Dr Gordon was long past his retirement age.

"No no, my dear. I am almost done too, it would take a mere few minutes more for me to jot down some observations on the session. You go ahead now." He brushed her away, his tone absent-minded.

She hesitated for a fraction of a second, throwing a quick look around the neat clinic. Dr Gordon was already deeply engrossed in his book, oblivious to her presence. She sighed, nodded to his bent, balding head and closed the door softly behind her, as she stepped out into the corridor.

His pen scratched on the sheet as he scrawled some notes on the latest hypnosis session. It had been riveting, to say the least. In fact, every session with his patients taught him something new. And not only because of the trust his patients showed in him. The beauty of their surrender and the way their minds opened up to him... All these sessions were mind-blowing. Eye-openers to a world beyond common human comprehension. The human mind was a hive and his research got more and more fascinating with every passing day and every unique session with his patients.

The door opened again and he glanced up absently. Then as recognition flickered on his face, he frowned.

"Oh, it is you again. What do you want now?"

"You know what I want, Doctor."

"And I have told you that I cannot reveal confidential information of my clients, to anyone."

"Can you at least tell me what is in it? I mean, is she—"

"No, afraid not. I can tell you nothing. You are just wasting your time, you know. I refuse to divulge confidential information."

"Then Dr Gordon, you leave me with no choice."

It was his tone that instantly alerted the doctor. But before he could fathom the meaning of the threat, gloved hands grasped his fragile old neck and squeezed it tight. He gasped, struggling wildly for breath, his frail hands trying to pry the deathly grip around his neck in vain, as he felt his life ebbing away from him. Within moments, it was over. Dr Gordon slumped forward, his head resting lifelessly on the desk.

One month before Christmas, Neuschwanstein Castle, Germany

The Swans... The best motif for love and peace...the opposite of blood and gore....

Leon stared at them, his heart racing. They were so perfect together, their beaks clinging to each other in the shape of a heart. Love, the all-encompassing emotion. An image of Rosy flickered into his mind. Rosy entwined in his arms, her soft breath on his cheek. The prefect love-couple. She would be there to appreciate his decision and this trip to Neuschwanstein would be so worthwhile.

The walk to the castle had been exhilarating and Leon had enjoyed every minute of it. The broad pathway, with piles of snow bordering either side, had wound uphill between snow-laden tall pine trees. The open horse-drawn carriages clip-clopped past the strolling visitors, the sturdy gleaming horses stomping their legs in the cold air as they made multiple trips ferrying the tourists to the castle.

His first sight of the spectacular palace had been the most breath-taking. Those deep blue, tall turrets rising majestically above the limestone walls of the five-storied fairy-tale castle were straight out of a magical Disney film. Perched royally on the Swan Rock, above the Alpsee Lake and near the deafening waters of the 45-metre high Pöllat Gorge. Some labelled it 'a fantasy realised in stone'. Leon preferred to regard it as the fulfilment of a gorgeous dream, like art from rock, or solidified magic dust. People of his time may have alluded to King Ludwig II as a mad king, but Leon was filled with admiration for the King's astonishing creation, for his megalomaniacal vision, his supreme love for art, his all-eclipsing obsession with beauty....

Winter touched the castle with an enchanting brush, Leon realised. Summers here were stunning of course, a competition of vibrant, contrasting colours. But the presence of this palatial beauty against the frozen backdrop, the snow a shimmering silver as far as the eye could see, was surreal.

As he had moved from room to room, he had sensed immense pride in his country. It was no wonder that millions of tourists flocked to visit this castle year after year. It was inimitable. The Throne Room, the Tower Garret, the Dining Room, the Bedroom—each an example of ostentatious marble and a gold-gilded expression of beauty. Dominating the walls and the tapestry were elaborate scenes of amazing detail from medieval German folktales, legends and scenes from Richard Wagner's stage compositions, most prominently Wagner's *Lohengrin*.

Leon had sensed awe as he climbed endless stairs and ambled from room to room, embracing the beauty and mentally making note of the architecture and the décor. But it was when he sauntered into King Ludwig's Living Room that a loud gasp escaped him. At last, he had found what he was looking for. A sense of wonder engulfed him as if he had found the lock to a long-lost key....

The world was aware of Ludwig's obsession for Lohengrin, the Swan Knight, who rescued Duchess Elsa of Brabant in a boat pulled by swans but it was never more evident than in this room. It was as if the Living Room was dedicated to the legend of the Swan Knight. 'The Miracle of the Grail' and 'The Arrival of Lohengrin in Antwerp' were proudly depicted on the murals. But what was striking was the way the motif of the swan was such an intrinsic part of the décor of the room, breathing life into the paintings on the walls, the ceilings and even on the silk upholstery and draperies. It was common fact that Ludwig was fascinated by Wagner's opera *Lohengrin*, considering it to be a 'form of enlightenment'. The King had led a lonely life and this had made him identify himself with the Swan Knight. It was said that the King had even dressed as Lohengrin from time to time.

Leon knew his history well but, standing in this room, surrounded by lush and crazy beauty, he could somehow connect to King Ludwig. His need to be alone, his need to cocoon himself with fantastical art, his need to self-obsess and play God. He understood it all.

His eyes had cruised over the chandelier with the candles, the blue and white drapes and rested on the beautiful white swan, encased in glass on a table. It was graceful in the turn of its neck and Leon's heart fluttered. Right beside the big swan were two smaller ones, facing each other, their black beaks touching and their necks arched gracefully to form a heart. They looked stunning in white and gold and Leon knew, with a rush of instinct, that his search had finally reached an end. *The Swans... The perfect motif for love and peace... the opposite of blood and gore...* And his symbolic gift to Rosy....

He would immediately make a requisition for paperwork and transfers. The Neuschwanstein Swans had to be their symbol of Love!

A month later, amidst tight security, the swans made their way to Feldafing at Lake Starnberg, near Munich.

21st December, late night, Feldafing (Lake Starnberg), Germany

The thick coat of undulating snow in thepark appeared pristine in the moonlight. The lake glinted silver in the distance, as the man cut across the snow-covered field, on the sludgy path. The night was surprisingly quiet. His shift in the bar was done and he was tired. Christmas time was always so busy.

It was at that minute that a sharp jerky movement far above in the deep grey sky caught his attention. He strained his eyes and stared at the smudgy nightscape.

Sliding across the sky, a tiny figure seemed to grow larger in size. It was elongated, floating white and seemed to have horns. The man's eyes widened in shock and his heartbeat quickened.

He gasped. *"Mein Gott... The Starnberg ET!"*

The man turned in panic and stumbled as the strange shapeless figure hovered above him, floating eerily over the low clouds.

Despite the biting cold, sweat broke out on his forehead. He broke into a desperate run, the spooky sight curdling his blood.

22nd December, Hotel Die Kaiserin, Feldafing (Lake Starnberg), Germany

Stefan glanced at the folder in his hand. *Imperial Sisi Congregation in honour of the Empress of Hearts.* The dossier contained the names and backgrounds of the five diplomats and financial tycoons of five countries—Austria, Germany, Italy, Greece, and Hungary. Maximillian Hartman, Leon Schubert, Carlo Pelle, Adria Gerodimos, and Harry Ramone. Five powerful countries with their influential representatives, already in talks for the past two days at the hotel. From morning to night, behind carefully closed and well-guarded doors. And on the 24th evening, they would together sign this historic treaty.

He stood outside, his gaze cruising the gardens of the Hotel Die Kaiserin. Shin-deep snow was layered with a fresh coat during the night and the hotel twinkled bright inside out. The usual winter bleakness was dispelled by the cheerful, soft music that emanated from the hotel. Through the large square windows, the Christmas tree beamed a cosy invitation. A merry atmosphere surrounded the old hotel and Stefan sighed, satisfied.

So far all seemed to be in order. The *Lohengrin* play and the gala costume dinner for the congregation, post the signing, would be well-attended with the administrative heads and special invitees of Lake Starnberg. The Swans were secure in the safe of the hotel, awaiting their grand display on Christmas Eve, in celebration of the Treaty. Stefan was in continuous touch with the different secretaries and police officers and everything was unfolding as per plan. He had heard that there were some disagreements and discussions between the congregation members were heated enough to melt the snow but Stefan hoped that all the heat would dissipate soon and they would come together with an ultimate consensus. He knew that almost all were in favour of the Treaty. Except perhaps Carlo of Italy. Carlo was hot-tempered and did not mince words. His unpredictable nature and quick-silver temper worried Stefan. But he couldn't think of all that now. The congregation members would no doubt handle any discrepancies, altercations and hot-headedness with the maturity of intelligent adults, he felt sure.

"Officer Stefan Weiss! Something has happened...," a high-pitched voice exclaimed.

Stefan turned towards Mrs Weber, the Chief Manager of the hotel. She was a hefty woman, with a blonde bob and black glasses. In her formal skirt and coat, she looked more like a strict school principal.

"What is it?" Stefan demanded.

"Please, could you come with me?" she requested, her tone breathless.

Stefan followed the lady to her office adjourning the restaurant hall, which was also serving as the German home team's temporary office. She pointed to the safe in the corner of the room, her face ashen.

"The swans are gone," she said, agitation in her tone. "As well as all your Treaty papers and seal."

"What!" Stefan looked stunned as he swung open the safe door. He stared at the neat pile of official books and stretched his hand deep inside the safe to double-check.

"How did this happen and when?"

"It was last night. The Junior Manager discovered it this morning. Never has so much as a pin gone missing in this hotel and in the ten years that I have been working here. We are so sorry..." She looked very troubled and her eyes were downcast.

"The Neuschwanstein Swans are priceless, historical pieces of heirloom—specially brought from the Neuschwanstein Castle. They were supposed to be the mascots of this Peace Treaty. I don't know what to say." Stefan sat down on a chair, a little shaken.

Mrs Weber appeared visibly upset, as she wrung her hands restlessly.

"How many people have the key to this safe?"

"Just me but it stays in a drawer in this office, which is supposed to be locked."

"So, someone forced open the drawer and took the key," Stefan completed.

"Like I said, our staff is trustworthy and we have never had reason to believe otherwise. Our monetary transactions almost always take place by credit cards and transfers," Mrs Weber explained.

"What's this?" Stefan extracted a piece of paper, tucked into the inside edge of the safe door.

It was a long strip of paper with a message pasted in newspaper words—a mix of caps and small alphabets. Stefan read it, a deep frown set in his face and a gnawing pit growing in his stomach. With all his years in the Police Service, he had faced several tricky situations. He was a man of action and liked to know what he was dealing with. Dark hints with unfathomable riddles made him uneasy, he confessed to himself. In that moment, Stefan knew what he had to do.

The German Police were efficient of course, but Stefan felt that he needed an insider to work with him. Someone he could trust beyond question. And he knew who could be the best person to understand the situation and solve this riddle. *Re Parkar.*

Re and Stefan had worked on cases before. The investigative journalist and detective had the brain of a scientist and the mind of a psychic and his flair for the arts blended both perfectly. Yes, he needed Re right now because Stefan sensed that something unknown to him was spiralling fast towards a cataclysmic denouement.

Paris

"Here's the perfume. Excellent choice. I am sure your mother will love it. Would you like something for your girlfriend too?" the manager enquired, eager to please.

"Ah, for my girlfriend," Re repeated, an amused smile on his face. A string of images ran in his mind's eye and he almost chuckled. "Perhaps in a couple of years?"

"I get it." The manager laughed.

Re stepped out into the shopping street which was a delightful array of twinkling lights, streamers of bulbs, a large Christmas tree that filled one half of the square, adding that touch of Christmas cheer. Strangely, the manager's casual question had sprung a leak of longing within him. Perfume for a non-existent girlfriend? He had many friends, of course, but none who would qualify as his girlfriend. Not one of the women he had met, had an energetic aura that aligned and matched his own. The fact that Re had been so busy in his cases, had not helped at all. Regardless, the manager's question had driven home the hard truth. Re felt alone.

The slushy ice melted with the rain, as Parisians and tourists alike huddled under umbrellas, thick jackets turned up till the neck and beanies comfortably on. It was a particularly nasty winter afternoon and hardly felt Christmassy to Re. No wonder he sensed a tightness around his chest, bordering on a yearning...deep and unfulfilled.

His cell phone rang and Re fumbled with his glove, as he extracted his mobile from his jacket pocket.

"Stefan! *Comment vas-tu*? Good to hear from you. Everything ok?"

"Unfortunately, everything is *not* ok, my friend."

Stefan's brief response put Re on alert at once.

"What's the matter?"

"Something very important and urgent has come up and I desperately need your help. But I can't explain over the phone."

"I get it. It can't wait until after Christmas?"

"Afraid not. The clock is ticking. It is a matter of international importance and you are the only person who can solve this."

"Right. Where are you?" Re asked.

"I am at Hotel Die Kaiserin, in Feldafing, which is at Lake Starnberg, 25 minutes from Munich."

"*Ça va*, let me check the flights."

"Grow wings if you must, but be here as soon as physically possible."

"I will," the detective promised.

He switched off his cell and tucked it into his jacket pocket again, his brow creased with lines. Stefan sounded worried. The matter had to be more serious than what the officer was letting on. Specially so if Re was being summoned all the way to South Germany on the eve of Christmas, at such short notice.

Lake Starnberg. The name stirred a flashing sense of unease. Had he been there? No immediate memory or image cropped up in his mind. And yet, the name generated something within him. A hazy emotion. Like a washed-out painting.

Disoriented, he glanced down at the bottle of perfume he held in his hand. A Christmas gift for his pretty, dainty mother. He was supposed to meet her for lunch the day after. He had been almost happy, selecting her favourite perfume and planning an evening of bonding. But now that would have to wait. He sensed an urgency, as he always did and he knew what he had to do. He had to forget all good intentions of a cosy Christmas celebration with his mother. Luckily, his *maman* was very understanding—had always been, on the numerous occasions he had cancelled their meetings. She knew that he was bound by a moral duty towards his profession. More than a moral duty, it was a personal promise. To help eradicate the poison of crime from the world. A noble promise ever since he had lost his little sister some years ago. With every case that he solved he felt an inch closer to his goal, but somehow the satisfaction eluded him. He knew he had tons to do. But every fraction was a personal marathon for him. And no matter what, he would continue to run these marathons....

He slipped the bottle of perfume into his coat and turned in the direction of his apartment. His attention was riveted by the majestic, cheerful presence of the Christmas tree. It was at that precise moment that the tingling began and coursed all over his body, like a tidal whirling wave.

The freezing water hit him and he gasped, as the ice enveloped him in a vice. He was being sucked down, deep down, the water gushing into his mouth and ears, choking and strangling him. His legs thrashed and he struggled, aware that he shouldn't but already the ice blocks were eating into his sensitivity and the pain had gripped him...

With a jerk, Re's eyes flew open. He stared confused at the shining tree and twinkling lights, even as he grappled with the pain of his frozen body. It was his *Vision* again! Strangely in the middle of the street and this time without a shade of warning.

He touched the five-metal Ganesha idol he always wore in a chain around his neck. His fingers still stung, as he felt the idol and tried to gather some emotional balance. The feeling of choking, with a tightness around his heart, was still real. His heart beat erratically in confusion. Before, his visions had always been about a place, about *a feeling*. About impending doom. He had been more an observer in his previous visions. *Never had he himself been involved in the scene.* But this time it was different. He had been a part of the vision, a participant...the drowning was real, the icy clutch all too painful. This was the first time that he sensed danger...to himself. Like a live, almost physical sensation of striking peril....

A dusting of snow was already being swept away by the rain and Re held his umbrella high over his head. With a deep breath, he slowly made his way down the illuminated shopping street.

1

23rd December, Bernried am Starnberger and Feldafing

Re felt as if he had stepped straight into an abandoned film set, as he glanced around him. He had been the sole person to alight from the Munich train and the station looked deserted at six in the morning.

Snowflakes drifted to the ground, merging with the dense white carpet on the station platform. It was freezing and Re could feel the snow slide down the neck of his coat. As the red train glided farther and farther away from the two-storeyed, quaint pink station into the grey-blue horizon, the investigative journalist zipped up his multi-pocketed black jacket securely. He pushed back his slippery silver-rimmed glasses, tucked his pony tail firmly under the black beanie, stuffed his hands into his leather gloves and clutched his small bag.

He made his way through the slimy ice sleet slope, into the street. A single light of the lamp outside Bernried am Starnberger station created a mysterious halo. A hint of peach-orange seemed to be streaking the dull sky in a faint glow. The taxi from the hotel ought to have arrived for him by now, he thought idly, to take him to Feldafing. He knew that there was a car park somewhere and a bus stop. Perhaps he should look for it and make some enquiries. Except, not a soul seemed to be visible in the rather empty station. He wished his phone had not died, he felt quite lost without it. The flight from Paris to Munich and then the train to Bernried am Starnberger had tired him. The biting wind stung his face as the snow fell softly and Re longed for a hot cup of coffee and a warm bed. He stamped his feet in impatient defiance to banish the cold.

Through the blur of snow, he caught a movement. Someone was actually on the street at this unearthly hour, he realised with a huge sigh of relief. Never had the hope of a human encounter seemed more appealing to Re as it did now. A short distance away, a figure paced slowly, illuminated by another lamp post. It was a woman and was that the bus stop? He wondered. The lady appeared to be biding her time, so perhaps it was. He dragged his small bag through the thick tracks, and plodded his way through the snow to the lamp post. Surely, she would be able to guide him to the Hotel Die Kaiserin?

With her back to him and in a white jacket, she seemed to merge with the snowy backdrop and only the trick of the light highlighting the shadows, seemed to alienate her from the surroundings. It was the manner in which she stood— the umbrella in her hand sliding gently unattended and her long dress dusting the snow—that arrested his attention. Graceful like a snow queen in her stillness, she seemed to be listening with keen intent to something, over and above the silence. Re tried to listen too. But only the eerie atmospheric hiss, broken by spurts of the wind through the snowy trees, reached his ears. Was she waiting for someone to arrive?

"*Entschuldigung…*," he began, feeling just a little guilty to intrude into her comfortable stillness.

She didn't turn around at once. Surely his luggage had created enough ruckus on the snow, to wake her from her reverie?

"Excuse me," he said again, a trifle loudly.

She turned then and her face glided into the light.

Re slapped away the snow hampering his vision and blinked. She was of medium height, with wavy brown, windblown hair. Snowflakes highlighted the attractive auburn streaks in her long hair and Re had the strangest impulse to brush them off. Blue-green eyes in a heart-shaped face studied him first with casual disregard, followed by a flashing spark of curiosity. Then, almost as if the pique of interest had been an illusion, a veil of shuttered indifference fell over her face. Suddenly aware of the softly falling snow, she hastily drew her umbrella over her head. Her white fur jacket slipped and she dragged it over a slim shoulder. Re inhaled sharply. Wild and stormy sea waves lashed in his mind and a strong, powerful energy rose to meet him.

"*Ya?*" Her voice was husky, strongly accented.

He drove his tongue over his dry lips. Something in her face struck him as odd. Perhaps it was the expression in her eyes. Unfocussed. Sad. Pensive eyes which seemed to look through him and beyond. He experienced a strange stirring of unease. Wasn't it a little odd for a lone woman to be standing by the station, at this inappropriate hour?

"Do you speak English?" he asked.

"Yes, I do." A half smile lit up her lips but it did not reach her eyes.

Before he could utter another word, the headlights of an approaching car cut through the dark.

"Ah, *c'est bien*. My cab is here." He indicated the vehicle with his hand.

She nodded.

"Would you like me to drop you some place?" he offered.

"*Nein*...it's all right, I have a car." She brushed him off.

With a strange reluctance, he tore his eyes away from her blue-green almost grey, steady gaze. Opening the cab door, he thrust his bag in and stepped into the cosy confines of the vehicle. The car moved and Re turned around for a quick last look. She was strolling towards the pink Feldafing building. Her head was lowered, as if occupied in deep thought and yet distracted.

"A double-egg omelette, toast and hot tea with milk please," Re placed his order.

The waiter retreated and the journalist relaxed against the thick cushions, realising that he was ravenous. He polished his silver-rimmed glasses and sent a tidying hand over his ponytail. He would enjoy his breakfast till Stefan turned up for his briefing. It had been a long night but a warm shower and a quick nap had proven invaluable. His room was cosy, all wood and rugs with a big bed in the centre of the room. He loved it—the contrasting cheerful atmosphere in the hotel, the well-lit carpeted passages and stairs and the presence of the Empress of Austria in the form of black and white photographs on the walls.

The corner seat was comfortable and secluded and afforded him a clear view of the hall. The warm sofas, upright cane-back chairs, laced tablecloths, stained glass partitions and wooden panelling with large windows which offered a splendid view of the frosty morning... The cheerful atmosphere in the quaint hotel in contrast to the bleak exteriors was very welcoming. Re relaxed against the red cushions, his eyes cruising over all the wall paintings. The big Christmas tree laden with lights and gifts was quite spectacular as it stood against the stained glass and snow fell softly outside in a blue sheen. The banner over the Christmas tree was particularly eye-catching. *Happy 180th Birthday, Sisi* (24 December 1837–10 September 1898).

Re knew enough German and Austrian history to know that Sisi was another name for the Empress Elisabeth of Austria. She had grown up in Possenhof and had returned to Lake Starnberg in search of the happiness of her childhood and to meet her cousin King Ludwig II. She had spent a lot of time over the years at the hotel until her beloved cousin King Ludwig II had been found dead in the lake. They had been close and she had been devastated by his death. After that, she had stopped visiting the hotel.

Re hadn't known that it was her birthday though and he liked the idea that the hotel seemed to be celebrating it in style.

Breakfast arrived and Re tucked into it heartily, intermittently glancing at his watch. It was almost nine. Stefan ought to be here any minute now, since they had agreed to meet for breakfast. Although the police officer hadn't given him any clue as to what this whole trip was about, Re was more certain than curious. Something large was at hand or Stefan wouldn't have summoned him.

When his table was cleared, he laid out a map. Outside the weather seemed to be undecided. The snowfall had ceased and a weak sun seemed to chequer across the window. Re took a sip of the hot tea and returned his attention to the map. *Starnberger See* was a large lake with towns from the south to the north tip. Feldafing was on Tutzing Road, about 5 kilometres from Bernried. He traced familiar names along the route...Possenhof, Tutzing, Berg, Rose Island Park...*Rose Island Park*. Somehow the name evoked the vision of that morning. The woman. Beautiful in white. Almost like an ethereal apparition...someone passing though this world. The elegance of a lady, but the spirit of a wild bird. He had sensed it all in that one fleeting moment... she was different...and he was surprised that he was still romanticising about her...a total stranger possibly already on some train to another part of Germany, or accompanying her kids and her husband to some ski resort on some snowy mountain, like one big happy family. The thought brought a knowing smile to his lips. Both the images were too clichéd and did not fit her aura by the longest shot.

"Here you are!" Stefan appeared and settled in the seat next to him. He was buttoned up in a thick deep-blue jacket and gloves which he removed and dropped in the chair. "So de-stressing to see you finally, Re! Coffee and some warmth, exactly what I need. Excuse me but I need to feed myself first," the officer mumbled.

Re smiled at his friend, as he quickly ordered some cheesecake and hungrily devoured it. Stefan was a handsome man with blue eyes and a lean jaw with a charming smile. When they had first met in Salzburg some years ago, they had started off on a wobbly footing amidst suspicions and accusations. But soon the misunderstandings and the antagonism had been laid to rest, and the special friendship had taken them on a couple of shared adventures. The pressure of the cases had cemented mutual trust as well as their combined love for justice. Re admired Stefan's steadfastness of virtue and he knew that Stefan depended on him for his insights. They made a good team.

"So, what exactly is happening here?"

The officer sighed. "Lots. But let me begin with the background because you need to understand the situation well. You have, of course, heard of the Empress of Austria."

Re nodded.

"Well, she grew up in Possenhof and always returned to it through all her married years. She wasn't a very happy person and somehow coming back here gave her joy. She was also close to her cousin King Ludwig II who was engaged to her sister Sophie but whom he never married. Anyway, that did not affect their friendship and she would visit Rose Island and Feldafing often to meet him. She felt that he was one person who understood her. She stayed at this hotel every summer for 24 years and it was only after Ludwig died, that she stopped visiting Lake Starnberg."

"Yes, I am aware of this bit of history. I have seen all the Romy Schneider movies too and love them. So, it's lovely to see all these celebratory decorations at the hotel. *Charmant.*"

Stefan took a sip of the coffee and threw a quick look around the hall. The weather outside seemed to be getting worse by the hour. Two of the tables were occupied. A youngish woman with her two children sat at a table, eating apple strudel and pastry with noisy appreciation. Two men in thick jackets were in deep conversation at the other table, filling the room with an occasional burst of spontaneous laughter.

"This hotel has a colourful history. In 1508, this was an inn with its own butcher's shop. In 1856, when Reichsrat Anton Ritter von Maffei, a large landowner in Feldafing, bought the inn with a vision for its beauty, he built another inn next to it with a grand terrace. When Empress Elisabeth of Austria began visiting from 1870, it was essential to expand the hotel. She would visit so that she could meet her cousin King Ludwig II and her family. She was here, when the devastating news of the king's death reached her on June 13, 1886 and she hastened to see him in Berg.

The Empress was here for the last time in the summer of 1894."

"Is that when they renamed the hotel, Die Kaiserin?"

"That was in 1900 when the Kraft-Bouchard family took charge of the hotel and in the same year they were granted permission to rename it. They made the hotel what it is today. Now, in honour of the time Elisabeth spent here, Die Kaiserin Hotel is celebrating her 180th birthday. But that's not the only thing." Stefan lowered his voice and Re leaned forward. "I have been assigned duty on a very special mission along with some other police officers from other countries. It is called Sisi's Imperial Treaty of Love."

"Intriguing!" Re exclaimed. "If it is what I think it is."

"It is. A special group of five financial, administrative, and political top honchos from five different European countries have been identified by the state who are deciding the fate of the Treaty. Germany, Austria, Italy, Hungary, and Greece. This is all rather low-profile of course, until it is splashed across the world by the governments tomorrow via social media. These representatives have come together to outline a noteworthy mission of love and peace amongst the five countries. Tomorrow evening is a very remarkable one for us. For the first time, Rose Island will be open in winter, if weather permits. An abstract of the play *Lohengrin* will be staged in honour of Ludwig II and his cousin Sisi, after which the Treaty will be signed amidst a lot of fanfare. Then, everyone will return to the hotel for a grand costumed dinner party. The theme would of course be the 1800s. The Treaty talks are on as we speak and I have been appointed on special duty to supervise the smooth interactions and implementation of the treaty signing, on behalf of the Austrian Government."

"This hotel is beautiful and ancient, just the right place to celebrate love, peace, and Sisi. Sounds exciting."

"It certainly is and would be a memorable day in the history of these five nations and in the future of world peace, if all goes well."

"So, what is the glitch?"

"Problems...multiple problems."

The waiter arrived to pour more tea and Stefan maintained a momentary silence. Re sensed his tension. He knew that Stefan wasn't easily frazzled and he couldn't wait to hear more. Stefan dug into his jacket pocket and extracted a folded newspaper. He laid it on the paper and Re could read the headline.

"*A Treaty of Love in the name of an Empress who never found happiness? Bad Omen?*" he read aloud.

"That was published yesterday in the local paper. Apparently, there's a group of interested parties who doesn't approve of this treaty in Empress Elisabeth's name. We were sent a letter requesting us to change the title because of her emotional and mental history."

"Oh, but this is in on behalf of her 180th birthday. And she *was* undeniably an Empress...*de l'Amour*."

Stefan sighed. "Exactly. But politically motivated sections will try to milk the situation, any which way they want. Anyway, that's the first of our worries. Read the news right below it. That's another of our concerns."

Re glanced at the article. *Ghost-like ET spotted over Lake Starnberg in Bernried.*

"I don't believe this!" He thrust back his glasses.

Stefan nodded. "This is shockingly real. A ghost-like ET is supposed to be disrupting the happy Christmas holiday atmosphere of the towns and that of the forthcoming Treaty. People are worried."

"Intriguing."

"Too many people have seen it to write it off as a figment of some highly fertile imagination. And what the reports claimed is true—it is white, floating and has horns or weird arms."

"Has this ET done anything to cause concern apart from frightening people?"

"Not yet but the sightings are eerie and have indeed sent a wave of fear through the people. This ET appears on some nights, mostly by the lake."

Re was quiet, as he skimmed over the article. "Has there been a pattern in his appearance? Like say alternate nights or any such thing?"

"No, no pattern noticed so far."

"And when was it first spotted?"

"About a fortnight ago and seen at least five times during this period."

"And why are you worried about it? Especially since no harm has been reported."

"Firstly, because it makes me uneasy *not* to know what it is and why it seems to be appearing in Starnberg. Also, it was first seen at the farthest end of the lake and since then, for some odd reason, it seems to be edging closer and closer towards Feldafing."

"Interesting."

"Yes, but that's not the reason why I invited you. You have a more pressing matter to attend to," Stefan said, his tone grave. "Follow me please."

Re rose at once and followed his friend out of the restaurant to the adjoining room. Mrs Weber, the hotel manager, was seated at her table and nodded as they entered her office. Stefan indicated a chair and they settled themselves opposite her.

"Mrs Weber, this is Re, my friend and an investigative journalist from Paris. Could you please re-narrate the details of yesterday's theft to Re?" the officer requested.

Mrs Weber nodded and brought Re up to speed on the incident—how her assistant manager had discovered the safe open, that the swans were stolen and a note kept in its place.

"A note?" Re repeated, instantly on the alert.

"Here it is. The main reason why I had to drag you away in the middle of Christmas."

Stefan placed the message on the table.

PEACE DOESN'T COME EASY. THE EMPRESS OF ROSE AND MOON MUST FOLLOW THE PATH OF HER POEM AND RETRIEVE THE SOUL SONG BY 5 PM, 24th DEC. OR THE WRATH OF THE SWANS WILL DESCEND ON LOVE AND PEACE IN STARNBERG.

Adler, dort oben in den Bergen...
Die Möwe bietet dir unser Lied in voller Blüte.
Auf dem Pfad der Kindheitsträume,
vorbei an dem See, der in Dunkelheit gehüllt ist.
Schweigend schwebten wir, doch tief verstanden wir
das Lied, das unsere Seelen einst sangen...
Nun bewacht es der Vogel in seiner stattlichen Haube,
inmitten des himmlischen Geruchs.

"A threat." The detective stated matter-of-factly. He sensed no surprise.

"Unsigned, of course. And the pasted letters render the message quite useless as a clue and make it untraceable."

"But what's this written in German?" Re asked. "I am afraid my German is very basic."

"It's a poem," Stefan said. "*Adler, dort oben in den Bergen... Die Möwe bietet dir unser Lied in voller Blüte.*"

"Wait...why did I not see this before? That poem sounds familiar. Can I take a look?" Mrs Weber cut in.

Stefan hesitated just the slightest, then handed the slip of paper to her. She was silent as she pored over the words. Re was quick to notice her sharp intake of breath before she glanced at them, her eyes suddenly wide.

"This is utterly incredible." She sounded almost breathless.

"What is?" Stefan asked.

Re leaned forward, studying the manager closely.

"This...this poem!" the lady shrugged, an incredulous expression on her plump face. "If it is original, which I think it is, since I have personally read her collection of poems in the public domain and we even have a collection here — this is a poem by the Empress of Austria. But how...and who found it? And what is it doing here? This is such an amazing discovery. It is historic and rare..."

Stefan and Re exchanged quick surprised glances.

"How can you be so sure the Empress wrote this?" Re asked, trying hard not to dampen the lady's excitement.

"It has the Sisi stamp, her distinct style. How can I explain...it is so beautifully expressed and it is so like *her*," Mrs Weber appeared a little frustrated, at the lack of her own articulation.

"How about if we first get the poem translated?" Re suggested. He whipped out his phone from his jacket. "I can do an online translate."

"You can do a *what*?" Mrs Weber looked flabbergast, her hand on her chest. "Sisi's poem from an automated translation site?"

Re couldn't help smiling, as he apologetically pushed back his spectacles. "It will help save time."

"Give me just half an hour. I will translate it and bring it to you."

"I am afraid we can't let it out of our sight, ma'am. It is evidence," Stefan cut in. "Could you do it here, right now?"

Mrs Weber hesitated momentarily, then nodded. "I will do my best. This is such an honour." She immediately extracted a pad from the drawer and set to her task with the eagerness of a school girl.

Re rose and took a closer look at the safe. It was sturdy and old-fashioned.

"This is definitely the work of either an insider or someone who is a regular here. Someone who knew that the key was kept in the drawer."

"The German Police have already questioned the staff and are covering the fingerprint route. Not that there were any on the safe or on the note. We have to be very careful. We don't want unnecessary panic nor any rash accusations. Die Kaiserin is a respected hotel and we wouldn't want to damage its reputation."

"I understand."

Mrs Weber rose from her seat, with a triumphant flourish. A look of immense pleasure and gratitude seemed to light up her ample face. Re couldn't help smiling. *The perks amidst the chaos,* he thought.

"Thank you for giving me this opportunity. I have no doubt that the Empress wrote this poem for her cousin Ludwig II." Mrs Weber's tone held a hint of awe. "She always addressed him as an eagle and he called her the seagull...they were both very fond of each other, which is why she spent so many summers here. They were kindred spirits you see, made from the same soul-fabric... This poem is so her style and as beautiful as her other ones. Here it is...

Eagle, up there in the mountains...

The Sea Gull offers you our song in bloom.

On the path of the childhood dreams,

past the lake shrouded in gloom.

Silent we soared but deeply we understood.

the song that our souls once sang...

Now the bird guards it in its stately hood,

in the midst of the heavenly tang."

She ended her recitation in a whisper of awe and reverence and both Re and Stefan responded with a respectful silence, allowing the lady her moment of satisfaction.

"Thank you, Mrs Weber. You have been immensely helpful, we really appreciate it," Stefan acknowledged, as he accepted the original sheet and its translation.

"It was a pleasure, although I can't help wondering who could have found this poem and where. And why has it been sent to you in exchange for the swans?"

"That is what we intend to find out. Can you infer anything from the poem?" Re asked.

"Difficult to say off the top. Sisi always had some context to each poem—mostly her deep reflections of life or an experience and since we have no clue when or how this poem was written, or anything about the background, it would be difficult to comment. However, I will look into the collection I have and try to find out if there is link in there," the manager offered.

"That would be great. Thank you," Re said.

Re waited till she exited the room, then read the note aloud again, allowing the threat to sink word-by-word into his mind.

PEACE DOESN'T COME EASY. THE EMPRESS OF ROSE AND MOON MUST FOLLOW THE PATH OF HER POEM AND RETRIEVE THE SOUL SONG BY 5 PM, 24th DEC. OR THE WRATH OF THE SWANS WILL DESCEND ON LOVE AND PEACE IN STARNBERG.

"Now you know what I meant. This situation is definitely more serious than the strange ET looming over Lake Starnberg or the unceremoniously raised objections to the Treaty being named after Sisi. This note is a direct threat to the Treaty and the unity of the five countries," Stefan remarked.

Re nodded as he glanced at Stefan, his face set in a deep frown. "The Empress of rose and moon of course signifies Sisi, we know that now. Sisi must retrieve the soul song mentioned in her poem before 5 pm tomorrow. It is 9:30 am now. Which means that we have exactly 31 hours to find this soul-song, whatever it is and wherever it is."

"But what *is* the soul song? Did the two of them share a special song which they secretly referred to as their soul-song?" the officer wondered, puzzled.

"Perhaps. We would need to figure that out. But don't you think we have overlooked a glaring problem? Sisi...

How is it possible for Sisi to retrieve the soul song? Sisi, the Empress of Austria has been dead for 119 years!" Re spoke slowly, his tone elaborate and his gaze fixed on the officer.

Stefan stared at the detective as the gravity of the situation sunk in anew.

For the first time Re experienced a huge shudder of apprehension.

2

Empress Elisabeth's room at the Kaiserin Hotel was exactly as Re had imagined it. Specially the polka dotted velvet blue walls and the one against which her polished copper-metal, four-poster bed rested. The white dots against the blue were like stars and the presence of the universe in the midst of a cosy room was overwhelming. A gold-edged oblong mirror stood on the floor beside an antique ornate wooden cupboard. Fresh sunlight streaming through the wide windows, added a surreal glow to the room. Strangely, despite the years since her visit, he could still sense her energy. It was balmy, suppressed, quite fragmented and fractured. The Empress had indeed been an unhappy woman. Or was it the lingering energy of her last visit?

Re knew that this room had specially been given to the Treaty members as their work space and right then, the atmosphere was charged with an uneasy silence. Stefan and the German policeman stared at the group of five people, as they read the sheet of paper and passed it forward without comment. Re leaned against the wall, glancing at the names that the Police officer had handed him before the meeting. Maximillian Hartman from Austria, Leon Schubert from Germany, Carlo Pelle from Italy, Adria Gerodimos from Greece, and Harry Ramone from Hungary—the five representatives who would decide the fate of European Peace. In another corner, stood a quiet little man, Klint, Harry's secretary. Re's presence in the meeting was more a way of lending quiet support to the two policemen and he awaited the explosion of protests he knew would soon be forthcoming.

"In all my years of experience, I have never encountered such a weird situation. How in heavens did this happen? How could the precious swans be stolen?" Leon Schubert expostulated. He was the last one to read the note and could barely contain his indignation.

Stefan turned to him patiently. "Mr Schubert, I understand that this is a big shock and a setback to us. But we are on it and we will find the swans."

"You better do that quick. We have just a day left for the Treaty to be signed," Carlo Pelle, the Italian business tycoon, spoke from the far corner of the room.

"Which means we also have a mere day to resolve our issues, Carlo," Maximillian Hartman reminded.

Carlo turned to face him; his hands deeply ensconced in his rather thick jacket. "You think I am not aware of it, Max?" the Italian sneered.

"If you were, we wouldn't be stuck with frivolous arguments," Leon Schubert snapped.

"*Ya*, by now we should have been skiing smoothly down the slopes instead of still trudging uphill," Max added, a chuckle in his voice.

The three men glared at each other while the other two looked on non-committally. The antagonism amidst them was palpable and Re wondered idly about the Peace Treaty. Surely a lot of air needed to be cleared before consensus for love and peace was sealed.

"I think what is important right now is to find those swans and the person who has sent this threat to us," Harry Ramone cut in smoothly.

"That's right, Mr Ramone," Stefan agreed instantly, glad that some sense seemed to prevail. "That is our prime focus. We will do our best. This Treaty means a lot to all of us and you can rest assured that we shall ensure swift action to get to the bottom of this matter."

"In the meanwhile, we will continue to sort our issues like adults and with an eye on the larger purpose of the Treaty," Adria Gerodimos added. She appeared suave with her immaculately coiffed hair, a creaseless business suit and light makeup on her tanned face.

Stefan smiled at her. "That would indeed be perfect, ma'am."

Re's gaze swerved from member to member, his gut instinct tuned into their energies. Max was youngish, clean-looking with an eager almost hungry-to-please look of a school child. But he was far from inexperienced and his career as a media baron showed a rapid growth to early and sure success. For some reason though, Re thought that he looked rather familiar. The pronounced jaw-line, slicked down brown hair, deep-set intense brown eyes... Had he met him before?

Leon Schubert was in his mid-thirties, handsome to the point of projecting an unabashed rakishness with his thick shock of blonde hair and a pronounced cleft chin. A devilish glint in his light blue eyes was what would draw the women to him, the detective concluded. Success had only added a glow of magnetism to his already self-possessed demeanour. A dangerous opponent without an iota of doubt, but a loyal lover?

Carlo Pelle, with his unruly black dishevelled wavy hair, seemed to be irrefutably the angry middle-aged man—his eyes were perpetually narrowed and his thin lips twisted in an unfriendly, sarcastic smile. Yet, Re read honesty in his face. Anger and strong emotion were often hallmarks of a clean and honest personality. Discourteous perhaps but upfront and straight.

Adria Gerodimos was in her fifties and had earned her name as the youngest equestrian of her time. She had been a natural, growing up on her father's horse farms. But she had taken the horse dream to a whole new international level with athletic trainings and corporate collaborations.

Harry Ramone, on the other hand, was now almost retired from active politics. But he was still on the eminent advisory committees world-wide, representing his country Hungary. Both appeared to be composed and unshakeable, smooth operators. If their non-committal reactions and mature approach to the situation was anything to go by, Re would treat them with utmost caution. He wouldn't trust them in eons. Even the thought brought on a deep crease to his forehead.

"I need a break," Max said, brusquely.

"Don't take too long," Carlo added.

"I'll join you." Leon picked up his jacket.

"I think I need a ride too. A quick one through the woods, but I shall take it just before lunch," Adria announced, flashing a general smile around.

"May I please request you to continue your talks as if nothing has transpired? Please don't let anything disturb the flow of your thoughts and decisions. I assure you that this will be sorted within no time," Stefan completed and the representatives nodded cordially.

Stefan flashed Re a quick look and a half smile and the policemen exited the room. Klint Capa had not budged. He had been a silent observer. Re followed Stefan quietly, still absorbing the disturbed energy of Sisi's room.

They were in the corridor when the police officer's phone beeped and Stefan glanced at the message.

"Something's happened. I have to be somewhere. Re, can we meet in an hour to continue our discussion?"

"Sure. I have hired a cab for the day, so I shall probably do a quick round of Starnberg to get the feel of the place," Re said. "But what's up?"

"Seems to be an emergency of some sort. Will share when we meet." Stefan hastened down the stairs.

The wooden door entrance to the Kaiserin Hotel was decorated in wreaths and twinkling lights—a prefect invitation to the warmth and cosy comfort of the ancient hotel. Re stood outside for a few seconds observing the hotel. Facing the road, it was three-storeyed and the green windows and the brown wooden balconies contrasted perfectly against the cream structure. He knew that on the other side was a long terrace, with steps leading down to a beautiful grand park, now under thick snow. In summer, this same park was a vision in startling bright colours, with striped umbrellas and visitors lounging in armchairs. The open sunny terrace was a favourite with the guests. That sunlit extravaganza was a far cry from the present snowy silence that hugged every corner of the park.

Re strolled in the driveway, his keen mind taking in the long row of rooms behind the parking lot and caught sight of his waiting cab. The cab driver was leaning against the car, chewing on something. Re approached him with quick strides and the driver straightened at once.

"Hi, I am Ben, your friendly neighbourhood driver." Ben lifted his cap to reveal a shiny, bald head and flashed a toothy smile. Attired in a thick black jacket, he was huge, at least a head taller than Re but displayed a cheerful, chatty countenance.

"Re." The journalist shook hands with Ben.

"As in a friendly neighbourhood Batman, Superman, Spiderman," Ben added, his smile widening.

"I got that!" Re grinned. "The Starnberg Superman, you mean?"

Ben laughed heartily. "*Ya*, I could pass off as one for sure, considering my parallel activities. Just kidding! Should we leave? Where to first?"

"What do you advise?" Re asked, casually.

"Sisi's route?"

"Sisi's route," Re repeated.

"The Empress of Austria grew up in these parts and often visited Feldafing, Berg and Possenhof—places of her childhood as well as to meet King Ludwig II, her cousin. So, folks call it the Sisi route and tourists love to see the many spots she visited."

"That sounds ideal."

"But I have to warn you that winter is not the season to visit Lake Starnberg. Summers are the time when everyone swims in the lake and the ferry is open to travel around the lake. But winters are kind of sad."

"More peaceful, less crowded," Re commented.

"And not good for business at all!" Ben laughed heartily.

"I have to be back in an hour, so Rose Island seems closest on this map."

"Rose Island is closed for visitors right now but you can stroll in the park. It is still beautiful."

Re nodded and opened the door of the car.

"Hey, that's my cab!" an accented voice hailed.

Re froze in mid-action. Even before he turned, he was aware of her forceful energy and his mind churned in shock.

"I believe that I had ordered this cab for the day," she repeated.

Re couldn't help staring. In stark daylight, she appeared slimmer, smaller. She was still in her white fur jacket and long dress and exuded the same elegance from dawn but the expressions on her face were like the sky in clear sunlight—unlined, sparkling without a trace of any shadows either personal or physical—and the authority in her voice was distinct. It was difficult to believe that she was the same woman he had encountered outside Bernreid station this early morning. The surprise he experienced was instantly replaced with curiosity.

"I am afraid *I* booked this cab," he said.

She raised a dainty wrist and glanced at the watch. "It's ten o'clock and this is the car number on my receipt." She swept a piece of paper under the periphery of his vision.

He frowned. "That's strange." He whipped out his phone and displayed his receipt to her. "Same number as you can see."

Their eyes locked in confusion as Ben blushed in embarrassment and intervened hastily.

"Apologies. I think there has been a mix-up. Perhaps the company thought that since the pick-up address was the same on the same day, Hotel Die Kaiserin, the car was booked by the same person in different names?" He offered, glancing from one person to the other, a little abashed.

"Lame explanation. And certainly, very irresponsible of the cab service. I guess I will take the car, since I have booked it for two days," she said, imperiously.

"*Excusez-moi.* I have booked the car for two days too." Re smiled.

For the first time, two clear lines in the semblance of a frown, appeared on her forehead.

"You can order another cab?" she suggested.

"Well, you can too, right?"

"Wastage of my time," she remarked.

"*Exactement!*"

"Well then, should we toss?" She returned the smile.

Re had to admit it. She had the most disarming smile he had ever seen on a woman. The corners of her lips and eyes crinkled softly and the blue colour of her eyes deepened with an inner smile.

"I have a better idea," he said. "Let's share the cab for the day. Perhaps tomorrow, one of us can order the second cab."

"Er... Perhaps there could be a shortage of cabs. After all it *is* Christmas time. The holidays are a big thing in Starnberg," Ben added quickly.

She considered the idea, with the seriousness of a woman on a mission. Her thinking was almost physical—head inclined towards the lake, a look cast in the distance, well-manicured fingers twisting a ring on the right finger. Re watched in fascination.

"I have work to do," she said. "I am doing a documentary on Sisi, the Empress of Austria and I need to visit the touristy spots."

"I am perfectly fine with that, *ma chérie*," Re replied.

She raised an eyebrow and held out her hand. "Call me Rosamonde."

Was that the slightest of rebukes? He wondered as he held her soft hand in a firm clasp.

"Re...as in the second musical note in Indian as well as western notes," he introduced himself.

"Interesting. Are you a singer?"

"A journalist with a flute for a companion. It keeps me sane on intense days and reminds me of life's priorities."

"So, a journalist who seeks solace in art and sports a ponytail—not so bizarre is it?"

"The ponytail is an indulgence and no, not as bizarre as I would like people to believe," Re said, a twinkle in his eyes.

"Ah, posturing is a game with you," she concluded.

"*Oui*, it is sometimes fun."

"Wouldn't be much fun when people begin to judge you for it."

"Quite right. But posturing isn't the vice. It is getting *caught* being pretentious that is the crime. And worse is getting caught playing at being pretentious."

"That would indeed be awkward," she agreed, her lips curving in an amused smile.

They glanced at each other for an infinitesimal moment and surprise flashed across her face. Re felt breathless. Like he had run through the knee-deep snow and needed to catch his breath.

Rosamonde was the first to look away.

"Where to first?" She swung open the door of the car and slipped in.

"Rose Island Park," Ben announced, grandly.

The car slid out of the hotel and Ben took the narrow, slippery roads with daring expertise. The quaint houses with their black and red sloping roofs draped in snow, white bare gardens shining with decorations in the dull grey light added a touch of melancholy cheer to the landscape. Rosamonde was silent beside him and Re could hear her slightly laboured breathing. She had shown absolutely no sign of recognition, no acknowledgement that they had met briefly early that morning, he realised.

Within a few minutes, the car turned into a clearing and halted in the parking of the Rose Island park.

"I have some shots to take. Back in an hour?" she asked, as she stepped out elegantly from the car.

She didn't wait for him to respond but set off at a brisk pace in the direction of the woods. Re had a funny feeling that she was running away from him.

He took the gravelly path through the park, still wondering at this encounter. There was a no-nonsense attitude about her, like a closed wall, which seemed to smother the lashing waves of the sea that he had sensed at dawn. Like she was deliberately shutting out some part of her. But in that one flashing second, just before climbing into the car, when their eyes had locked, something had stunned them both. The look of surprise on her face was evidence that she hadn't expected it. More importantly, *he* hadn't. He shook his head, puzzled. It was very unlike him to give too much thought to people who passed through his life....

He hugged his jacket as the biting cold seeped under the skin. The trees seemed to tower over him, lanky and straggly but bearing the weight of the layers of snow rather bravely. The path made its way through the trees and a statue of Jesus on a tree caught his attention. And soon another one. Fresh flowers were placed in little cane baskets at the foot of the statues. How strange that the park seemed to have these small shrines of worship and that someone actually came often to pray in this biting cold. The path curved and the lake came in sight, almost white and still like a painting. In the distance, Rose Island appeared like a clump of haze-washed trees, seemed to emerge from the lake like a solitary presence. He had heard so much about this island which was the fairy-tale king's abode of solitude. And he knew that he wanted to visit it soon. But it wasn't the island in the distance that grabbed his attention. It was the signs of the policemen, the ambulance and the brisk activity near the jetty that instantly perked his attention. He saw a familiar tall figure, in a blue jacket, deep in conversation with the uniformed experts at the far end of the jetty. Stefan... So, this was where he was summoned.

Re's footsteps quickened. What had happened? Going by the presence of the police, he sensed what it was. The yellow tape which cordoned off a part of the jetty confirmed his suspicions. As he approached the jetty, he could spot the man on the edge of the pier, sprawled lifeless, his one leg almost dipping in the water. Re stood inconspicuously aside as the police did their job with an efficacy that rose out of practice. The stiff body was laid on a stretcher and carried to the waiting ambulance. Re caught a glimpse of his face as the sheet that covered him, slipped. His eyes were partly open, almost as if he was struggling to stay awake and alive. But was that a look of surprise on his ice-layered face? Almost as if he didn't expect to die but had been dealt a terrible blow—not just a physical blow but a blow to his belief? As if someone had betrayed his trust. It wouldn't be the first time that such a thing had happened, Re thought. *The world of crime was full of surprises, unexpected betrayals and spontaneous expressions of greed.*

Re was aware of the police procedure and as a rule did not interfere with their work. The hard truths were being evaluated with competent brains. It was the layers of the unobvious and inconspicuous that surrounded the spot of crime that interested him. Like the proximity of the crime to Rose Island and the fact that the man had been lying sprawled on the jetty, as if he was lying causally, idly staring at the sky and at the apparently deceptively peaceful and still landscape. Except that there wasn't anything peaceful about what had happened...something and someone had assaulted him with savagery and taken his life. Another lost soul...no matter what his crime.

Stefan spotted Re and raised a hand in acknowledgement. A couple of minutes later, he detached from the group of German Police and strode towards the investigative journalist.

"Awful business here, Re, especially in light of the Treaty," Stefan said.

"What happened?" Re enquired.

"Head thrashed by a hard object. Not sure of the motive although we should know soon enough. I am just an observer, of course, but the German Police are identifying the man. Officer Karl Schmidt is in-charge. But I don't like it at all. This, on top of everything that is already going on. Anyway, I need to head back, but we will meet as planned."

Re nodded.

Stefan appeared to be under a great deal of pressure and Re wasn't surprised. The cryptic code message, the theft of the precious swans and the blatant threat were bad enough to give restless nights. But murder was infinitely worse. Was it in any way connected with the Treaty? There were missing links and Re hoped that Stefan would bring him up to speed soon enough with the details. The investigator's senses were now heightened and alert and he was raring to begin his journey into understanding and unravelling the scene, puzzle by puzzle.

As Stefan returned to the group of officers, Re turned around and headed back in the direction he had come. The sight of the body in the beautiful landscape had touched a raw nerve inside him. Some evil mind had just taken a valuable life, with no fear of the consequences. And no matter what the motive for the act, no reason was justification enough for crime and most certainly there was none for murder.

The path uncoiled parallel to the edge of the lake, which appeared glazed and sparkling as far as the eye could see. Two ravens skimmed over the surface of the ice, pecking at dead insects. The frost-laden trees looked like lanky creatures with white hairy arms bordering the lake and catching the dull light in melancholy patches. And yet there was a touch of pristine stillness to it all. Like nature had paused in its journey, to rest and admire its own tranquillity... Re stared at the landscape, extracted his camera from his jacket and took a few pictures and videos. Then he strolled along the path, completely in tune with the silver countryside.

It was when his camera was panning over the icy, near-frozen lake when a scarf suddenly floated into view. Re lowered the camera with a jolt. Wasn't Rosamonde supposed to be taking shots for her film? Yet, there she was, standing motionless on the bank of the lake, between the overgrown bushes, a beautiful apparition in white. His pulse began to race with an excitement he couldn't understand.

He tucked his camera in the jacket pocket and without the slightest hesitation, plunged into the patch of snow between them, his boots sinking deep into the thick softness. She continued to stare out at the lake, arms loose by her side, the umbrella half inclined and the wind flapping wildly at her shoulder-length, loose hair. He noticed that she barely moved, so oblivious was she to her surroundings, to any kind of disturbance, or sounds. Once again, wild sea waves lashed in Re's mind and he sensed the tug of a strong, powerful energy around her.

He approached her silently, as if afraid to frighten her and without a word, joined her. Sensing company, her head angled. Momentarily, her eyes flicked over him, almost without recognition, to turn back to where her sight was glued.

"Such a beautiful lake. Has always inspired me... A smaller version of the seas of my travel. When you are young and vulnerable, life can be exciting but also scary," she said. "But the sea and the lakes and mountains gave me more peace than...than people. Which is why I always sought solace in nature, in my travels."

Re nodded. She seemed to be rambling, or was she? He frowned.

"And then there's death, the biggest betrayer of life. Takes away loved ones. *Precious* loved ones...you think you can't live without them and then one day, just like that they are gone.

Oh Death, you must atone,

for the blow that you coldly dealt my heart

I sob, plead and moan—

Bring back the soul that you forced to part!"

"That is so beautiful," Re said, softly.

"When he died, my whole world crumbled. I knew then that life as I knew it was over. My best friend was gone.

So sudden, so painful... The pain of loss is so deep and so throbbing, it takes away any other emotion or thought. Those who have never lost anyone, don't understand this... never will unless they lose someone." Her voice broke with deep emotion.

"I am sorry...I know what you mean. I understand this loss."

She turned to face him, seeing him for the first time. Her eyes smouldered in some kind of recognition. Of a kindred spirit.

"You do..." She searched his face with a direct, searching gaze.

He could see the clear blue of her eyes, the hint of grief in them. He knew that she would find the same mirrored in his eyes. The grief of having lost his young sister and the pain of having to live without her.

"I do," he reconfirmed.

A swift look of confusion flashed across her face and her eyes widened. As if sudden realisation had physically slammed into her rambling state of mind. As if she had snapped out of one mood and was hurtling into another.

"I am sorry. Did I say something? Is...everything all right?" she stammered. Her hand flew to her mouth as she tried to grapple with an inexplicable inner turmoil. Her glazed eyes searched his face for answers, hoping against hope that he wouldn't have them.

"Everything is fine, Rosamonde," Re reassured, promptly.

He sensed her inner agitation. Her need for assurance. Her attempt to tamp down whatever emotion had taken hold of her moments ago. He understood it all and longed to hold her and pacify her. His hand reached out to steady her, in a spontaneous reaction but she backed off.

"I need to get back to the hotel. Do you mind?" She didn't wait for his response.

Without another word, she picked up her long skirt and brushed past him, her long white dress trailing behind her, gathering icicles along the way. Re had a crazy urge to lift her train—the image of a beautiful princess racing off into the forest floating into his imagination.

He experienced a twinge...of anxiety, concern and something else. He couldn't place his finger on the concern. This was a completely different Rosamonde from an hour ago...the intelligent, rather practical, no-nonsense lady who was keen on doing a film on Sisi. The truth was also that he scarcely knew this woman. Yet, he experienced this odd twinge of concern for her and Re was a little taken aback.

He watched her hasten through the trees in the distance, as if some invisible hand was propelling her to do so. A smudge of elegant white gliding over the spotless snowy landscape, occasionally merging in, occasionally detaching itself. He waited till she vanished down the path between the trees. He had to let her go. He had to refrain from following her at once...she needed some time to collect herself...from whatever she had been going through. She needed to take time to be herself again. How strange that he had already met her thrice in such a short span of time and in rather odd circumstances. And each time, it had been as if he had met her for the very first time. It was like meeting three different women...Rosamonde was beginning to interest him in rapid strides. What exactly was she doing, roaming the cold country lanes of Lake Starnberg, under the pretext of making a film? First at Feldafing station, and now here by Rose Island. Who *was* she? And what was she searching?

Curiosity was an asset for Re and he usually milked it to his advantage. But this was more than curiosity. He was intrigued. This lady in white, who called herself Rosamonde, had slowly and steadily begun to tantalise the investigator in him. And he knew that he wouldn't be able to rest till he unearthed her story. But could he? What with a threat against the Treaty and the search for a 'soul-song' claiming top priority? Re experienced a tearing sense of frustration at being trapped between two intense choices. But then he didn't really have one, did he? And he sure hoped that he wouldn't have to make one....

3

All through the car ride, Rosamonde was silent and Re respected her need to be so. Ben kept the atmosphere light with a low whistling of a rather unidentifiable song. As soon as the car turned into the snowy slope of the hotel drive, Rosamonde turned to Re.

"You know what, why don't you go ahead and use the cab for the rest of the day? I think I will take my brother's car if available. We just have varied things to do and I don't want us stuck...," she began, her accent prominent.

"How do you know?" Re cut in.

"How do I know what?" She floundered, her resolve shaken momentarily.

"That we have varied things to do?"

"Well, I am assuming that you would like to use your day better than just trail around with me following Sisi's route." She glanced at him full in the face.

She is trying to avoid me, he guessed instantly. Feeling awkward for being caught? Vulnerable for having shared too much too soon? Uncomfortable with a stranger who seemed too perceptive? Or was it something else? He had to think fast and sharp before she made up her mind.

"Sisi's route is a prominent attraction, featuring on my to-do list. Besides, I would be interested in seeing how you plan to utilise this in a film. I am a filmmaker myself you know." He shrugged.

"Well," she hesitated and Re sensed the scoring of a dent in her resolve.

"However, I don't mind a quick cup of coffee before we proceed," he added, rubbing his gloved palms. "It's freezing and my lips are already too blue for my liking."

A faint smile flickered on her lips. "And a cheesecake. Shall we go in?"

As Re led the way into the warm ambiance of the hotel restaurant, he felt as if he had surmounted an invisible wall of resistance. For some reason he couldn't explain right away, he sensed the need to keep Rosamonde close. He needed time to figure out the essentials, especially her energy.

He found his favourite corner seat again and they settled down awaiting their order. In a corner, he noticed Klint Capa, Harry's secretary sitting alone, sipping coffee. He glanced up just then and nodded at Re in acknowledgement. Re smiled back. He removed his beanie and shook out his ponytail. Rosamonde did the same, her long hair a healthy brown crown, cascading gently to her shoulders.

"Have you produced many documentaries?" he asked, leaning against the red cushioned sofa and observing her in the light of the chandeliers.

"I don't know how many is many." She smiled. "But I've been producing documentaries for the last ten years. It's my passion. I am fascinated by facts, research and anything to do with history and representing them is the honour and privilege I give myself."

"Ah, sounds like you have found your calling." Re remarked, as he pushed back his sliding glasses.

"I do think I have. With every film that I make, I feel more fulfilled," she agreed.

The waiter brought the cheesecakes and coffee pots and receded. The room was full of people, huddled in warm clothes, enjoying a quiet winter morning. Klint picked up a folder and exited the room.

"And what made you choose the Empress of Austria as your next subject?" Re continued, sipping the coffee.

Rosamonde took her time to respond. Re noticed her delicate but capable fingers as she toyed with the spoon.

"I like her. A lot," she replied, simply.

Re was a little surprised. For some reason it felt more like a confession.

"In fact, I have liked her all my life. Ever since I was a child when I would come to these parts with my family. She has fascinated me as no other historical figure. My mom used to think my interest in Sisi was quite morbid and even a little unhealthy. Max, my brother, would tease me about it. Anyway, being her 180th birthday, I thought I would make a film as a tribute. She was after all the Empress of Love and Beauty and quite unlike anyone I have read about before."

"So, you must have undertaken a great deal of research and visited Sisi's route often?" Re confirmed, an idea beginning to form in his head.

"Sisi's route, no. I am returning to these parts after several years. I know about it of course and am looking forward to filming it but I haven't really frequented it as much as I would have liked to. But yes, I *have* done tons of research, so much so that you can rouse me from my sleep and ask me just about *anything* about her and I would respond in a snap." Rosamonde smiled, a twinkle in her blue-green eyes.

Re nodded.

"So, your brother Max, is he the one—"

"Yes," she cut in, briefly. "He is *the* media baron and he suggested that I time the filming of my documentary with his official trip."

"That makes sense."

Stefan strode into the restaurant hall, just then and spotted Re. He hesitated as his gaze took in Rosamonde but Re nodded and the officer walked towards them. Oblivious to him, snow still clung to his shoulders.

"Hi there...I am not sure if you two have met. This is Rosamonde Hartman, Max's sister. And this is Stefan Weiss, the officer supervising the Treaty on behalf of Austria."

"Oh, we've met briefly." Rosamonde smiled. She rose. "Why don't you sit? I'll go to my room for a short while. We leave in half an hour?" She glanced at Re who nodded.

Stefan took the sofa, as Rosamonde headed towards the stairs.

"You two seem pally. Rather quick work too. Where do you plan to go in half an hour? Is there anything I should know?" Stefan raised an eyebrow.

Re grinned. "Trying to get my bearings still and using all possible resources."

"And Rosamonde is a resource?"

"She knows a lot about Sisi—could prove useful. And I have a gut instinct about her. Just need to sift through some mental mist first."

"Have you had a chance to think about the note?" Stefan asked, as he ordered a cup of coffee.

"I have." He extracted the note he had copied that morning. "PEACE DOESN'T COME EASY. THE EMPRESS OF ROSE AND MOON MUST FOLLOW THE PATH OF HER POEM AND RETRIEVE THE SOUL SONG BY 5 PM, 24th DEC. OR THE WRATH OF THE SWANS WILL

DESCEND ON LOVE AND PEACE IN STARNBERG. The more I think of this note, the more I realise that there's more to it than meets the eye. Immediate questions arise and the first one, to state the obvious is, who sent this note to us and what does he or she hope to achieve? Secondly, he has set off a timer. We need to find the song and the swans by 5 pm tomorrow, before the Treaty is to be signed. Or something terrible would happen that would disturb the peace of Starnberg. Clear threats. Also, assuming that the poem has genuinely been written by Sisi, the next logical question is: Where did he find it?"

"All valid questions and analysis," Stefan agreed.

"What is quite evident, is that someone wants the 'soul-song' desperately—so desperately in fact that if we aren't successful in finding it in the stipulated time, the Treaty faces the menace of dissolution."

"And that is an eventuality we will oppose at any cost."

"Exactly. So, this mysterious person *knows* that we will take no risks with the treaty and hence we will undertake every necessary measure to ensure its occurrence. Even go to any length to find the song. The timing and the window of opportunity are perfect."

"That's right."

"That means that the song, or whatever it represents, is extremely important for this person. More important than the Treaty," Re concluded. "Let me construct a little background and character sketch for you. Going by the clue that has been given to us, it is obvious that Mr X is an educated person. He probably found this poem by Sisi and realised its worth. He realised that he needed to encash on it, since he was smart enough to understand the poem.

He probably also knows a good deal of the Sisi history, so perhaps he is German or an Austrian? Also, he is well-versed with the Treaty, which means that he is in some way connected with it. He knew where the swans were kept and the other material and he could steal them with the ease of an expert. Or with the ease of a local person?"

"Rather good so far. Except that a good number of people are involved with the Treaty signing, many governments, the media, so it would be difficult to narrow down on a suspect on those grounds alone."

"I agree. There is also something that puzzles me immensely. The insistence and demand that the Empress of Rose and Moon must not only *follow the path of the poem* but *retrieve the soul song*. Like it is lost and needs to be retrieved. The word 'retrieve' is indicative of a search. And therein lies the major problem! Unless Sisi still lives incognito, in some secret German cave, how would it be possible for her to bring the soul song? How is that even possible?" Re scratched his head, pushing back his steel-rimmed glasses.

Stefan was silent for a few moments, as he sipped his coffee thoughtfully.

"Perhaps he doesn't mean Sisi as in a real person, but in some kind of a symbolic way?" he suggested.

"Possible...or a person who is a descendant of Sisi? Or perhaps someone who looks like—" Re broke off, a sudden idea surging through him like lightning.

Stefan saw the look of excitement in his eyes. "What?"

"Empress of Rose and Moon..."

"Yes, that's Sisi."

"Unless, she is *not* Sisi?"

Stefan frowned. "What do you mean? The Empress...."

"Yes, that part is correct. I mean rose and moon...it's like an anagram, *almost* like an anagram for..." Re paused, deliberately, awaiting that spark of recognition on Stefan's face.

Stefan stared at him, intrigued. "Rosamonde!"

Re nodded, a triumphant smile on his face.

"The Empress of Rose and Moon is *Rosamonde!* Someone wants Rosamonde to find the soul-song."

"But why would anyone want her involved in this entire scenario? What does she have to do with it all?" Stefan frowned, a little bewildered.

"She is Maximilian's sister. A documentary filmmaker, here to make a film on Sisi. There has to be something about her that we don't know that would fit into this puzzle, I am sure," Re suggested.

The image of Rosamonde wandering at dawn near the Bernried station rose in his mind. Royal, almost ethereal. And then a while ago, as she spoke about death...the poem...the grief over losing loved ones. Whom had she lost? Whom was she grieving?

"But can we trust her?" the officer wondered.

"I haven't a clue. And the only way to find out, is by inviting her to be a part of the swan-and-song search team. And I sincerely pray that she agrees."

"I am going to leave the magic of persuasion to you." Stefan smiled. "Use your charm, Re."

Re laughed. "That is more your domain, *mon ami*. I am just an ordinary investigator."

"Oh yes?" Stefan's blue eyes twinkled. "If I hadn't seen how quickly you two have hit it off, I would have been fooled. Here she is now."

Re saw her in the corridor, speaking to a waiter.

"Stefan, could you ask one of your guys to dig up whatever they can about her? I just want to know where I stand with her."

Stefan nodded, just as Rosamonde approached them with a smile on her face. She appeared fresh in a deep green faux-fur coat which accentuated her blue-green eyes.

"I am ready. I have brought my camera along too and will begin filming as we go," she announced.

"I better get back to work. See you soon, Re, we'll stay in touch," Stefan excused himself, with a meaningful look at his friend.

Re waited till the officer had left, then turned to her. "How good are you with poems, puzzles and songs?"

Rosamonde raised an elegant eyebrow. "Is that some kind of a trick question?"

"No."

"Well then, very good if I may say so myself. I write poems; besides films, they are my power of expression. And I enjoy a good puzzle, of course. But why are you asking?"

"Why don't you sit down. I need to talk to you."

Rosamonde frowned, flashing a quick glance at her watch. Although she readily perched onto the sofa, Re sensed that her guard was up. The early afternoon had brought on a festive crowd to the hotel. A group of youngsters was chattering and giggling in the centre of the restaurant. Re noticed the way a spontaneous expression of annoyance crossed her face as she angled her face towards them.

"We would need to hurry. I want to catch the beautiful light for my filming." Her suggestion was mild but firm.

"Rosamonde, how deeply are you associated with the Treaty?"

"Not at all deeply. I am simply accompanying my brother. He is the one appointed by the Government. I mean, I do accompany him on diplomatic missions from time to time and I am the VP of Hartman Media, but I rarely interfere. And only offer my opinion if it is explicitly sought. Why do you ask and how are you connected with it?"

Re explained his position briefly, sticking to the bare minimum facts.

"You are a detective!" Surprise flashed in her eyes. "Well, you don't look it."

Re was tempted to ask whether she meant it as a compliment, but refrained and forced himself to focus.

"Yes, and am here by Stefan's express invitation. Something has happened. Something disturbing and time-bound and we need your assistance." Re went on to explain about the stolen swans and the note.

"Intriguing." She commented. "What do you need from me?"

"You are an expert on Sisi. I need your help in deciphering Sisi's poem and to help find this 'song'."

Rosamonde was silent, deep in contemplation for long moments, staring at an embroidered flower on the table cloth. Finally, she glanced at him.

"I understand the gravity of the situation and I am sorely tempted to decipher Sisi's original poem but honestly, I would rather not get involved," she said with a shrug.

"Why not? If this situation gets out of hand, it would affect the future of five countries. Doesn't that mean anything to you?" Re's tone was a trifle sharp.

"It does but I cannot lose sight of the reason I am here—I have a commitment to my producer and I need to focus on my documentary. Besides, I feel you would be better off seeking the assistance of a person more qualified than me. A historian maybe? I would rather not be a part of something that doesn't directly concern me."

Re inhaled a deep steadying breath. "But it does concern you, *ma chérie*, very much so."

"It does? How so?" Rosamonde straightened, a hint of haughtiness in her stance.

Re extracted the note and placed it on the table. "Your name is an intrinsic part of this threat note. Perhaps you can explain why?"

She scanned through the sheet of paper, her expression non-committal.

"I don't understand. This note is neither addressed to me, nor have I been mentioned in it."

"Initially when we read the note, we felt that the Empress of Rose and Moon was supposed to be Sisi. But for obvious reasons, Sisi cannot retrieve the song because she isn't alive. Which meant that this note was referring to some other person...someone whose name has been turned into something of an anagram..."

"Rose and moon," Rosamonde whispered, almost in awe.

"Now you know." Re leaned against his chair, folded his arms and observed her keenly.

"No, I don't. What does all this mean?" Two deep lines of a frown etched between her eyebrows.

"It means that someone had kept tabs on your movements, knew about your arrival at Feldafing and now wants you to find Sisi's song before 5 pm tomorrow."

"But why me?"

"I was hoping *you* would be able to answer that question."

Rosamonde shook her head. "I haven't a clue. The first time I heard about the Treaty was some months ago and although making a documentary on Sisi has been on my cards for long, I haven't been to Starnberg in ages. In fact, since my childhood. So, I see no connection whatsoever between this note and me. Are you sure you have interpreted it right?"

"Positive." Re's voice held complete conviction. "There has got to be a reason, why you have been chosen to find the song, Rosamonde. Think. Have you ever read this poem before? Discussed it with anyone? Do you know anything about this 'soul-song'? Or where it is?"

"Stop!" Rosamonde raised a hand imperiously. "Barraging me with questions is not going to help. I will repeat—I don't have the faintest notion about a 'soul-song' or why I am so important in finding it."

Re sighed. "In that case, *ma chérie*, our path is chosen... we have to find out the truth behind the matter. *Together*."

She glanced at him and their eyes locked. He noticed the blue-green specks deep inside her eyes, the faint crinkles around her lips and the way the fur coat sat elegantly on her shoulders. She was beautiful. In a cold, haughty kind of way. And yet when she spoke there was an inherent softness to her. A mix of contradictions. A criss-cross of energies that seemed to elude solo identification. More like an energy trapped within another energy...Re sensed it all. Was she withholding something? Something she ought to share with him? Even perhaps unknown to her? The more he thought of it, the more he became convinced. Rosamonde was a vital clue to the unravelling of this knot. Perhaps, to give her the benefit of the doubt, she just didn't know it yet.

Re's heart began to race in anticipation...and the excitement of an opportunity to explore and find what lay behind that intriguing and suave façade. Which was perhaps a vital key in unlocking the mystery of the soul-song and the swans.

4

"Let's get down to action. Where do you want to begin?" Rosamonde shrugged off her coat and dropped it beside her on the sofa.

Re placed the note on the table. "Let's start at the beginning.

PEACE DOESN'T COME EASY. THE EMPRESS OF ROSE AND MOON MUST FOLLOW THE PATH OF HER POEM AND RETRIEVE THE SOUL SONG BY 5 PM, 24th DEC. OR THE WRATH OF THE SWANS WILL DESCEND ON LOVE AND PEACE IN STARNBERG.

> *Adler, dort oben in den Bergen…*
> *Die Möwe bietet dir unser Lied in voller Blüte.*
> *Auf dem Pfad der Kindheitsträume,*
> *vorbei an dem See, der in Dunkelheit gehüllt ist.*
> *Schweigend schwebten wir, doch tief verstanden wir*
> *das Lied, das unsere Seelen einst sangen…*
> *Nun bewacht es der Vogel in seiner stattlichen Haube,*
> *inmitten des himmlischen Geruchs.*

And here is the English version that Mrs Weber translated for me:

> *Eagle, up there in the mountains…*
> *The Sea Gull offers you our song in bloom.*
> *On the path of the childhood dreams,*
> *past the lake shrouded in gloom.*
> *Silent we soared but deeply we understood.*

the song that our souls once sang…
Now the bird guards it in its stately hood,
in the midst of the heavenly tang."

Re allowed her to study the note, his mind working in silence as he observed her. When he thought she had had a good look at the note, he leaned forward.

"We need to begin with the obvious inferences, step-by-step. But first let's give this mischief-maker a name, shall we? Any suggestions?"

"The thief," she shrugged.

Re laughed. "Very original."

"The villain," she suggested with a smile.

"Don't treat this so frivolously. It is a matter of crucial consideration, as this will lay the foundation to the identity of the brain behind this chaos."

"Right. My skills are being judged and my reputation will turn to ashes if I cannot rise to this occasion," she agreed, in a grave tone but the twinkle in her eyes gave her away.

"Now you understand me perfectly, *ma chérie*." Re smiled.

"Yes, surprisingly, I do." She glanced at him, a shade longer than necessary. "How about Mr Virus?"

"*Oui c'est ça!* More apt, Mr Virus who has thrown our best laid plans into a tizzy."

Re gave a thumbs up and Rosamonde laughed. He liked her melodious sound that rose like a low tinkle and peaked into a crescendo. For that matter, he was beginning to like a whole lot of things about her. Her eyes…deep and intense, her wide mouth with the imperceptible fine lines, her shapely forehead and the way she held her head, her poise. Re stopped himself short. *What was he doing?*

"Right, so Virus it is. What's the next step?"

"The precious swans have been stolen, along with some Treaty material, so no guesses for concluding that Virus isn't too keen on the Treaty. Also, if the Empress of Rose and Moon—who we initially thought was Sisi, but then concluded was you—doesn't follow the path of the poem and find the soul-song in time, something rather terrible is bound to happen in Starnberg. What that would entail, is something we need to figure out by and by. But the threat is undoubtable and imminent. Some pertinent questions arise. One is, as we said before, why you? Why would Virus single you out? How did he know that you would be here? Why does he want you and only you to find this soul-song? Do you have any enmity with anyone who may want you to be involved in an international conspiracy?"

Rosamonde was silent for long moments. Re was surprised. He had expected a quick rebuttal of his suggestion, but her thoughtful expression as she contemplated her response in careful consideration, made him realise that perhaps something murky lurked in Rosamonde's life. *Was he hoping that something did?* He wondered? *Was he deliberately hoping that something would come up so that he would be forced to regard her with disdain?*

"Of course, there's always something in everyone's life," she murmured. "But I don't see anything that warrants being embroiled in a conspiracy of this magnitude."

"So, no person comes to mind or event..."

"Afraid not." Rosamonde shook her head. "Don't you believe me?"

She searched his face and Re blinked, trying to maintain an impassive face. He wanted to reveal nothing. Neither his suspicion, nor his instinctive leanings. He wanted to remain fair.

"As of now, I don't have reason to not believe you, *ma chérie*," Re retorted, drily. "What we need to find out is why Virus has so much faith in you and believes that you are the answer to his search. Perhaps it's your expertise on Sisi? Do you know anything about a soul-song that Sisi and King Ludwig II shared?"

"Well, they did share a special bond, so I wouldn't be surprised if they had a secret soul-song. But I haven't come across any. And I doubt if anyone has, if it is not in the public domain. She wrote beautiful poetry but mostly about her musings, her loneliness, nature and such."

"Mrs Weber is convinced that this poem has been written by the Empress herself. She very kindly translated the poem for us. Which is why we have this English version for my understanding. Why don't you read it again to see if it makes sense?"

Rosamonde nodded and he angled the note towards her. While she pored over it, Re glanced around the hall. The chattering youngsters were leaving and a group of elderly men took some sofas. Waiters dressed in a white uniform hovered around patiently, serving the guests. The Christmas tree shone bright and merry. The snow outside glinted against the windowpanes and the light reflected on to the stained-glass images in the hall. The atmosphere of lazy holidays was rampant and yet Re knew that all was not as it seemed.

Finally, Rosamonde glanced up. "I tend to agree with Mrs Weber. This indeed seems to be something that Sisi would write. Her poetry was inspired by Heinrich Heine, the German poet and a radical political thinker. She liked to refer to herself as Titania, from Shakespeare's fairy queen. I am also assuming that it is hers because of that tone of melancholy in it. It's so graphic, it touches the heart. Elisabeth used her romantic poems to express her deep thoughts and desires and they were almost like a secret diary. She wrote about her wanderlust and journeys, on classical Greek and romantic themes and her writing an ironic commentary on the Habsburg dynasty. So yes, this could be written by her. I wonder where Virus found this. He was smart enough to understand that this poem is not just something Sisi wrote to her cousin. The first two lines—*Eagle, up there in the mountains... The Sea Gull offers you our song in bloom*—instantly suggest that Sisi would like to give King Ludwig something."

"And Virus wants that 'something'. Obviously, it's not really a song. He has concluded that it must be something precious and worthy of putting a cog in the wheel of the Treaty."

"Yes, but there's no way of really knowing it, unless Virus is in possession of more information. But in that case, he should have shared that bit of information with us."

"Let's assume that Virus does indeed have more information and it is indeed a 'thing' which represents Sisi's 'soul-song'. Mostly because the second-last line—*Now the bird guards it in its stately hood*—is a clear indication that a bird is guarding a 'thing'. I just wish we knew what the *thing* was." Re frowned. "Isn't there a museum here in Starnberg? Sisi's museum?"

"Yes, there is. All those artefacts may give us a clue as to what the 'song' really means! I am sure that the museum will be a good start." Rosamonde's eyes shone.

"Perfect. That's where we will begin then." Re couldn't curb a spring of excitement.

"And it will give me a chance to take some shots too." Rosamonde patted her bulging handbag. "I have an important meeting tomorrow before the Treaty signing regarding the film and I would like to be well-equipped with my shots before that."

Re shrugged his jacket on, as he rose. From the corner of his eye, he spotted Max appear in the corridor. Something about the manner in which he threw quick furtive looks in the hall, caught the investigator's attention. Max opened a side door and slipped out into the terrace.

"Do you mind waiting for a few minutes? I'll be right back."

Rosamonde nodded, whipping out her cell phone. Re hastened into the corridor and opened the door to the terrace which overlooked the dense snow-covered park. In summer, this was a sunny and warm place, but at the moment the tables and chairs were all clustered together, upside down as snow seemed to carpet the floor. Re sensed a movement and a jacket flashing at the end of the terrace and he hastened after the figure. As he approached, Max's hushed but clear and angry voice carried through the stillness of the morning.

"Don't you dare try my patience! A bargain is a bargain. I did what you wanted, didn't I? What more do you want? ...I really don't care...all I know is that you have to stand up to your side of the promise and give me what is mine. Do you understand? I won't tolerate this, I won't!"

Re sensed Max moving again, so he quickly retraced his steps and slipped back into the corridor. He had heard enough, to realise that Max was in trouble of some sort. But was it in anyway connected with the Treaty? Who had Max been speaking to? What had he done for this person? Why had the deal soured? The questions crowded in his brain. Re had a sudden image of a well of water covered with thick moss. This entire case was something like that...drinking water choked under a thick coat of poisonous moss.

Stefan was in the office going over the itinerary for the next day, when Chief Inspector Karl Schmidt walked in with Felix, another official associate. Both were tall men with blonde hair and mild expressions. But Stefan knew that they were hardcore policemen who wouldn't allow any criminal to escape.

"We have news. Finally, we have a lead on the murdered man," Karl spoke in German.

"What is it?" Stefan asked, feeling hopeful.

"There was no identification on his body, as you already know. But we found his phone, which had probably slipped into the water during a scuffle. It was literally frozen and dead of course, but Felix here has done his best to revive it. We called the first number on the phone and you know it turned out to be his wife's. His name was Hans Becker and he was a journalist. Also did a lot of odd jobs on the side for extra income. We are heading over to talk to his wife. Would you like to join us?"

"Of course, I would!" Stefan replied instantly. "I shall just inform Mrs Weber first. She can handle things here while we are gone."

Karl nodded. "We will wait for you outside."

"Elisabeth was born on 24th December 1837 and she was the fourth child of Princess Ludovika of Bavaria, Duchess in Bavaria and Duke Maximilian in Bavaria. A very sensitive girl, who married Emperor Franz Joseph when she was only 16. He was actually supposed to marry her sister Helene, but instead he fell in love with Elisabeth," Rosamonde said, as Ben drove past the snow-laden lanes towards the Possenhofen railway station.

"Yes, I am aware of how romantic she was and that somehow Franz could not live up to her romantic expectations," Re agreed.

"He was too busy and practical and his mother too dominating. Life with her was quite a torture especially since she completely took over the care of Elisabeth's first two children, without her consent. Ah, here we are..." Rosamonde broke off as Ben turned into the station parking. "It is said, that this station was built by King Ludwig II. Isn't that right, Ben?"

"That's right. It's a historical station, first opened in 1865 in the community of Pöcking. The Empress first came here in her wagon car in 1869. She would wait in the grand waiting room before heading to her childhood home Possenhofen Castle on the shore of *Starnberger See*. The museum was started in 1998 and is fascinating too with its unique collection of items. About ten years ago, it was renovated and now the rooms are really something. You will find beautiful exhibits on Sisi's roller-coaster of a life." Ben smiled.

"Precisely why we are here." Re nodded, as he stepped out of the car.

The Possenhofen Station, now a museum, was a peach-orange, single-storied, modest building with large, cream, rectangular windows. But Re's attention was instantly riveted to a dark grey statue of Elisabeth just outside the station. It was a full figure of the Empress, standing tall and graceful and her head held high, looking straight at Re. In a high-collared dress, with her hands held demurely, the expression on her face was calm yet haughty. Something about it made Re pause. He glanced at his companion who was taking quick pictures of the grey-black statue and almost smiled. Rosamonde reminded him of himself. Re was the one who usually carried his camera everywhere and took as many photos and videos as he could. More like a record of his adventures, many of which were turning into unique memories. But this time, he had resisted the urge. He didn't wish to get in the way of Rosamonde and her filming.

"Isn't it a lovely statue of her?" Rosamonde enthused and the investigator agreed.

At the entrance of the museum, they were greeted by an elderly lady, with a sleek bob and rimless glasses.

"Good afternoon, I am Mrs Heinsen. You must be Re and Rosamonde." She shook hands with them. "I have come specially to show you the museum. You see the museum is usually closed in December and it's Christmas tomorrow."

"Thank you! We really appreciate that you made this a special case. I assure you we won't take too long. Just a quick peek at the items and her history," Re said.

Mrs Heinsen nodded and took them past doors into the station. The museum was a chronological display of Sisi's life history, her clothes, articles, photographs and paintings, most enclosed in glass cabinets. Paintings were hung on the papered walls. As Re moved from item to item, listening to Mrs Heinsen's explanations, he had a sense of a vast overview of a fascinating personality. The Empress of Austria was a prominent figure—as royalty, as well as a human being.

"Elisabeth was a very accomplished woman. She was an excellent Equestrian and a wild horse rider, quite inappropriate for those times. And she was obsessed with her diet, her looks and her long hair. When loose, her tresses would trail on the ground and it was a major task to keep it tied around her head. That is why she stopped posing for pictures in her mid-thirties. She always wanted to retain her youthful beauty in the eyes of the public," Mrs Heinsen explained. "Unfortunately, she got tragically trapped in her own imagination and romanticism."

"She was a lady who knew her own mind. She was talented and creative... I mean look at her poetry. Her love for nature. She was a vagabond in spirit, but tied to her royal duties," Rosamonde cut in.

"So vagabond in spirit, that she barely stayed at home, travelling all over Europe, leaving her husband behind."

Re and Rosamonde glanced at each other, aware of the curator's censorious tone. While she continued to point out the family history, Rosamonde moved ahead, reading the placards, taking shots, admiring the silver, gold and black gowns of the Empress on display.

"And this is the portrait of King Ludwig II, Elisabeth's cousin. He was, as you probably already know, called the 'mad king'."

The portrait of a young, elegant man on a sleek black horse, did no justice to the title of a mad king. Ludwig looked handsome and royally in command.

"Ludwig and Elisabeth were really good friends. In fact, they were very similar in nature, with their love for freedom and art and poetry. Both non-conforming to the dictates of society. Their relationship became rather intense after he became the king. Too intense for some," Mrs Heinsen shrugged, as her glance transferred to another portrait.

It was Elisabeth on a black horse in a black riding gown and hat, against a gloomy but luminescent backdrop of a mansion, staring straight and unabashedly into the eyes of the viewer. Even as Re stood glancing from one portrait to the other, he felt as if he could reach through the paintings and into their hearts. A slow, violin played at the back of his mind, the notes long and drawn into a heavy sadness. He shook his head, to fend off the melancholy energy, that seemed to clog inside him. It felt sad and unfulfilled. without a sense of closure.

"There was an eight-year difference between the cousins..."

"Oh, the dogs." Rosamonde sighed, cutting into the curator's sentence.

Re and Mrs Heinsen glanced in her direction. She stood before four portraits of Sisi posing with her dogs. One shaggy haired large dog, lounged by her feet, as Elisabeth sat upright in a chair, his leash in her hand.

"1867...I remember this sitting... Shadow was an Irish wolfhound, so loyal and lovable. In fact, all the dogs were such good friends—Houseguard, Dragon, Diana, Roma, Hamlet, Plato but Shadow remains a favourite being the first. Without them life would have been really lonely in the royal palace," she said.

The wistfulness in her tone propelled Re towards her. She was staring at the portraits—Sisi in different poses with her dogs lounging by her feet. In another portrait, a little black dog stood on the table, forcing Elisabeth's attention. But it was the expression on Rosamonde's face that arrested Re's attention. Mrs Heinsen glanced at Rosamonde, a puzzled frown crossing her face.

"The Empress was very fond of dogs. She would say, 'I fear a dog breed large enough for my tastes, does not exist!'" Mrs Heinsen remarked. "The Irish Wolfhound was one of her favourite dog breeds. 'Shadow' was her first Irish

Wolfhound puppy and would follow her from room to room. Later, two other dogs were also named Shadow."

"Franz was not animal lover. He never liked animals and more so dogs. I think that may have made a kind of negative impression on my mind," Rosamonde continued, as if Mrs Heinsen had not interrupted her.

"Rosamonde..." Re gently nudged his companion by the elbow.

"Mercifully, Rudolf inherited his mother's love and passion for animals. Do you know that he made provisions for his dogs in his will? He ensured that they would be well-cared for." Her voice broke and she glanced at the floor. "Excuse me...Re, do you mind if I step out? Just feeling a little claustrophobic in here..."

Without completing her sentence or waiting for his response, she hastened out of the hall.

Re stared after her, surprised. Mrs Heinsen glanced at him, looking perplexed.

"Rosamonde...is she—I mean, I don't understand..." the curator began but Re cut in smoothly.

"I think you will have to excuse us, Mrs Heinsen. Thank you so much for the tour. May I call you again if I need anything?" Re was apologetic.

"Of course," the lady responded graciously. "Call me anytime."

A short, sharp scream from outside the hall, cut into her sentence. Re was startled as was Mrs Heinsen. *Rosamonde!* Re rushed out into the open, followed closely by the curator. He was prepared for the worst, his imagination rife with images of Rosamonde in danger. But a strange sight met his eyes. It was Elizabeth's statue and for a few seconds the sight and state of the statue startled him. Rosamonde stared transfixed, her mouth open in shock. The statue was covered from head to toe with lingerie. The graceful statue now looked hideous in its cheap display of multiple-coloured bras, snatching away the royal sanctity of the majestic Queen. It was a disturbing sight—the blatant display of insolence and the clear message of disrespect.

"*Mein Gott*!" Mrs Heinsen exclaimed, looking faint.

Re strode towards Rosamonde. "Are you all right?"

"Who could have done this? So vile, so disrespectful... How dare they!" Her face was red with fury, tainted with a haughty air. "Whoever did it should be caught and punished severely. Such dastardly acts cannot be condoned. I won't have it!"

Re glanced around. The winter afternoon was cold and wet and not a soul seemed to be around in the station yard. He saw a bunch of youngsters slipping into the station from the side entrance, laughing and shooting glances in their direction. Without another word, Re strode towards them. Vandalism wasn't new to him. He had seen a lot of variety in his time as an investigative journalist. It was the manner in which it had been done that bewildered him. Why Elisabeth's statue? For what purpose? And why the lingerie?

"Hello there!" he called out.

The four youngsters were high-school kids and looked at Re curiously.

"Did you just put all those clothes on the statue?"

"*Nein*!" one of the kids declared. "No speak English."

"Ya...so what?" another one spoke, insolence in his tone.

The other three frowned at him and nudged him in warning.

"A man gave us 20 Euros and asked us to decorate the statue. So, we did."

Re studied his face to see if he was lying. The kid was blond with an impudent expression on his face.

"What did the man look like?"

The boy exchanged a few words with his friends. Then he turned to Re again.

"Like any other old man. White beard, sunglasses and a brown beanie...bundled up...," he said.

"But it was all just fun. We didn't intend any harm," another kid added hastily.

Re didn't want to argue the merits of respect and demerits of vandalism with the kids. He turned around and walked back to the statue, taking some quick pictures of the sullied statue. A couple with their two children walked by, horrified looks crossing their face. The mother quickly hastened the children in the other direction. Mrs Heinsen was speaking on the phone, urging immediate attention to the insulting incident. Rosamonde leaned against the wall, looking pale and shaken.

"It was just a joke...some foolish kids... Let's head out of here," Re said.

With a wave at Mrs Heinsen, he led Rosamonde to the car. She was still breathing heavily and he was puzzled. Rosamonde had reacted rather out of character. There was no permanent damage done to the statue. It was more like a foolish statement of dissent, if anything at all. Then why had she reacted with such vehemence, almost as if it was a personal insult? Also, her reactions to the dogs in the museum, the familiar manner in which she spoke... He remembered how he had sensed the strong energy in the museum. Perhaps Rosamonde had picked up the same energy? She was already so attuned to Elisabeth and her life... When she had said that he could rouse her in her sleep and she would still be able to tell him anything about Sisi, she had really meant it... Her research on Sisi was deep and she was very focused. Perhaps a little too much? If she wasn't careful, she could jump the thin line between research and imagination and confuse history with reality.

Thoughts were crowding in his head and he knew that he had a lot to figure out.

"The next stop should be Possenhof Castle," Ben announced. "That is where Elisabeth lived."

"That sounds logical," Re said.

It was as Ben reversed from the parking lot, that Re saw the woman. She was heavily cloaked, with a thick hood but he could see wisps of hair flying in the cold wind. She stood just by the entrance like a casual by-stander. But was she? Re wondered.

Mrs Becker was sobbing her heart out and Stefan felt uncomfortable. He hated being the carrier of bad news but in their job, it was inevitable. Karl had done all the talking, explaining the situation to her in a soft voice and consoling her for her loss and Stefan felt deeply sorry for her. Felix stood a little away, quietly jotting down notes.

They were seated in a cosy sitting room which was rather tastefully decorated in reds and gold. Stefan caught sight of a family photograph on a low cupboard. Hans and his wife with a young boy between them, all smiling at the camera.

"I kept telling him that it wasn't good to go off in the night whenever he was called. That we should be content in whatever he earned as a freelance journalist. He was a good writer and could sniff a good story, you know. But no, he wouldn't listen to me, he had to keep doing all sorts of jobs—we need the money to raise our son, he kept saying," Mrs Becker spoke between hiccups.

"What kind of jobs?"

"Oh everything. He was a cab driver on a shift and he would go boating with his friends in the middle of the night. Fishing in Lake Starnberg, he told me but I just didn't believe him."

"So, when did you last see him?"

"Last night. He had his meal. Then he got a call and left immediately. He said he would come back soon, but he didn't return last night and all morning I have been wondering what to do and whom to call, because Hans wasn't picking up the phone."

"Do you know who phoned him?"

"Must be one of his friends. I don't know, Hans never shared details. But I think one of them owned the boat they went out in some nights. Do you think one of those people did this to him?" she asked, suddenly aware of the implications.

"We don't know yet, but we will find out who killed him," Karl said, grimly. "Can you describe any of these friends?"

Mrs Becker shook her head. "I never met any one of them. Hans never brought them home or ever introduced me to them. Which I found strange initially but thought that they were his professional friends and I didn't need to know them. Sorry, but I am of no help. I...I...feel as if my husband is a stranger!" She burst out into fresh sobs.

Stefan and Karl exchanged quick knowing glances. It was time to allow the woman some time to grieve in private.

It was such a relief that the snow had ceased falling for a short while, Adria thought, as she scampered across Rose Island Park on her horse. Blake had been restless and Adria had sensed it. That was why she had excused herself from the meeting for an hour, requested Gunter, the stable-hand, to saddle Blake, and had set off across the park. He needed the warmth of a brisk canter and she needed some breathing space to think, Adria realised. The meetings were very passionate and although she understood the necessity to tweak and straighten every clause to a fine shape, to justify and glorify the end cause of the benefit, she felt the need for a breather.

The horse snorted and the cold puffed out in the form of smoke as the lady spurred the horse on. The sting of the icy wind flying through her hair was enough to set Adria on fire. Oh, how she loved riding. Which was why she mostly travelled to places where she could ride. Blake belonged to the hotel but the animal had bonded with her from the moment go.

It was as she was cantering speedily across the park towards the hotel, that she heard the snap. Like a throttled thunder clap. Almost a whip cracking in dead silence. Her instincts drove into a warning, emergency mode. But too late. The saddle slithered from under her, dropping to the ground and dragging soundlessly on the snow. Adria teetered dangerously over the horse, clutching at the reins, desperately trying to gain control as her heart pounded in fear. The next instant, she was flung to the ground, landing with a painful, thundering thud.

5

Surrounded by a huge garden and lawns, the house carried an air of quaint dignity. The shuttered green windows, the pointed, sloping brown roof, the cream walls gave it a striking look. A tall fence of thick bushes bordered the garden, cutting the house off from the shore and the lake.

Rosamonde and Re stood by the closed gate on the paved path, gazing at the house where Elisabeth had lived in her childhood. Ben was trailing behind, talking on the phone.

"THE EMPRESS OF ROSE AND MOON MUST FOLLOW THE PATH OF HER POEM," Re read the note.

"And the 'path of the poem' says *The Sea Gull offers you our song in bloom... On the path of the childhood dreams...* So here we are, our second stop on Sisi's route, her childhood home—*a part* of her childhood dream," Rosamonde announced.

"What a lovely place to grow up in," Re remarked. 'She must have had a happy childhood."

"Yes, I believe that she was quite a happy, carefree child and grew up without any compulsions to etiquette or conventions of the time. This was the summer residence of Maximilian Joseph, Duke in Bavaria and Sisi's father. Her parents had a troubled marriage and while her mother had to take care of eight kids, her father travelled extensively. Possenhofen Castle was Elisabeth's favourite home. She learned to fish, ride, climb and swim and to connect and be with nature. I believe her love for nature originated here and that lasted her a lifetime. I would have loved to see the house from the inside but unfortunately, we cannot, since it is now a private residence."

They strolled away from the house, following the path between the long rows of bushes, which opened into the shore of the Starnberg Lake. The house peeped from between the trees and Re guessed that once upon a time, Possenhofen Castle had been right on the shore.

The early afternoon sun glinted on the still white stretch of water, so still in fact that the clouds seemed to reflect and shine over it. The trees were like sentinels covered in snow and a cold biting wind pierced through Re's thick jacket and beanie. Overgrown frozen brown grass bordered the shore, occasionally rising from the frost-grey water.

Rosamonde parked herself on a bench, huddled in her thick furry coat, her hair completely hidden inside the black beanie. Re studied her from a distance. What was the purpose of this meandering? Why did Virus want Rosamonde to follow Sisi's route and where was this headed? Doubt crept into his mind rather treacherously. Had he misread the clue? Could he be wrong? Perhaps the note had nothing to do with Rosamonde at all and the Empress of Rose and Moon had indeed been a reference to Sisi? But then he was back again at square one and the one pressing concern—Sisi was dead...she could *not* walk down her own route. No, he had been right. All he had do was be patient. Someone had pre-empted Rosamonde's moves and all Re had to do was trust his instincts and follow her cues.

Re strolled to the bench and settled down beside her.

"We went to the museum hoping to get an idea what the soul-song could be. But there was nothing there to indicate an answer, right?"

"No...in fact, if anything at all, the museum blocked my thinking. I felt stifled..."

Re nodded. "There was a strong energy there, I felt it too. I guess, following Sisi's route seems to be the right thing to do. Do you want to talk about what happened back at the museum?" he asked.

"What happened at the museum? Oh, you mean those kids dressed up the statue in those cheap clothes! It was abominal, the way they behaved."

"I was thinking more about the way you reacted."

"How did I react?" Rosamonde frowned. "I reacted as any history-loving, principled person would—indignance at such a horrendous act."

"Right." Re continued to glance at her, aware of her defensive tone. He searched her face as she stared out at Lake Starnberg. She seemed composed, as she brought out her video camera and began taking some shots of the lake.

Perhaps she was right and he had over-imagined it. He knew by now that she was intense and perhaps what he felt was a reaction out of character, was probably her *natural* reaction to the statue episode. After all, he had barely known her for a few hours. Perhaps *he* was the one who had somehow gained a coloured vision and was over-analysing her reaction.

"That across the lake there, is Berg Castle." Rosamonde pointed to a hazy building rising from amidst trees in the far distance. "That's where King Ludwig II would stay when he came to Starnberg, it was his summer residence and he invited his special guests there, including the composer Richard Wagner. And that castle, his precious home, was where he was also locked up in those final days of his life."

Re strained his eyes to observe the conical roof and a rust-coloured structure surrounded by white trees, right across the lake. He knew it was a private residence now but did the association of history and grief ever leave a house?

Rosamonde suddenly turned to the detective. "Can I see the poem again, please?"

Re nodded and brought out the copied sheet of paper from his pocket.

> *"Eagle, up there in the mountains...*
> *The Sea Gull offers you our song in bloom.*
> *On the path of the childhood dreams,*
> *past the lake shrouded in gloom.*

Right now, we *are* on the path of her childhood dreams... Sisi's childhood dreams grew here on this shore and right in this castle, by this lake shrouded in gloom," she confirmed.

"Yes, we are," Re agreed.

"You know, now that I am here, some of my childhood memories seem to be surfacing too. I remember coming here often. We lived somewhere close by, on the two trips that we stayed here. This was my favourite view, right by this lake, in fact exactly where we are sitting this moment. I was fascinated by Possenhofen Castle, imagining Sisi living in it, climbing trees in the garden, walking these shores, swimming in the lake. My mother thought my obsession was morbid and she had to put an end to it." She smiled wryly. "In fact...wait..."

She suddenly rose and strode briskly to a large tree. Re followed her, as she frantically circled the tree, scratching away the snow from the branches and trunk, till she finally halted. Then she dropped to her knees on the cold bed of snow and cleared the trunk with her gloves.

"It's still here...," she whispered, looking up at Re in awe.

Re dropped down beside her and touched the deeply carved initials on the trunk of the tree. RH.

"Rosamonde Hartman... Wow!" he exclaimed.

He was a little taken aback that she had remembered the exact spot, after all these years. But then, with her own admission, she had been deeply involved in her visits to Possenhofen. And some childhood memories tag along invisibly all your life and pop up when you least expect it.

"Oh, that's funny." She frowned. "I had thought that I had carved Elisabeth's initials here..."

"It was a long time ago, wasn't it? Perhaps you got confused."

"Time has flown. You are right, perhaps I got mixed up," she said, doubt still thick in her voice. She touched the letters again, a little absently, unaware of the cold ground.

It was as she was rising that her coat got caught in the prickly bush and she skidded.

Re's arm shot out instantly and he steadied her.

"Oh, I am sorry..."

"The ground is slippery. You need to be careful," Re admonished.

As he slid the coat back onto her sleeveless top, he noticed the tattoo on her upper left arm. It was like a ship anchor.

"That's an unusual tattoo to have. Is that an anchor? Why an anchor?" he asked.

"That's not a tattoo. It's a birthmark," she corrected, buttoning up her coat firmly. "At least that's what I was told. I have never really thought about it. It does seem like an anchor, doesn't it? I have often joked with Max. If I ever got lost, this is how he would recognise me."

"Very ingenious." Re smiled.

"Do you mind if we return to the hotel? I happen to know that they are specially cooking recipes from Elisabeth's recipe book for lunch."

The impish smile on her face took Re by surprise. It wasn't just the smile that reached her blue-green eyes and hit him directly in the stomach. It was her sudden change of mood. She seemed almost happy, different and even carefree. Almost as if the memories of her own childhood had brought on some semblance of cheer to the cold snowy day. And it was a very infectious smile. It seemed to light up his gloomy day too and that surprised Re more than anything.

He held back as she walked on ahead, and for a few moments stared out at the lake, stretching to the far corners of the landscape. A sudden chill crawled up his back. The dried trees formed a border around the banks, the branches gnarled and laden with snow. The shore appeared lonesome, uninhabited and slippery. In the distance, Berg Castle, the house where Ludwig II had been held captive, seemed to be nestled in a hazy, white sheen.

Sudden tingles began up his finger and before he knew it, the vision had engulfed him.

The freezing water hit him and he gasped, as the ice enveloped him in a vice. He was being sucked down, deep down into the lake, the water gushing into his mouth and ears, choking and strangling him. His legs thrashed and he struggled, even as he knew that he shouldn't but already the ice blocks were eating into his sensitivity and the pain had gripped him...

With a jerk, Re's eyes flew open. He stared confused at the scene before him, as he grappled with the pain of his frozen body. Everything was just as still and ice-covered as before. And yet, although it had lasted for just a few fleeting, painful moments, the vision felt so real. Had the lake triggered the vision? But earlier, he had always got visions of places he had previously visited. This time, why was he getting a vision about a place *after* he had visited it? He racked his brains, for any sense of familiarity, for any memories of past trips to the Bavarian lake. But nothing showed up. His steps quickened, as his shoes slithered through the slush on the street towards the car. Something had brought up the vision and a near panic attack. For the first time, Re felt bewildered. This was neither the time nor the place for the vision. And yet...

Rosamonde had reached the car. As he trudged through the snow towards the vehicle, Re caught a glimpse of a black coat between the trees. Was that...he whipped around. A figure slipped behind a tree and hastened in the direction of Possenhofen Castle. Re inhaled deeply and hastened to catch up with Rosamonde. She seemed completely unaware that someone was following them. Was it the same woman who had stood outside the museum? Re didn't have an iota of doubt.

Stefan stood by the window of Adria's room, staring out at the hotel park, a long stretch of thick undulating snow. He turned from the window to face the diplomat; his forehead creased in thought.

"Would you have any idea, why anyone would want to cut the strap of your saddle?" he asked.

Adria met his gaze candidly. Her leg was rested against the pillows and only the red and black bruise on her forehead indicated any sign of her recent harrowing experience.

"So, you mean to rule out that it was an accident?" She raised an eyebrow in enquiry.

Stefan nodded. Felix was sitting by the table, a pad in hand.

"The police have concluded that the strap was neatly cut in half. It only took some pressure and some galloping for the saddle to give way. It has got to be the work of someone who knew of your love for riding and was aware that you ride no matter where you go."

"Everyone knows that I love to ride! I am a National Equestrian champion, for God's sake," Adria retorted, with candid impatience.

"Given that, we cannot rule out that it has got to be someone who has a personal vendetta with you. Someone who wished you harm," Felix added, quietly.

"True. I could have died. But an enemy who would follow me all the way from my country? I seriously have no clue," she said, her voice strong but nonetheless affected by her ordeal.

"Never estimate the power of hate, jealousy and greed," Stefan said, drily.

Adria sighed. "I agree. I don't wish to take names, but have you considered that perhaps someone didn't want me to weigh in on the Treaty? An injury would mean one less vote in favour of the Treaty?"

She was clearly hinting at Carlo of course, he realised. The Austrian officer nodded. "The thought did cross my mind. Do you suspect anyone?"

"Not really but it is an angle well worth pursuing, I would say. It was an unpleasant experience, to say the least, and certainly startling on a trip like this one. That is why I expect that you would get to the bottom of this affair."

"We will," Felix assured, at once.

"In the meanwhile, you would need to be careful, be with people and don't venture out alone," Stefan cautioned.

"You mean, someone may want to finish his unfinished job?" Adria sounded a trifle troubled.

"Not necessarily. Specially because we don't know yet why someone did this in the first place. This is just a precautionary measure for a couple of days." Stefan explained.

"Anyway, one thing is for sure. No riding till I return home. I guess, I should just feel relieved that I got lucky and escaped with a minor sprain. I would have regretted not being able to complete my duties for the Treaty."

"We are all glad too. But rest assured, we will find out who did it. The German Police are already questioning the stable hand and making other enquiries," Stefan said.

"Thank you. I appreciate it. Now if you are done, I think I will return to the discussions in the Conference Room." Adria rose.

"Are you sure...would you not rather rest that ankle a bit?"

"I am fine. It would take a lot more than a sprained ankle to keep me from my duties." She grimaced.

Stefan stepped forward to offer help but she raised an imperious hand.

"I have a stick. I can manage, thank you. I shall meet you all for lunch in the hall at 1 pm."

Stefan nodded and he and Felix left the room.

6

The snowfall began thick and unrelenting, just as the wine was being served. Lunch was organised in a private room specially for the guests associated with the Treaty. Re sat in a corner, observing the general banter across the long table. The five diplomats were exchanging some light moments. Harry was narrating one of his stories from his coterie of experiences and the others were listening in rapt attention. Except Carlo who listened on with a look of disdain. Adria had an amused expression on her face and Max was trying to hide a look of admiration. Leon was seated next to Rosamonde, his head bent towards her, almost speaking into her ear. Re frowned. Leon's familiarity towards Max's sister was way too obvious to go unnoticed.

Klint, Harry's secretary sat by a window, all alone, completely focussed on his meal. He was aloof and his demeanour did not invite casual conversation.

The entire group had maintained a calm front so far, not getting bogged down by the pressure Stefan and the German Police were facing. Perhaps it was more to do with the belief that the custodians of law would handle the needful.

Re watched the heavy snowfall from his window seat, as it blinded vision, his mind spontaneously going over the day's events. The room had an airy charm, with red drapery and two black-and-white photographs of Sisi on horseback. The chandelier threw a spot on the plush red rug on the floor and Re stared at it detachedly.

Stefan slipped into the chair beside him.

"Time to exchange notes and some news," he said, in a low voice.

Re nodded. "Looks like you have some."

"I do," the officer agreed and went on to share the news of Adria's accident.

"*Mon Dieu!* That is serious indeed," Re remarked.

"It is. She took it very sportingly and didn't create a scene but it was a breach of security. We shouldn't have let her out of our sight or at least sent someone to keep a watch on her when she went riding."

"Except that you didn't know there was any such danger," Re reminded, gently. "This case is very unusual, Stefan, don't get carried away with self-accusations. We need to focus our energies on finding the truth and not focus on the guilt."

"I know but I can't help thinking what if the damage had been something more permanent? What if Adria had died?"

"I don't think she was meant to... I mean whoever cut that strap, didn't really mean to kill her. It was supposed to be an accident. The more I think of it, the more I feel, it was supposed to injure Adria with the objective to incapacitate her temporarily. Any luck with the stable hand?"

"No. His name is Gunter and he claimed that he knew nothing about it and said that he hadn't noticed if the saddle strap had been cut. It sounds believable because the cut was indeed quite fine and inconspicuous. It was meant to snap when she rode."

"And the body from the pier? Any more news on that front?"

"Yes. The dead man was Hans Becker. Worked as a freelance journalist. The German Police have taken over the investigation, and we met his wife a while ago. It wasn't a happy meeting but I believe that we do have a definite lead."

Re listened gravely as Stefan narrated the exchange they had with Hans's wife.

"Poor woman. It was difficult to console her although Karl did a good job. We are now trying to track down people who own boats in Starnberg."

"There would be quite a few I think?"

Stefan nodded. "Yes, but we have a list of Hans's friends from Mrs Becker and we will match our list with hers. Once we find a match or find the slightest connection which I hope we will, our search will become easier."

"But is there any connection between Hans and the Treaty case?" Re wondered.

"I don't know. But it *is* too close to the Treaty venue and the timing too seems a bit weird. Starnberg is a relatively safe place. Anyway, tell me your news. Any luck with finding the swans?"

Re shook his head. "I am not even sure that we are on the right track. I have never felt more disoriented about this search than before. So completely out of control and it is *not* a good feeling. Bringing Rosamonde on board was a good idea but the whole point of it is eluding me right now. I feel I am missing some big link."

"I have never heard you speak like this before," Stefan flashed him a quick concerned look. "Are you sure you are feeling ok?"

"I *am* ok, or perhaps not. I feel as if there is a whole lot going here…much more than we know. I get this image of a huge abyss and we are gradually allowing ourselves to get sucked into it without understanding anything about the abyss. And I don't like it. I don't want to enter an abyss blindfolded. I want to shine a bright light so that I can see a path. And moreover, what bothers me is that the light I am shining is falling *outside* the abyss, not inside. What's inside the abyss, do you think?"

Stefan did not respond, aware that Re was thinking aloud and it was a rhetorical question.

"Too early in the investigation to get frustrated, don't you think?" he asked, wryly.

Re nodded. "It is. I feel like I am gazing at a modern art painting hung upside down on the wall. From my viewpoint, there are lines where they shouldn't be and rounds where there ought to be squares. And the squares and rounds can't be plugged into each other!"

"Stop. That's enough of your expert analysis of the painting and abyss." Stefan raised a hand. "For the Re I know, these are minor hurdles and in no time, the squares and rounds will be logically plugged, light will shine at the bottom of the abyss and the painting will stand right-side up and make sense."

"So be it. Cheers to your confidence." Re raised a glass, his face solemn.

They clicked their glasses and sipped their wine.

"And besides, we don't have a choice. The clock is ticking, pressure is mounting and the swans have to be found."

"I know," Re said. "Now tell me about Max."

"What about him?" Stefan asked.

"I overheard him speak on the phone, this morning." Re quickly narrated to Stefan what he had overheard.

"Sounds like he is being blackmailed." Stefan frowned.

"Right. But does that have anything to do with the Treaty? With this current business? Or is it something from his past that has caught up here?"

"I know what you mean. Should we talk to him?"

"No, let me do it. I want to chat with him anyway."

Re glanced at the long table where lunch had been served. Leon was still leaning over and engaging Rosamonde in conversation. The two seemed to be really hitting it off well.

"Oh, by the way, here it is." Stefan pushed forward an envelope on the table. "All the info you needed about Rosamonde. She seems to have a squeaky-clean past."

A wave of relief swept over Re. Almost as if he had held his breath under water. Why was he so worried? But then he didn't need to ask himself twice, he *knew* why. Deep inside he was struggling to understand Rosamonde. She was smart and intelligent, well-read and alert. And yet, he had witnessed certain slips in her behaviour. Had they been involuntary or deliberate? He had no reason to believe that they were deliberate because he didn't know her well enough. Then why had the thought even crossed his mind? *Because he couldn't gauge and sense her energies clearly.*

"Go ahead and read it. Anything else you need from my side?"

"What about Leon? He seems pretty pally with Rosamonde."

"Leon is practically a family friend. He and Max go a long way and I guess Rosamonde knows him well too. Why, do you suspect anything?"

"No, not just yet. I am trying to keep myself updated on their equations. For example, it is obvious that Carlo is sticking out in that group like a sore thumb. He is an outsider for some reason. Harry and Adria have something in common—their astuteness and their advantage of age. And they both recognise that in each other. Leon and Max can tune into their entrepreneurial tales and are open to the law of experience. Not Carlo...their dynamics interest me, that's all. Specially with Rosamonde in their midst."

"Do you think any one of them may have something to do with the theft of the swans and the message?" Stefan frowned.

"I don't know yet. It is obvious that someone doesn't want the Treaty to go through. Why can it not be one of them?"

"If one of them did not want it to go through, he/she could have stayed away and sent in their excuses."

"And risk having a falling out with their country? I don't think so." Re shook his head.

"Just to play safe, I shall bring you some notes on them too. We don't want to rule out anyone as too much is at stake."

"Thanks. What about Klint?" Re's glance flickered to the corner table.

"Harry's secretary?" Stefan asked, surprised. "As far as I know, Harry trusts him explicitly. Klint has been working with Harry for many years now. Why do you ask?"

"Just curious," Re brushed it off. He noticed that Max was helping himself to some coffee. "Excuse me, I think I am going to join him there."

Stefan nodded. Re rose and headed to the coffee table and Stefan turned to the buffet for lunch.

As Re approached him, Max smiled. He looked young and impressionable in his blue suit and yet Re knew that he was a shrewd businessman.

"I believe Rosamonde is helping you out with the message," he said in a low tone.

It was just the opening Re could have hoped for.

"She told you?"

"We share everything. We are quite close, you know. In fact, I have always looked out for her. Call me the protective older brother." He laughed.

Re led him towards a corner table. "Which is why you insisted that she accompany you on this trip and complete her shoot for the film. Isn't that kind of extreme protective behaviour?"

They settled down by the table and Max shrugged. "She has had a kind of difficult and strange childhood."

"What do you mean by strange?" Re's interest was piqued and he leaned forward in anticipation.

"Please keep this between us but she has not had a normal childhood. And I think one of the main reasons was that she got immensely obsessed with Empress Elisabeth. She watched the Romy Schneider movies over and over again and I believe that subconsciously she connected so deeply with her that she began acting, thinking and behaving like her. Once she even listed the common things between herself and Elisabeth and we teased her about it, saying it was more wishful thinking but she was dead serious."

"What were the similarities that she listed?"

Max shrugged. "Oh, I don't quite remember now. But things like how she loved to travel and indulged in sports of all kinds—Rosy is also an excellent swimmer and rider like Elisabeth or how both had a poor digestion, didn't like crowds and dabble in poetry. And a host of other things that she painstakingly jotted down. Now when I look back, for a child of 12, she was rather well-researched."

He took a sip of the coffee, his eyes gliding spontaneously to his sister at the round table.

"I remember we stayed in Starnberg for two summers and she would go missing for hours. One day, our local governess couldn't find her and when she did, Rosy was drenched wet and cold. We never knew what happened. She wouldn't speak and she seemed exhausted. My parents packed up on the same day. Our governess was fired and she was very upset because she really loved Rosy. But after that I have never allowed my sister to visit this part of the world alone."

Both fell silent. A tiny ray of understanding began to flicker in Re's mind. Finally, he was beginning to get a glimmer into Rosamonde's mind...a glimmer that was fast turning into a strong beam.

"I noticed a tattoo on your sister's arm. She said that it was a birthmark," he prompted.

"It's an anchor and it isn't a birthmark. She insisted on getting that tattoo made when she was a child, watching the Romy Schneider movies. She had discovered that Elisabeth had an anchor mark on her arm and she was determined to get one too, in solidarity with her hero."

Somehow the knowledge came as no surprise. Re had kind of guessed that it was a tattoo and yet Rosamonde had explicitly told him it was a birthmark. Why had she lied? *Or had she?* What if she genuinely believed that it was a birthmark? Re shook his head in confusion. This revelation threw a different light on things.

"What I don't understand is why my sister is the sudden focus of this investigation. What does all of this have to do with what's happening here?" Max frowned.

Re leaned against his chair, finishing off his coffee. "Someone wants your sister involved in the search for the song. We don't know why and that is why I am trying to glean as much information as possible to figure out the reason for her involvement."

Max nodded. "I understand. I wish I could be of more help. All I know is that I don't want her to be involved in anything dangerous."

"I won't let anything happen to your sister," Re promised.

Max stared at him a moment and something flickered in his blue eyes. "You like her, don't you?" he asked with sudden insight.

Re met his gaze head on. "I want you to share with me, every tiny detail that you think may be important in solving this mystery. Anything at all."

Max wet his lips with his tongue nervously and glanced at his cup. "I will."

Re waited for him to continue, hoping that Max would mention the talk Re had overheard that morning but he didn't.

"Excuse me...I think we need to head back to the meeting room," the media honcho said, indicating the sudden bustle at the long table.

Re nodded. The moment was lost. Max had refrained from confiding in him about that morning's telephone conversation. The investigator leaned against his chair and watched as the group dispersed. Adria was leaning on Harry's arm, followed by Klint Capa and Carlo was lagging behind. Leon was still talking to Rosamonde, reluctant to leave her side. Max joined them and swung an arm around his sister's shoulder. It was obvious that he really loved her. Re sighed and headed to the buffet table. His stomach was suddenly growling.

7

It was two o'clock when Re got back to his room. The first thing he did was open the envelope that Stefan had given him, his heart beating in anticipation. Although the officer had assured him that Rosamonde was squeaky clean, Re was unashamedly curious about her. In fact, there existed an abnormal craving to know more about her.

He laid out the single typed sheet and the newspaper clippings on his writing desk. He thrust back his sliding spectacles and scanned the contents with an eagerness which rivalled all his earlier investigations.

Born in Munich on 14th December, daughter of wealthy parents, the Hartmans. Father, a brain surgeon and mother, a software consultant. Brother Maximillian Hartman, owner of media conglomerates. Rosamonde was accomplished in a stunning variety of fields—a qualified documentary filmmaker with at least nine films to her credit, some of which had won awards at international film festivals, music composer who played the violin, a good horse rider, excellent swimmer, had published a book of poetry titled *Yearnings* when she was 21, had travelled widely and even been to a spiritual retreat in India. No criminal record, not even a parking ticket. Had an array of boyfriends and been engaged for a short while, before it had been called off. A steady group of university friends and some professionals that she kept in touch with and met up occasionally. Had suffered from depression when she had been in her early twenties. Re paused. *Depression?* He found it hard to believe or imagine. She was such a vibrant person, poised and confident... But there had to be some truth to this comment although a quick background check on paper could hardly justify the true experiences of a person, specially someone who was as active and dynamic as Rosamonde. What could have led to the depression? He wondered.

Re glanced at the newspaper clippings attached to the sheet, with a sudden sense of reserve. Out of the blue, he felt guilty of the knowledge he possessed. It was unfair to Rosamonde, this in-depth and surreptitious peeking into her life. Almost voyeuristic. Almost unethical. But then, of course, it wasn't. He was doing his job and it was a professional hazard. He wanted to eliminate all chances of mis-interpretation of the situation. In fact, he was doing her a favour, wasn't he? He was trying to assemble a logical reasoning for her involvement without actually criminalising her presence.

Re collected the clippings and the info sheet and thrust them back into the envelope. He opened a drawer and dropped the envelope into it, closing the drawer with a deliberate push. He had seen enough. He had no reason to suspect Rosamonde of anything. She could not be involved in this criminal activity of her own volition, of that he was sure. Now it was up to him to delve into the mind of Mr Virus to decipher his desire to involve Rosamonde in his conspiracy.

His cell phone beeped and Re glanced at it, surprised. It was his mother.

"*Maman*, just the person I was thinking about."

"*Mai oui, mon cher*," Maria said. "I got your message. What did you want to talk about so urgently?"

"Do you remember if we ever visited Lake Starnberg? When I was a child or..." he began.

"Of course, I remember. You were ten when your father and I took you on a holiday to the southern part of Bavaria," Maria said, her voice as clear as if she was in the same room with him.

"Oh, no wonder, I had this feeling of déjà vu—" Re said, frowning. But strangely, he had no concrete recollection of this holiday.

"Yes, it was quite a trip. I have mixed memories about it. It was on the last day of the trip that you got lost for hours... We looked everywhere for you. We were almost on the verge of reporting to the police, when Arthur, a waiter from the hotel, found you. You were gone for more than five hours and they were the worst five hours of my life."

"Where was I?"

"We don't know. You were sitting by the lake apparently, by this 1,000-year-old oak tree, in a park. You could barely speak, you were so drained and frozen."

Re's frown deepened. He could remember nothing, but he felt that he ought to. Like it was important. The blank space in the place of his memory suddenly worried him. Why did he not remember such an important incident in his life? But at least now he understood that the water from the vision, had to be Lake Starnberg. It *was* the lake in his vision.

"But why do you ask?" Maria asked.

"I am not sure but I think I was at the same shore of Lake Starnberg today... Probably being there again sparked a vision... It was strange. Anyway, do you remember the hotel we stayed in?"

"It was very pretty, near the station. I'll find the exact name and address and send it to you."

"*Merci, Maman.* I'll talk to you soon."

"Re, whatever it is you are on, be careful."

Re couldn't help smiling. "I'll be fine. Don't worry. And *Joyeux Noël, Maman*."

"*Joyeux Noël, mon cher. Je t'aime.*"

Re was thoughtful as he switched off the phone. His mind was a whirlpool of confusion.

The conversation with his mother had at least cleared one mystery. He had been to Starnberg as a child. But why could he not remember the exact details of the trip and specially the day he went missing? Something odd had transpired during the trip. Something unpleasant—in fact, it must have been so disturbing that he had sub-consciously removed all reference to it from his brain. What he did know now though, with the certainty of the rising sun, was that he *had* to find exactly what happened that day. He had to find the hotel and Arthur... Perhaps that was the place to begin.

So far, his visions had only been about the places he had visited and it was then that he actually revisited the place in an effort to find a solution or protect it or even prevent disaster from happening. Like he had visited the Schloss Leopoldskron in Salzburg or Lund University in Sweden. But this vision was different. Was it a warning or a reminder? A premonition or an awakening? Was something going to happen at Lake Starnberg, or was it just a recreation of something that had happened to him in the past? Re felt confused. He had never experienced this kind of a duality in his mind before. He had always been sure...that the vision was leading him to a place which needed him. But here he was already, almost as a prelude to his vision. Why had the chronology changed? And what exactly was leading to it?

For the first time since he arrived, Re wondered at what he really was doing here. Was he here because Stefan had invited him? Or was he here because destiny had led him to discover something—something that he had to revive, investigate and reinstate? Some energy had beckoned him back to the spot and he had arrived here, unaware that he already shared a strong connection to this place. It was now time to figure how that connection was to fit in the present lay of things. Where did the treaty and Rosamonde fit into all of this, if at all? Rosamonde with the haunting blue-green eyes and windblown hair and with words that seem to come from some weird reserved secret place within her. And why was he even thinking of her? He had work to do...he was here to assist Stefan... Re shook his head in frustration. *If only he could remember something...anything!*

"This is our final round and chance of discussions. By evening we have to lock this Treaty," Harry announced, as they took their places around the table.

"That's right," Adria agreed. "We already have a list of pro-opinions. We just need to begin eliminating the contentions."

"Since the Treaty focusses on arts, culture, borders and opportunities, I say we each write down, what is explicitly non-negotiable for their country," Carlo added.

"For God's sake, Carlo, there can be nothing non-negotiable at this stage. Each one of us here is accomplished and already represents these fields in our full professional capacity—I am a wood carver and my shops and companies offer jobs to hundreds. You do a number of things, apart from being politically inclined. I happen to know that your designing is excellent. Adria here needs no introduction. You won't find a more skilled rider in her country and she has changed the face of equestrian history. Max here is a media magnate and handles PR companies for his country and Leon is a researcher and a historian and his educational institutes are not just a family legacy, they are important landmarks in German academic culture. We are here to turn the non-negotiable to negotiable. It is important to have just the right mindset for it." That was the longest speech Harry had given and Adria looked at him appreciatively.

"This Treaty aims to join our forces in peace, open opportunities and sharing of resources. Co-existence and harmony are the key factors," Leon added.

"Don't forget that the EU has strengthened the continent in the face of a hugely bipolar world, making it unipolar due to the fall of the USSR and fragmentation of communist thought," Adria cut in.

"Also, this Treaty could be a foundation for a larger one among all the EU members, so each one of us should support it unconditionally," Max remarked.

Carlo pursed his lips. "And what about history? And the past..."

"That has to be overcome," Max retorted. "That is the basic objective, isn't it?"

They all glanced at each other and nodded.

"So shall we begin with the final shortlist?" Adria asked.

She opened her folder of notes and a small slip of paper flickered to the floor. She frowned as she picked it up and her eyes widened in surprise as she read the single line.

Ask Carlo what he did and if he doesn't tell you, look into his room.

❄

It was 2:30 pm when Re and Rosamonde slipped into the back seats of the cab.

"Did you have lunch, Ben?" Re enquired.

"*Ya*, I did. The hotel has been kind enough to welcome me into their kitchen. Where to next?" Ben asked.

"What comes next on Sisi's route?"

"Rose Island. But you should keep it for a sunny day," Ben said, casting a glance at the shadowy sky.

"Let's go to Berg Chapel," Rosamonde suggested.

Re glanced at her. "You mean near Berg Castle, where King Ludwig II was imprisoned and died."

"That's right. The chapel was built in memory of him. I would need some time to take a few shots as well."

"The chapel is called Votivkapelle Memorial Chapel. It will take us about half an hour to reach the place. I need to go slow, as the roads are very slippery especially near Ferdinand-von-Miller-Straße and Schatzlgasse on the way to König-Ludwig-Weg," Ben explained. "Are you sure you still want to go?"

"Of course," Rosamonde glanced at Re and nodded.

Ben drove out of the Kaiserin Hotel on to main road and Re angled towards his companion.

"Tell me more about how Ludwig II died."

"As you already know, King Ludwig II spent tons of the royal money building his castles and these amazing structures in the most picturesque spots. He was fond of art and was a lover of beautiful things but in the process, the state treasury was emptied into these lavish structures. That is why he was called the mad king. He was a loner and had very few close friends. One of them of course was his cousin Elisabeth," Rosamonde explained. "It was on

June 13th, 1886 that he died. He was already in captivity at Berg Castle during that time. It is said that it was in the afternoon that he suggested that he and his doctor, Von Gudden, go for a walk, without his attendants, around the Schloß Berg Park, and along the shore of the lake. They were supposed to be back by 8 pm but they never returned. It was a stormy night and a search party went out from the castle. They searched for three hours in the rain and it was around 11:30 in the night, that both the king and his doctor were found floating very close to the shore. The king's watch had stopped at 6:45 pm. There were signs of blows on the head and neck as well as strangulation marks on Gudden's body and this led to the suspicion that Ludwig had strangled him. Strangely, officers patrolling the park hadn't heard any sounds or anything and hence it was declared that the King had died by drowning."

"Tragic," Re remarked. "Does anyone know what really happened?"

"There are theories of course and lots of opinions. But basically, two main theories can be considered. The first one is of course suicide and the second is that the King was murdered. The autopsy report revealed that there was no water in his lungs so the suicide theory falls apart. Also, he was an excellent swimmer, so how could he drown? On the other hand, some say he was shot while he was trying to escape but there were allegedly no bullet holes in his jacket. That afternoon, Sisi was staying on the opposite bank of Lake Starnberg, at Possenhof. Earlier in the afternoon apparently Ludwig had sent her a note, perhaps to let her know the time of his walk around the lake. It is said that she had been walking along the shore all afternoon and had a carriage waiting to transport him to Munich or Austria. A boat was supposed to bring him to the shore. This came out much later, in 1933, when his personal fisherman Jakob Lidl claimed that he was hiding in the bushes with his boat to help Ludwig II escape. But allegedly, just as Ludwig was about to climb into the boat he was shot. We don't know what really happened, but the fact is that unfortunately, Ludwig never arrived on the other side of the lake and Sisi kept waiting for him. And that is the end of the sad story. So you see, there is a lot of speculation but no real answers."

Re was silent, as her words sank in. Ben manoeuvred the car expertly on the white slippery curves, as they passed snow-laden trees and houses, the early afternoon sun dull and uninspiring.

"And why do you think it is necessary that this should be our next halt?"

Rosamonde smiled. "The Empress and Ludwig were very close and were even alluded to as 'soulmates'. I think it would be important to explore that part of the lake because of what the poem read—*Silent we soared but deeply we understood, the song that our souls once sang...* We need to cover all the areas which suggest the soul connection between the two. And what better place than the one where he allegedly drowned?"

A spark of interest ignited in Re's eyes. "Of course, it makes perfect sense. Also, those lines in the poem about the lake shrouded in gloom—in reflection, I don't think it means the Possenhofen shore at all. I think it meant the Berg side of the lake...cloaked in perpetual gloom because King Ludwig II lost his life there."

"You are absolutely right!" she agreed promptly. "Although admittedly it makes me nervous—this whole Ludwig drowning episode. Elisabeth was naturally devastated. He was the one person she connected with. And suddenly he was gone. I can imagine that she must have almost lost her mind too. She did speak out against what happened but it was already too late. She had lost her dearest friend and she didn't know what to do anymore. After that she stopped coming to Lake Starnberg. Somehow, when you think of it, the whole affair leaves a terrible taste in your mouth."

Re nodded. "Would put a suspense novel to shame. Two cousins from royal families, as different from the rest of their royal family and kin as they can be, free-spirited, artistic and poetic, lonely, misunderstood — soul-mates in every sense of the word. I can't help feeling sorry for them."

Rosamonde stared out of the window, her head poised and for the second time Re noticed how she thought with her body.

Stefan was in his office, his mind occupied with the interview with Mrs Becker. He still felt sorry for her and her son. But consequences had to be faced... Consequences of communication gaps, over-ambitions, stress and even irrational acts. His cell beeped interrupting his flow of thought and he was surprised to see a message from Adria.

"Could you please meet me in 5 minutes outside the conference room? It is urgent."

Instant curiosity clamped Stefan. Now what was up? Some new development? He rose promptly and hastened up the steps towards the conference room. Adria was waiting for him and without a word handed him a slip of paper. The expression on her face was stern but calm.

"It was between the pages of my folder," she said, calmly.

The officer studied the slip—the single line was pasted in caps and small alphabets. Somewhat similar to the message they had received. Had the same person issued this suggestion?

"Any idea, who could have access to your folder?"

"It is on the table when we leave the room for lunch or tea and the room I believe is always locked."

"What about in your room? Could someone have slipped into your room and done it?"

Adria reflected for some moments, then nodded. "Yes, that is possible."

"So, what you do you plan to do? Confront him outright?" the officer asked, as he reread the note.

Adria shook her head. "I don't think so. I think it is your job to find out the truth. I am entrusting it to you."

"I get it. But do you really suspect Carlo? Do you think he may have had something to do with the accident?" he asked, searching her face.

"I barely know that man. I must have met Carlo a couple of times at a conference and a rally but that is it. If he did it, I have no clue why. But I will say this. That man is capable, if that is what you mean to ask. Also, when I announced that I would go for a ride before lunch, he was very much there."

Stefan nodded. "Let me look into it. I will revert if I find anything."

Adria nodded and slipped back into the room.

She had appeared calm and collected and just the tiniest bit anxious. Stefan marvelled at her cool. She had had a close shave with death which this mysterious note had hinted at as foul play. Yet, she had kept a tight hold on her emotions. The officer couldn't help admiring the gutsy lady.

Ten minutes later, Stefan was in Carlo's room on the second floor. He threw a quick look around, everything seemed as it should. He hadn't expected Carlo to be a neat person, yet his room was in perfect order. Stefan stared at the note: *Ask Carlo what he did and if he doesn't tell you, look into his room.*

Stefan had no idea what he should be looking for. An article that shouldn't be in the room, something that would stick out of the place like an oddity. Could this be a red herring to throw the police off form the real culprit? He wondered for a moment. Even if it was, he couldn't let a lead pass without investigation. He had to be doubly sure. The words in the note displayed confidence and an inner knowledge of the incident. Which was why Stefan was positive that he would indeed find damaging evidence. He looked under the bed and in the cupboards, in the toilets and on the writing desk. Everything seemed in order... except...he paused at the desk. On a tray lay a pen, paper cutter, some pins and a pair of thick scissors. Stefan picked up scissors with a gloved hand. He studied the half-open blades and his eyes narrowed. Some fine strands of hair were caught between the grip of the blades. They were the hair of a horse.

Karl and Felix were in deep conversation when Stefan returned to his office.

"Here you are," Karl said, glancing up from the table.

"Any news?" Stefan asked, instinctively.

"Yes, we have narrowed down to three people who own boats in this area," Felix chipped in.

"And?" A sliver of excitement shot up Stefan's spine.

"One of them is Gunter, the stable-hand at the hotel."

"The one you had questioned earlier this morning with regard to Adria's fall."

"That's right. We also did a bit of research and found out that he is actually a freelance journalist, between jobs and is a temp here."

"Sounds like he could be Hans's friend."

"That's what we plan to find out now," Karl replied, his tone grim. "He has already left for the day, but we plan to visit him wherever he is. Want to join us when we trace him?"

"Of course! Unfortunately, it just brings it all uncomfortably closer to the hotel and the Treaty," Stefan said.

If Gunter was connected to Hans, it could mean that the murder was connected to the incidents with the Treaty. That would make matters infinitely worse for this case... Anxiety stung the officer. *Where was Re and what was he doing?*

The cross stood in the water like a lone figure, a gentle reminder of the lonely demise of King Ludwig II, who was found dead on that exact spot. The sky darkened over the lake and yet a small glimmer of the sun's rays sparkled around the cross, almost as if isolating darkness from happiness, beauty from truth and imagination from reality. The sounds of the gently lapping waves seemed to fill the cold winter silence and Re sensed a heightened energy—of solitude, of sadness and regret. Bang opposite, separated by bushes and a small lawn, rose the cream-stoned chapel with its green turret-style roof, simple and elegant in contrast to the flamboyance of the King, memorialising one of the greatest mysteries in German history. Grey stone steps led from either side to the chapel which stood right across the memorial cross by the shore.

Rosamonde stood staring at the glimmering water, the frost more like choppy brush strokes on a canvas. The cracks on the frozen surface around the cross appeared like gnarled cold fingers on the lake.

"There was a big funeral on June 19, 1886, six days after he was found dead. He lay in the State Royal Chapel at his Munich Residence Palace with a posy of white jasmine plucked and placed by Empress Elisabeth, who was completely devastated at her cousin's death. But although his remains are in the crypt of the Michaelskirche in Munich, his heart was put in a silver urn and placed beside his father and grandfather's as per Bavarian tradition, in the Chapel of Mercy at Altötting," Rosamonde stated matter-of-factly. "It marked the end of their very special friendship."

Re was quiet. Somehow the evening, overcast sky seemed to agree with the sombre mood.

"Oh Death, you must return,
My life and my heartbeat...
Don't let my love burn
And turn to ashes in the heat..."

Her voice was soft and her words lingered as if she was coaxing them to float across the skies to willing ears.

Re stared at her, intrigued. In her green fur coat, black beanie and an absent look in her blue-green eyes, she appeared aristocratic and distant. The early evening light seemed to single her out. Re felt strong vibrations from her...a swirling energy he was finding difficult to pin down.

"Elisabeth was staying at Possenhof after his death, when one night, he appeared to her. He stood by her bed and looked sad and asked her not to be afraid. He told her that death had not given him peace. He also told Elisabeth that she had much to endure before she joined him. When she asked what if he was a dream, he asked for her hand and the cold wet grip of death touched her. She understood then and begged him not to leave her. But he disappeared..." Her voice was a whisper and displayed just the slightest tremor. "He even predicted that her death would be quick and she would not suffer. That's exactly how Elisabeth died, ten years later. A swift knife wound..."

A chill ran down Re's spine. Every word that Rosamonde spoke, dangerously exposed her involvement with the royal couple. It made him simultaneously curious and uncomfortable.

"Would you find it odd if I tell you something?" she asked, suddenly.

"Very few things fit into the definition of odd for me nowadays. So, go ahead," Re replied.

"For long now, I have had the strangest feeling. Quite incredible actually. This unique connection—very deep connection to King Ludwig II."

Re maintained an impassive expression. "You have done extensive research on Empress Elisabeth and King Ludwig for your film. It's natural that you feel a kind of affinity for them."

"You remember the placard on the boathouse on the way here which said that King Ludwig II took the boat to go to the other side of the lake to meet his soulmate, Elisabeth? That's exactly how I feel—like they are my soulmates. I feel so close to them, so perfectly aligned to their emotional journeys. As if their journey is entwined in mine. As if we are indeed soulmates."

"It isn't impossible because soulmates can reach out through many life times. An instinctive sense of connection is not uncommon."

She was quiet and Re knew that more was coming. He sensed a deep-seated excitement uncoiling within him. He wanted to know as much as he could about this enigmatic woman. It was more an instinctive curiosity to understand this complex woman, than anything else, he told himself. And perhaps now, slowly she was beginning to trust him, to open up....

"I can *see* him, you know. And *feel* it all...his feeling of helplessness, the struggle to break free, his breathlessness... I can see him gasping for breath and I want to reach out and help him...jump into the water and try to save him, bring him back to the shore safely..." She whispered.

Re noticed her tight clutch on the railing of the wall and her knuckles shone white.

"You have an active imagination," Re said, caution in his voice.

She continued to stare at the wooden cross in the water, her body strangely still. "Is that what you want to call it? My imagination? Well, it's not."

"Tell me what you feel," he commanded, in a soft tone.

She took time responding, inhaling deeply as if fortifying herself with the cold, snowy breeze. When she spoke, her words flew out like hot lava.

"It's like I am right there, waiting, waiting for him to appear but fearing deep in my heart, that something awful is going to happen. That he may not escape. But he deserves to. He can't live his life as a prisoner in his own house. He is a free spirit like me. We need to be together, we understand each other. We share things...we create poetry together... such a precious gift...such warmth of emotion...such free spirits, unbridled by custom, and brave enough to see it and live it... But now he is drowning and I can't help him. Oh, the maddening frustration! I can feel it in my gut...he is sinking, he is dying and I have this feeling of having lost everything in life, everything that means anything to me... this immense wave of grief, this choking in my chest—" She broke off, her hand on her heart, her head sunk in volatile emotions, she seemed to have no control over.

Re leaned forward swiftly and rested his hand firmly on her arm. Her breathing was laboured and tears were streaming down her cheeks.

"Rosamonde..." He tried to hide his deep concern. He didn't wish to frighten her away.

She turned to stare at him, a wild look in her eyes. "Don't you see him? He is drowning!"

For the briefest moments, her tone of conviction made him falter. His attention was riveted to the lake. Was someone actually in there? Had he missed something? But the waters were still, frozen and undisturbed. Relief locked with an unease he couldn't immediately explain. His gaze returned to her anxious, angry face, studying her closely.

"Get a grip, Rosamonde. No one is drowning, I can't see anyone in the lake," he assured.

"Of course, there is... Let me go!" she struggled.

He released her hand instantly but stayed close, worry gnawing at his insides. She whipped back to the lake with urgency and self-doubt. For long moments, she stared at the still lake and then suddenly, her body slumped. Re instantly reached out and steadied her by the shoulders.

"It's all right... I am here," he said, softly.

"I... I am sorry...I thought... I..." she stammered, shaking her head.

"You thought what?" Re was concerned.

"Ludwig...he drowned here, right on this spot... I know it sounds irrational to you, but I thought I saw... I saw him thrashing in the water, struggling... I am sorry. You think I am quite insane, don't you? But I am not." She straightened and her head titled proudly, as she met his gaze unflinchingly.

He noticed the pensive look in her deep blue-green eyes and yet her face emanated a stately glow. Re could sense the coiling and uncoiling of energy, strong and high-volt and suddenly, for the first time, he recognised it. In a flash, he understood why he had felt this immense magnetic pull towards her. It was because they were kindred spirits. Their energies were alike and aligned. He had sensed it at first sight but it had confused him then. He hadn't expected to meet anyone like Rosamonde on this trip. As a matter of fact, he had never met *anyone* with the same throbbing energy before and it had taken him aback... He had refused to acknowledge the truth that had been facing him ever since his first meeting that morning with Rosamonde. It had taken him the whole day to fully grasp it and post a name on it. But at that moment, standing against the cold frozen lake with the isolated cross and the darkening sky and streaks of pale sunlight, Re knew.

Rosamonde had captivated him. The three encounters he had with her were of the oddest nature. She seemed to be in a perpetual, delirious state of mind. And yet, she seemed to know what she was talking about. She wasn't rambling. She was lucid and in grip of her emotions. Had she really seen Ludwig drowning? Some would call it hallucinating.

Re's experience of the psychic and un-natural was deep and he was not above believing that such an experience was possible. He rarely brushed something off as a mere product of imagination. It wasn't a common occurring, of course. And often, with him, they were just an occasional flash of vision. Was Rosamonde from the same category as him or was she experiencing something different? A strong suspicion was taking root in his mind. It wasn't impossible. He had heard many tales of reincarnation. Could Rosamonde be the Empress of Austria's reincarnation? Her 'hallucinations', the way she slipped from third person to first person, her reactions in the museum—all made sudden sense. Were flashes of her past life encroaching into her present life and confusing her reality? Was Rosamonde indeed Sisi from last life? Re didn't dare voice his suspicion aloud. If there was even a one percent chance of him being wrong, he could wreak havoc in her life. And he didn't wish to inflict more suffering than she was already enduring. His theory would remain a secret within him. If necessary, forever.

"Do you think I am insane?" she asked again, the slightest tremor to her voice.

"No, not in the least." He was quick to reassure.

"You don't? You believe I saw Ludwig in the water?" She baited.

She looked at him straight. Re faltered. It was difficult to avoid the direct gaze, honest and daring. No, she certainly did not seem insane. But this continuous talk of Ludwig...

"Rosamonde, I wouldn't pass a casual judgement on something this serious. Specially not until I know any relevant background information. You claim you saw the King, but I didn't see him and it's a fact that he isn't there. So, then what makes you stake a claim for sanity? Obviously, you possess some inner knowledge that you need to share with me before I assess your claim, don't you think?"

"Re, any sensible person would accuse me of hallucinations, you know that."

"I am not 'any person'. And I sense this deliberate attempt on your part to force me to admit to your insanity, highly objectionable. It's as if you want me to admit that you are insane. Why?"

"Because even if you don't, I think *I am insane*...or *something*! And have been for many years...this obsession with two dead people, it's madness... I should have stopped this nonsense long ago...my mother had warned me, my doctor had told me... I went through depression just thinking that I was going mad...I don't know what to do anymore... It was a bad idea to come here to Starnberg...to this place which has been haunting me all my childhood...to Sisi...why doesn't she leave me alone!" Her cry of anguish was deep, as tears began streaming down her cheeks again and she sobbed with her head in her hands.

Re moved forward swiftly and held her in his arms, allowing her to release the storm inside her. His heart was thudding with an emotion he could barely understand. All he knew was that Rosamonde was in pain and she needed him. And he would be there for her. No matter what.

The snow began to fall softly around them and the sky darkened. A sharp wind picked up and seemed to whittle between them, creating a space of awareness. Re continued to hold her in a gentle embrace as the wind whistled around them and the snow sprinkled on their coats. Gradually, her sobs tapered into hiccups and she raised her head.

"I am really sorry... I don't know what overcame me. I am normally not like this...high-strung, babbling..."

"Shh...it's all right," he said in a soothing tone. "I think we are done with this place. It's freezing. Let's go find some hot coffee."

She shivered. "Coffee would be good."

She sniffed, looking small and vulnerable and Re had an impression of a young innocent girl, struggling to be an adult in a complex world.

"Rosy?" a voice interjected into their cocoon of camaraderie.

Startled, Re and Rosamonde turned around to face a woman in a black cloak. Her face was partly hidden by her hood. Re inhaled a quick sharp breath. She was the same woman he had seen lurking in the background, on the previous occasions.

8

L eon stared at the single line taunting him from a half sheet of paper. It had been tucked into his folder and it was while he was making some notes that the slip of paper had peeked out. His heart raced at the implication of it. Who could have written it and what did he or she want? More importantly, what did he know and how much?

The treaty meeting had adjourned for tea and they were in the breakfast room, pouring themselves steaming cups of tea and coffee. Leon dropped the note into his pocket, passed a restive hand through his blonde hair and glanced around for Max. He was talking to Harry and Adria, his face animated with the conversation. Leon took his cup of coffee to the window. Staring out into the pristine snowy landscape, he sipped the coffee, a little aloof, his handsome face creased in deep thought. He had to get Max alone somehow and quickly, before they headed back to their final round of discussions. Max was his best friend. Being a media baron, he had some fantastic ideas and they had worked together on several projects and liked and did similar things including his passion for the latest media acquisitions. It was one of the reasons why he had taken so much interest in the Treaty. Max and he had dreamed of creating something huge like that. They had played a major role in the initial discussions for the Treaty. Max was the reason he had met Rosamonde. Leon trusted Max completely…until now…

And Rosy—she still made his heart flutter…if he was entirely honest with himself, he knew that his choice of the swans as symbols for the Treaty, were completely influenced by his feelings for Rosamonde. The swans were his way of expressing his love for her. He wondered if she still wore the swan ring he had gifted her. Studded with diamonds, it had been a birthday gift for her. And she had loved it. The swan was their soul bird—a shared secret just between them, but then they had had their differences and she had stormed out of his life...but not forever... He still cared deeply for her and he was positive that she was aware of it and deep down in her heart, reciprocated his feelings.

With a deep sigh, he turned for a second cup of coffee, caught Max's eye and beckoned him. Max murmured something to his colleagues, detached from the group and approached his friend with a cocked eyebrow.

"You look intense," he remarked.

"That's a relief, I thought I looked murderous," Leon mumbled.

"Why?" Max frowned.

Leon extracted the single line note from his pocket and handed it to his friend. "Tell me what games you are trying to play."

Max glanced at the paper. *I know what you did!*

"Mein Gott!" he expelled. "Who wrote this? And why do you think I am playing games with you?"

"Because it's written on your letterhead. Can't miss the embossed emblem. And who else knows my...my secrets?"

"Goodness Leon! I wouldn't be so stupid as to send you a note, would I?" Max thrust the paper back to Leon, clearly irritated. "You better show that to the police."

Leon faltered, glancing at his friend. "You mean, you..."

"I didn't and I take mighty offence that you even thought of it. Don't let your anger colour your trust. How and why would I ever do this to you?"

Leon sighed. "You are right. You wouldn't. But I saw your letterhead and was just so angry and upset..."

"Anyone can steal a letterhead. It's lying in my room on the desk."

"You are right. But then who and why?"

"Better share that with Officer Weiss. Strange things are happening here. The theft of the swans and that bizarre note involving Rosamonde... Adria almost died this morning and now this. It's obvious someone is determined to upset the Treaty."

Leon nodded. "I guess you are right. I'll show it to the police."

Almost as if on cue, Officer Stefan Weiss walked into the room, his gaze cruising the room to rest on Leon. He looked tall and dignified and Leon liked his quiet yet determined demeanour.

"Can I have a quick word with you?" Stefan asked.

"Of course, Officer. I have something to talk to you about too."

"I'll see you in the Conference room," Max cut in and excused himself.

"As you know the swans that you so painstakingly brought from Neuschwanstein have been stolen. And we are trying our best to retrieve them but there is no trace of them yet," Stefan said.

"Oh no! The swans are invaluable and precious pieces of history. I gave it a great deal of thought and had to justify how apt they were as perfect symbols of peace and love.

And I did have to move many papers for permission to move them here for the Treaty signing."

"I am aware of that. And I do know that eventually the German Police will find them. Probably just not in time? Or just in the nick of time? Which is what I wanted to talk to you about. In the eventuality that we fail to retrieve them in time for the signing tomorrow evening, I was wondering if we could have a Plan B. Do you know of any other castle where we can find a similar swan?" Stefan asked, keeping his tone low.

"That would be a real pity," Leon said. "It can be very difficult. Neuschwanstein was where King Ludwig's love for Lohengrin and swans came together. He ensured that it was imbedded into his decors and I am not aware if that is the case with the other castles. But, more importantly, those swans were our mascot. I am responsible for them. We have to find them."

Stefan nodded, pursing his lips, his expression thoughtful.

"Officer, I have something I want to share with you too. Look at this." Leon handed him the slip of paper.

Stefan's face registered surprise. Another note?

The café was empty and the quaint bell jingled over the door every single time some local walked in to buy some bread. It was cosy and the small Christmas tree in the corner, added the necessary Christmassy cheer to the café. The wooden décor and the shelves displaying an assortment of wooden deer felt warm as opposed to the biting cold outside.

Re observed the lady who sat opposite Rosamonde. She was middle-aged with peppered hair drawn tightly back from a tired forehead. Her face displayed deep lines and as she smiled at Rosamonde, she appeared a little resigned and pensive.

"I don't expect you to remember it all, of course," she said gently, her English heavily accented.

Their conversation slipped between German and English and Re strained to catch the flow.

"Oh, but I do, Mrs Merwelt...I mean at least parts of it," Rosamonde said. "I am just feeling terrible that I am the cause of so much suffering."

"You cannot blame yourself, my dear. What happened was not your fault. Matty was my sister, but she was partly to blame of course. She was too attached to you and felt responsible for you. She felt she allowed you to play games that affected your mind. That day when no one could find you, she was convinced that something had happened to you. What a relief it was when you returned, safe and sound. But Mrs Hartman, your mother, dismissed her from service for irresponsibility. Matty was mortified. She had looked after you for years and she was heartbroken that she was dismissed so easily. She tried to reach you several times and even years later she wrote to you and tried to call you, but you didn't respond."

"She tried to reach me? But I didn't receive any phone calls or letters." Rosamonde frowned.

"She did. And when you didn't respond, she kind of gave up. I believe that the thought that she would never see you again really broke her. And the guilt that she had somehow been careless and played with your life. She passed away last year and I believe that was her only regret."

"I am really sorry to hear this. I would have loved to meet Matty again. She was soft and gentle and she encouraged me to be me."

"Anyway, when I heard that you were coming, I wanted to meet you one final time and explain things. I hope you don't blame my sister for what happened."

"I don't and nothing has happened. I am fine. I am a healthy, hardworking woman, none the worse for my highly imaginative mind," Rosamonde assured.

"Is that why you were following us?" Re cut in.

Mrs Merwelt glanced at Re and nodded. "I wasn't sure how and when to speak to Rosy. All I knew was that I was determined to meet her."

"Sorry to hear about your sister. I am sure that the entire incident was a misunderstanding."

"And a little harsh on Mrs Hartman's part to cut Matty off from Rosy's life. Even if she was just the Governess. She had really loved the child."

"How is Conrad?" Rosamonde asked.

Mrs Merwelt smiled. "You remember my nephew?"

"Yes, of course I do."

"He is a writer now and lives in Munich with his girlfriend, but comes for the occasional holiday. Anyway, I would have to leave now. I do hope you will forgive my sister, if at all there is any ill-will."

"I assure you there is none." Rosamonde was quick to respond.

"And I wish you good luck! Goodbye..."

Mrs Merwelt rose with a half-smile, and Rosamonde embraced her warmly. Then the senior lady walked out of the door into the cold and the bell jingled merrily, announcing her departure. Almost as if it was celebrating the successful closure of a long pending affair. Her mug was half-full, the coffee barely touched. Rosamonde stared at the closed door for a few minutes before turning to her companion.

"Poor Matty. I wish I had known. But I was too involved in my own world. I vaguely remember Mama telling me that Matty would come no more and I feel that I may have protested. But Mama being Mama, hot-tempered, always had her way. I guess I must have just given up. Who knew that the poor woman had been riddled with guilt all these years, had suffered and the consequences would be so severe," she remarked.

"They say a string of actions and reactions make life. But it's not only your own actions. It's a combination of actions—of the people around you, people in your circles and outside your circles, sometimes random people who happen to cross your path or deliberately cross your path... so many permutations and combinations of actions and life is a sum of all them. That is why it is always so difficult to get to a root of any problem. The roots have spread and entangled in criss-cross tentacles, so much so that finding the beginning and end is humanly impossible."

"Put like that life does seem infinitely complicated." Rosamonde smiled.

Re smiled back. "It does, doesn't it? The trajectory of human foibles."

"Do you think Sisi's route has revealed anything other than my weaknesses, since morning?" she asked, raising an elegant eyebrow.

"It certainly has, although discovering your 'weakness' as you say, has been quite an interesting journey and an enlightening experience for me."

"I am glad you are amused. But your quest is for the soul-song, not my soul-search."

"And what if both can be found on the same path?"

Rosamonde caught his excited tone. "What do you mean?"

"We have known since morning that Virus wanted you to revisit Sisi's route. Earlier, I thought it was to assist you in finding this soul-song, but we aren't any closer to it, are we? On the other hand, what if it wasn't merely for the soul-song, but also to revive your memories of the past? Revive your insecurities, your so called 'obsession' with Empress Elisabeth?" Re could feel his heart thumping. Was he right? Was he heading towards a breakthrough in the investigation?

"But why? Why would someone want to rake up my past, my emotional connection to the Empress? And who would know about it, anyway? I mean other than Max and perhaps Leon, there isn't anyone..." Rosamonde broke off, staring wide-eyed at Re.

Re stared back at her, his eyes bright and suggestive.

"Max?" she frowned. "But Max is my brother!"

"I am *not* saying Max is the culprit. But he knows you well and he could have shared that knowledge with someone else. He did insist that you accompany him on this trip and suggested that you produce your documentary while he was here with you."

"He was just being a protective brother."

"Perhaps. I am just speculating to understand your involvement in this entire Treaty affair." Re shrugged. He did not mention Max's phone conversation he had overheard that morning. Someone was blackmailing Max perhaps. What had he said on the phone? *I did what you asked me to...now you have to complete your side of the bargain.* What if bringing Rosamonde to Starnberg was Max's part of the bargain?

"What about Leon? He knows me well too," Rosamonde added.

"I am not sure, yet. Stefan told me that it was Leon who selected the swans as the mascot of the Treaty and ensured that they were transferred to Starnberg. It was also Leon who suggested that a play on Lohengrin, the Swan King, be presented before the Treaty, followed by the ball. He seems to have invested a great deal of time and energy into the Treaty. Perhaps more than even Max."

"All the more reason why he would ensure it's safe implementation."

"Right now, all I can say is that someone is using your fondness for the Empress to their devious advantage and I plan to find out what that is," Re said, grimly.

"Did you notice the gathering group outside?" Rosamonde remarked, suddenly.

The investigative journalist turned and glanced outside the glass windows. A purple darkness seemed to be descending rapidly over the street and the street lamps were already on. A couple of men crossed the windows and one of them tried to peer in.

"Time to leave anyway. Let's head back to the hotel and discuss this after dinner." Re rose as he dropped some euros on the table and flung on his jacket.

He experienced a niggle of worry as he escorted Rosamonde to the café door. They had just stepped out into the cold biting wind, when a group of people hustled forward. Bulbs flashed from all directions and Re raised a hand to shield his eyes. What in heavens was happening? He didn't have to wait long to know.

A young man asserted his way between the jostling group and stepped forward, pushing a mic towards Rosamonde even as another young man trained his camera on her.

"Miss Rosamonde Hartman, you claim to be a reincarnation of Empress Elisabeth. Do you have proof?" he demanded in German.

Another man shouted above the din. "Ms. Hartman, what makes you feel that you are the Empress reborn?"

Re's blood curdled, as he braced to face the surging sense of shock. This was beyond anything he could have expected. And the worst scenario Rosamonde could have ever experienced. The questions came hurtling towards her in German and English and he could catch the gist through the sharp and accusatory tone. She glared from one journalist to other, shock and embarrassment written large on her face, as she found her unable to respond coherently.

"Is your claim supported by the Government and politicians?"

"Rosamonde, will you play a major role in the Treaty now that the Government thinks you are a reincarnation?"

"Please share some of your past life details with us."

"Rosamonde, you do know that your claim for reincarnation can change the face of German history and its future?"

The questions were pouring in on her from all directions. But Rosamonde stood frozen and bewildered, her eyes shining bright, the camera flashes stunning away all sense of reality.

"Stop it," she shouted, suddenly, over the din.

But no one seemed to want to listen. The group of journalists was closing in on them like vultures, waiting for their piece of meat, indifferent to any discomfort or pressure. They were joined in by curious passers-by, their snow-covered jackets and beanies a blur of black and white in the gathering dark. It began to snow lightly and the cold in the wind nipped up, sending a shudder down Re's spine.

"Will you please back off?" he cut in sharply. "Ms. Hartman does not wish to comment. Excuse us, excuse me, *Entschuldigen Sie bitte...*"

"But Ms. Hartman...Rosamonde..."

Re clasped Rosamonde's hand in an iron grip and thrust his way brutally through the pack of journalists, cameramen and blinding flashes of the camera. The questions sprung around them as he held on tightly to her and shoved through the crowd. His only thought was to get his companion to the safety of the car. The snow began to make vision difficult and he tried to spot Ben. He hoped against hope that the driver had stayed glued to his parked spot and would rush to their rescue. The journalists followed, stepping on each other's toes, scuffling for some pictures and firing questions like bullets. Rosamonde's hand in his hand was limp and soft as she allowed herself to be led and struggled to stay close to Re. He caught sight of Ben near his car and waved hard to get his attention. At once, the driver straightened, immediately got into the car and turned on the ignition.

Re opened the door of the cab hastily.

"Ma'am, respond to one question, please. Are you a reincarnation of the Empress?" one lady insisted, her camera rolling.

Rosamonde halted. The scrambling crowd suddenly paused. A hush fell on the journalists as the mics strained to reach her and the cameras were trained on her. Everyone waited with bated breath for her response. The snow fell softly but the energy of the moment could have whipped up a snow storm.

Re pressed her hand, warning her to stay cool.

"Ma'am, are you the Empress reborn?" another journalist asked.

"No. I am not," Rosamonde declared, her voice clear and strong.

"But you claimed..."

"I have claimed nothing! I am not the Empress of Austria reborn. I am Rosamonde Hartman and please stop bothering me."

"Rosamonde...one more question...."

"Ms. Hartman..."

Re ignored the volley of questions and nudged Rosamonde. She ducked into the car and he followed suit, shutting the door with a bang. The paparazzi walked along as the car glided, like a frenzied mob trying to take pictures from the windows, their feet crunching in unison on the snow-covered ground. Ben picked up speed and within seconds, the jostling crowd dropped back and merged into the snowfall.

9

"What in heavens just happened!" Re expostulated, as the car headed towards the hotel in the dusk.

"I wish I knew. It was a nightmare," Rosamonde's voice was low.

Re glanced at her quickly. "I don't understand what it all means. How did they get hold of this news and is it even true?"

"You heard me Re, it's not true. And, I can't imagine who must have played such a dirty trick on me."

"Obviously someone who knows your fondness for the Empress and wanted to get you into trouble. And even if it was true…why make the fact public? Why send the paparazzi on you?"

"It's not true, Re, you have to believe me. I am nothing like her. She was an amazing woman, ahead of her times in many ways, but she was also self-obsessed, vain and like a trapped bird in a golden cage…brimming with love, so much love, she didn't know what to do with it. And her poems, they touch my soul as nothing ever, almost as if I have written them—" she cut off mid-sentence, suddenly aware of what that would imply. "I am spiralling…I am so confused, I don't know what I am saying anymore. I need to breathe."

Re was quiet. For moments, when he had pulled her through the crowd, a nameless fear had gripped him. Was it the fear of the mob pressing in on them rather ominously or the startling dread that his worst doubts were being confirmed? That Rosamonde was indeed a reincarnation of the Empress? The thought that had crossed his mind earlier and which he had been determined to suppress at all costs, for everyone's sake, was now exposed in the open and paraded like some cheap piece of meat. If he was so rattled, he could only imagine how the experience could have affected poor Rosamonde.

He turned to her on an impulse and held her hand in his.

"Are you okay?"

She nodded. "It was...unexpected and in a way terrifying. I am so glad you were with me. Thank you for bringing me out of that nightmarish experience. But I shudder to think what would happen if this should pursue."

"It's a nuisance for sure and would certainly create a hindrance in our investigation. I hope they got the message and won't mess with you again," Re assured, trying more to convince himself than her.

"I hope so too."

The car suddenly swerved and began to slide off the road, the headlights like two orange, crooked ribbons on the tar and snow.

"What's happening?" Re frowned, leaning forward to talk to Ben.

"The weather is worsening and the road is slippery, I drove too fast, trying to escape that crowd. Sorry about that, need to slow down," the driver responded, gripping his steering wheel with resolve.

Re nodded. "It's best you stay at the hotel till this messy weather mellows down or clears, Ben. And have a hot meal."

"If you say so. I have many friends at the hotel and I know the kitchens well." Ben glanced at Re through the mirror and smiled wryly. "Sorry to see what happened just now. It was unpleasant indeed. Journalists can be such crazy hounds, chasing blood... I hope you are okay, Miss Hartman?"

Rosamonde nodded. "I am...now. Thank you. But I shall feel a lot better when we are back at the hotel."

"We are almost there." Ben said, his grip firm on the wheel.

"Excuse me, sir...something strange has come up," Felix reported.

"Now what?" Stefan glanced up from his notes.

It was dark outside and the snow reflected white on the window panes. A low hum reverberated outside indicating the rising wind.

"Intelligence has intercepted an odd message. Because it mentioned Feldafing, they instantly contacted Officer Karl. We think you should see it."

He thrust forward the paper and Stefan read the message.

'Treasure confirmed transfer. The dove will fly at 1600 hours, 24/12 Feldafing.'

"Treasure—*mein Gott!* Another puzzle to decode. It seems the pile is growing. This weekend is fast turning into a nightmare." Stefan sighed. "Does Karl have any ideas?"

"I am not sure. This case has all of us stumped, sir. All our leads seem to be coming to a dead end."

Stefan nodded. "I know what you mean. And given the gravity of the situation and the Treaty, it is not a good sign at all."

Re glanced at his watch. It was almost 8 pm. Dinner would be served in half an hour. He needed to sit quietly to think. His room was the perfect haven right now. Quaint and particularly cosy as the snow fell outside in the dark of the evening. He could hear the wind whistling and rising slow and long in a melancholy wail.

His mind was crawling with thoughts. Ben had driven them to the hotel in silence. Re liked his restraint and his control over his curiosity. He had not asked any further curious questions regarding the paparazzi incident or offered any comments. He had minded his own business and Re had sensed a wordless support. Re was glad that Ben had some friends at the hotel and felt at ease that the cab driver would be safe indoors.

As soon as they had arrived, Rosamonde had also gone to her room. He had been hesitant to leave her alone, but she had appeared composed. Much as he was concerned about her, he also didn't wish to appear overtly worried. After all, he had known her only for a day. But what a day it had been...fraught with the strongest energy that had warned him as well as attracted him to her. He was intrigued and yet at the same time, a warning bell seemed to be jangling relentlessly in his brain. *This was just a case*, he reminded himself—the reminder like a harsh record inside his head. *Just a case*. Rosamonde was simply another person he had met on a case. Nothing more. She *couldn't* be anything more. He didn't know her at all. And when he allowed his agitated mind to still a bit, he had to admit that deep down inside him, he didn't trust her. He felt a rush of relief to admit it. He had felt stifled and had self-censored the thought. But now it felt like a huge relief to acknowledge that he did not trust Rosamonde completely. She was smart, beautiful and very intelligent. They even shared their passion for filmmaking and history and in any other circumstance, he would have bonded with her instantly. But right now, he couldn't forget the images that thrust themselves between any excuses that he could form for her. The image of her that dawn, strolling in trance at the station, her talk of death by the lake, her extreme reactions to the vandalised statue of the Empress and the way she spoke about Sisi's dogs and her son...and most importantly the anchor on her forearm, which she claimed was by birth but Max had confirmed was a tattoo... Her talk of connecting with Ludwig and seeing him drowning in the lake...her volatile emotions laced with self-indulgent nudges of insanity...conflicting evidence and images and even more conflicting conclusions. Was Rosamonde indeed a reincarnation of the Empress of Austria? The day's events pointed a strong finger towards its actuality and if it was indeed so, what would be the consequences? To her, to her country, to Austria? Even a mere hint at it had driven the paparazzi hounding after her. What would happen if she indeed turned out to be the Empress in her last life? And, most importantly, what did all of this have to do with this case, with the soul-song and with the signing of the treaty?

Re absently touched the Ganesha idol on the chain round his neck, feeling the cold metal against his fingers, deriving a strange kind of energy from it. His mind was completely in tune with it, sensing it, feeling it...he needed answers... and he knew they were coming....

He sat up suddenly, as a thought clamped on his mind. Had someone already guessed that Elisabeth was Sisi and that is why had entrusted her with the task of finding the soul-song? Because someone *knew* that only Sisi, who had written that poem, would know where it was? That was why Rosamonde was chosen to walk Sisi's route. *Because she was supposed to know where the soul-song was!*

A strange kind of excitement gripped him. If he was right then his search narrowed down instantly to two people who seemed to know Rosamonde intimately. Max and Leon. And both were a part of the Treaty congregation.

He would have to sit up that night and do some more research, he realised, but right now they had a dinner to get through.

Re pulled on a jacket and opened his door. The corridor was empty but as he sauntered towards the staircase, he heard voices from a room. He instantly recognised Max's voice and Re paused.

"You don't think I would put my own sister at risk, do you?" Max hissed. "This was all supposed to be just a kind of a game. I never thought it would come to this."

"You could have consulted me," another voice cut in. It was Leon. "You know I care for her."

"We both do. But you know what a fiasco your last attempt was, don't you? I didn't want to repeat any of that. I didn't want her anywhere near danger..."

"And now you've put her bang in the centre of it!"

"I haven't. It's just...let's wait and see what happens," Max concluded.

"Max, we are playing with fire here. Lives could be at stake. Someone sent me an ominous message from you. Adria has narrowly escaped with her life. Who knows what else is cooking. We can't afford to take risks. You really need to take a call."

"What about you? You brought the swans here, for a reason..."

A door closed loudly in the corridor and Re instantly dropped to his knee, pretending to fiddle with his shoes. It was Harry. He walked down the corridor, a parcel under his arms. Re recognised the man with him—a small figure in a suit and neat tamped down hair, with a thin moustache and a wiry mouth.

It was Klint, Harry's secretary. Their low talk drifted through the silence in the passage to him.

"Make sure it goes first thing tomorrow morning, Klint," Harry said, handing the parcel over to his companion.

"I will personally ensure that, sir," Klint assured.

"Good, because you know how important this is to me. It has to be dispatched at the earliest."

"I do."

"I appreciate it, Klint. I am sorry that you have to spend Christmas away from your family."

"Don't mention it, sir. Anything for the nation and you. My wife and daughter understand this."

Harry smiled. "Thank you! I will make it up to you and them, once we return."

"Thank you very much, sir." Klint sounded pleased.

Re rose, nodded at them and strode briskly down the stairs towards the dining area. His mind was whirring with the conversations he had just overheard. It was amply clear that Max was worried about his sister and didn't completely trust Leon either. What was it that was worrying him so much? Harry's conversation with Klint brought a slight smile to Re's lips. It was a pleasant exchange and Re liked the hint of loyalty and camaraderie in it. But what was in the parcel that Harry had given to his secretary to post? What could be so urgent? What was so important that it had to be dispatched despite the weather condition and the holiday season?

The dining room was a separate conference room, specially designated for the Treaty members. It was carpeted and compact with a long oblong table, the traditional red draperies, two ornate chandeliers and a buffet on the side. Re paused at the large entrance door monetarily, taking in the bustle of the evening, in a sweeping glance.

"Re, just the person I needed to see." Stefan accosted him instantly and holding him by the arm, led him to the farthest corner of the dining area.

"What's up?" Re noticed his serious tone at once, as he seated himself across the table.

"I have some news. But first, tell me if you are any closer to finding the soul-song."

"I don't know. It has been a strange day and I am not at all sure that if any of it is directly relevant and yet I feel as if it is. I am waiting. Almost like something or someone has kept me on hold, on a pause, before releasing the big grand reveal on me. Like a wave of creativity or knowledge unloading on me."

"It all sounds too vague," Stefan frowned. "We need to find the soul-song before tomorrow evening, Re."

"And we will. Trust me. I may not have concrete proof or a lead yet, but I feel it in my guts that I am very close to the crux of the issue."

"I sure hope you know what you are talking about. Because complications just seem to be growing."

"Is it the Treaty?" Re asked.

"Actually, that is finally going surprisingly well. They have reached a consensus and are now drafting the final document. I guess it's going to be a late night for some of them while they complete it for tomorrow. Something else has cropped up. We intercepted a coded message this afternoon. It is cryptic and yet quite to the point."

Re leaned forward, his brown eyes focused on Stefan from behind his glasses.

"The message read: *'Treasure confirmed transfer. The dove will fly at 1600 hours, 24/12 Feldafing.'* That is tomorrow and an exact hour before the Treaty signing at Rose Island."

Re was thoughtful. "Wow! Lake Starnberg seems to have come alive with intriguing happenings. Protest, ET fear, stolen swans, a mysterious soul-song and now this treasure... And, I am assuming that you have no idea *what* the treasure is."

"Not a clue. I mean it could be anything. It has got to be something really precious otherwise it wouldn't be called a treasure, right?"

"*Mai oui*. It could be a code word for documents and articles or a cargo or a parcel. And it could be just about anything and anywhere in Feldafing—here at the hotel or anywhere out there. We need to have some more information, Stefan."

"I am aware that we have very little to go on and yet we cannot ignore the coded message. The German police is keeping a sharp eye on anything suspicious. I am positive that it has something to do with Sisi's Imperial Treaty."

"But you said that the treaty has been kept low profile until it actually happens?"

"Yes, I did. But information can leak. We both know that security has its limitations. Luckily, Intelligence picked up the message by chance and re-directed it to the police here. I can't help feeling there is a connection between the treasure and the Treaty and for that matter, all of what seems to be suddenly happening at Starnberg. I am a little uneasy and that is why I needed you here. To help speed things up and for you to use your psychic instincts and your energy readings to help me figure out the tangle. I feel that it is imperative for us to find the 'the treasure' *before* it is transferred to God knows where, but it is equally imperative that nothing stalls the Treaty. *Nothing*."

Re stared at Stefan, comprehending his anxiety and the gravity of the issue.

"*Bien sûr*... I am here and we will see this through successfully."

"We have until tomorrow evening to decipher what the treasure is. I will get some officers to make a list of possible items that count as treasures in this area. But be warned that the weather is not going to help. Heavy snowfall has been predicted tonight and the next two days and perhaps even a snowstorm tomorrow."

"I love the snow!" Re shrugged.

"Trust you to connect with nature in the midst of a tempest. And I agree, it is stunningly beautiful. Got to go, I need to make a quick phone call before dinner. Let me know if you strike gold."

"And you, if you hear more music."

Stefan paused and a smile lit up his handsome face, displaying his dimples. "Thank you for being here, Re."

"*De rien, mon ami*... Wild snowstorms wouldn't have kept me away." Re returned the smile warmly.

A sudden commotion arose at the entrance of the dining hall.

"How dare you! I have never been more insulted," a furious voice echoed through the hall.

Re rose instantly. He had never heard or seen Harry so angry.

10

It took a few moments for Stefan to firmly nudge the small group to Mrs Weber's empty office. Harry's face was flushed and his usual suave impassiveness was rudely ruffled. Stefan took the Junior Officer aside.

"What happened, Felix?" he asked, in a low tone.

"Sir, we received an anonymous call, saying that the stolen swans were in a parcel that belonged to Mr Harry."

"What? I hope you got the number and have sent it for tracking."

"We will do it, sir. But as per instructions, in any case, we don't allow any parcels to leave the hotel unchecked. And now specially after the anonymous tip, we couldn't ignore the fact that his secretary Klint was carrying a parcel to his car. We stopped him and Mr Harry was furious. I was just doing my job."

"Absolutely," Stefan agreed, glancing at Re.

"We need to see what's in the parcel," Re confirmed.

"Right," Stefan nodded.

Re turned around to glance at the elderly gentleman. He remembered the parcel that he had just seen Harry hand over to Klint. How quickly someone had tipped off the police. Who would have known that Harry had the swans and that he would parcel them off to some place? What was the likelihood, in the first place that such a reputed gentleman would steal the swans, however precious, keep them in his possession and naively parcel them off in front the entire hotel? Harry was too experienced and worldly wise to do any of the said things. And yet, someone had the audacity to accuse him of theft and of secretly getting rid of the antique swans. Would someone do that without proof? And if this mysterious someone already knew that Harry had the swans, why tip off the police at this last minute? Why now? That Harry's ego was hurt and he felt grossly offended at being requested to show the contents of the parcel, was one thing. The possibility of being *wrongly* accused was infinitely worse. Re wondered what would emerge as the truth. The swans in the parcel or Harry's indisputable innocence.

"We are extremely sorry, sir," Stefan pacified, his tone soft but firm.. "The situation is delicate and volatile. Because the swans are missing, the Officers have standing instructions to examine every parcel that goes out of the hotel. We are just being thorough and we mean no insult."

"You can't seriously mean that this parcel would contain the stolen swans?" Harry snapped, with deliberate, icy coolness.

"No, not at all. But we would still have to check. It is now routine."

"But your officer said that they got a tip off," Klint spoke up.

"We did," Stefan admitted.

"What tip off?" Harry's eyes narrowed.

Stefan glanced at Re, a little anxiously. Re knew that if Harry heard of the direct accusation, he would blow his top and the situation could escalate out of proportion, affecting the Treaty.

"I am afraid we can't reveal that. I request you to submit the parcel for a quick appraisal. It would barely take a minute," Stefan said.

"But it contains personal, sensitive material that I wouldn't want to expose to the world."

"No one will know what it contains, except us, I promise."

Harry glanced at his secretary and nodded. Re felt a rush of relief and he sensed Stefan exhale a slow breath. Felix brought the box-like parcel to Mrs Weber's table. It made a jangling noise as he deftly slit the wrapping paper. Re and Stefan waited with bated breath. The moment of truth was here. Felix tipped the box and something slid out. It was an intricately carved wooden crown.

Re whistled spontaneously. "*C'est exquisite!* Did you do this yourself?"

Harry nodded. "It's a mould for an administrative purpose for the State. I just finished working on it. I carry my tools everywhere with me. It's my passion," Harry shrugged.

"*Magnifique,*" Re repeated, as he took a closer look at the crown.

"And as you can indisputably see, it's not the swans," the ex-politician reminded, his tone dripping with sarcasm.

"Thankfully not," Stefan agreed, looking a little abashed. "We are sorry we had to put you through this trouble."

"I don't condone but I will try to understand."

Re wondered if he would. Either condone or understand. Felix handed the cello-taped parcel back to Klint who looked dour and unhappy. Harry nodded stiffly and headed out of the room without a word. Stefan glanced at Re and shook his head.

"That did not go well. Whoever tipped us off was way out of line."

"Or deliberately misleading us," Re added.

Stefan nodded, frowning deeply. "And this weather isn't helping."

Re understood what he meant. As he stood in the corridor, he listened to the low wailing of the wind on the outskirts of the hotel, enveloping it in a circular energy. Re didn't quite like it himself. There was uneasy air about the hotel—inside and outside. As if something was waiting to happen. Something more sinister and disturbing than all the incidences put together. For some reason he felt that he was in the midst of it, not on the fringes of a case, like he usually was. But right in the middle and he couldn't see how or why. Except for his dream—the sinking and sucking into the ice-cold water of the lake...

A strong gust of wind blasted in through an open door. Someone shut it at once. Even in that short interval, a drift of snow had blown in, covering the carpet with a thin layer of white sheen. The receptionist continued his work undeterred and a couple of guests huddled on the sofas of the restaurant hall, drinking coffee. Re saw the waiters carry the dinner for the Treaty members to the private hall.

The investigator followed the waiters through the ajar door and observed the scene inside with a great deal of interest. A general chatter filled the room, as the guests chatted with wine glasses in their hands. Harry was in deep conversation with Adria, probably sharing with her his unpleasant experience with the German Police. Carlo and Max were listening as Leon narrated a story with an intense expression on his face. Rosamonde stood by the window, staring at the snow lashing against the glass pane. Re strode across the room and joined her.

"Getting wilder by the minute," he commented.

She didn't turn. "Starnberg char and trout and Hollandaise sauce with potatoes."

"What?" Re pushed back his sliding glasses.

Rosamonde turned away from the window and looked at him. She appeared freshly showered and her face was glowing. In a maroon-red dress, she looked as if she had stepped out of the cover of a magazine.

"Asparagus, veal cutlets with rice, quark pancake roulade, lemon and cream strawberries and chocolate cake."

"Sounds delicious, is that the menu for dinner tonight?" Re confirmed.

"It was also the menu the day King Ludwig II died, June 13, 1886. Or at least part of it. And although I appreciate the effort and the theme, don't you think it's a bit morbid?" she asked in a conspiratory tone.

"I look at it as more like celebrating his memory? I mean that's what the Empress ate the day her closest friend died. So..." Re shrugged.

"You are right. I am just being silly. Nothing morbid about it. Nothing to worry about."

"Worry? Why do you say so?" Re's interest was piqued.

"Just like that, given the circumstances. Don't you sense an unease in the air? I feel like a kite in mid-air waiting for the wind to fall and for me to drop down to earth... I mean not literally but you get my point. It's like waiting...waiting for something to happen..."

Re stared at her. Rosamonde was voicing his exact thoughts. How strange that they were so well-tuned in frequency and that she spoke his thoughts.

He nodded. "I know what you mean. Your words resonate with my thoughts and the weather ...*si melancholique*...but it is surely our hyper imagination at work. The hazard of a fertile creative mind."

"Oh, the easy escape of labelling everything as hyper imagination." Rosamonde sighed.

"You do not agree with me?"

"Certainly not. The situation is grave enough, don't you agree?"

"Yes, but an over-active imagination can only cloud clear judgement. We may question, dissect and even anticipate to a point but not jump the gun imagining the worst."

"That's true. But when I think of the paparazzi hounding me outside the café, my imagination takes on a very real, creepy and terrifying appearance. I felt as if they were trying to force a mask over my head, a mask I did not wish to wear or claim...a mask the mere idea of which scares the worst nightmares away and all I can do is struggle to breathe and to yank the mask off my face. But I can't yank it off, instead it sinks lower and lower into my skin, burning and melting into my face like a flaming hot second skin."

Once again Re was struck at the choice of her words and the expression. How had he not noticed before that their conversation was made of layers of content. It was almost as if they spoke in a subtle, code language which probably just the two of them could understand and read, between the words and lines too.

"Fear was never better expressed in graphic, brutal words," he remarked.

"That is because it is governed by an emotional reality more graphic than imagination."

"But the wise use fear as a tool to leash the emotional reality."

"I am afraid I wouldn't call myself wise by a long shot."

"The wise rarely call themselves wise." Re smiled. "It is the hidden power and knowledge within that speaks and vouches for them."

"Thank you for the show of confidence. But the fear of the mask is too real right now for me to be wise."

"For personal record, I wouldn't have let anything happen to you back there, *ma chérie*," Re said, suddenly. "I would have protected you with everything in my power."

Her blue-green gaze met his over the rim of her glass and she nodded.

"I know. We share the filmmakers' honour."

A smile twitched at his lips. "Right. Filmmakers stand by each other no matter what."

"As do friends."

"Are we...friends?"

"Are we?" she repeated, her smile-less blue gaze meeting his over the glass. She had an air of gravitas that demanded attention.

Re felt sucked into the gaze, spiralling long distances into it. It made him breathless and yet vigilant. He had to be careful. *Rosamonde was just a part of a case....*

Dinner had been arranged and the guests were gravitating towards the buffet table.

"The Sisi menu awaits us. Shall we?"

"I can't wait to relive the past." Rosamonde smiled.

It was just as Re had taken a plate that he saw Ben and a waiter in a white uniform approaching him hastily. He stood taller than the rest and his bald head gleamed in the light. Re stiffened, his senses on automatic alert mode. What was Ben doing here?

"Can I speak to you for a moment? This is urgent," Ben whispered.

Immediately Re took the driver and the waiter aside.

"What is it?"

Ben shot a quick glance at the waiter, who looked nervous. He dug into his pocket and extracted a transparent bag.

"This is Charles, my friend in the kitchen. I was helping out my friends in the kitchen when he found this in one of the cooking utensils. It was in the sauce."

Charles nodded vociferously.

Re gasped. He took one look at the poison bottle wrapped in a kerchief and he wheeled around sharply.

"Stop! Don't eat the Hollandaise sauce anyone. I suspect that there could be poison in it," he announced.

11

Shocked gasps burst into the room, as plates clattered and commotion broke out. Stefan turned to Re, his eyes wide with astonishment.

"Are you sure?" the officer strode towards the journalist.

"No, but Charles here found this in the sauce and I don't see how a poison bottle can find itself at the bottom of a utensil by its own," Re remarked.

Stefan glanced at the bottle in his hand, then without another word, he turned to the members of the congregation. Carlo and Leon appeared stunned. Harry and Adria had slipped into their seats, anxiety written on their faces. Max had immediately taken Rosamonde's plate and returned it to the table.

"There appears to have been some tampering with the food. We have found an empty bottle of poison in the sauce. It is best not to touch anything at all," Stefan confirmed.

"This is preposterous!" Carlo expostulated. "Poison in the food! Someone wants us all dead!"

"I have to admit, this is an extreme we had not expected," Leon added.

"I quite agree. It's one thing to steal and quite another to want to take a life," Max remarked.

"Ladies and gentlemen, let's not panic. We will send the food to the police lab first thing tomorrow morning. It's quite likely that a bottle fell in by mistake in the sauce and the rest of the food could be safe. But I suggest, we allow this food to go back to the kitchen and kept safe in containers till we know if it is indeed poisoned."

"In the meanwhile, I am sure the kitchen can whip up some sandwiches and soup for all of us," Re spoke up.

"I will go tell Mrs Weber," Ben offered, hastening out of the hall with Charles.

"How can we eat any meal here anymore when there is a danger to our lives?" Adria asked.

"We will keep a policeman on continuous guard in the kitchen from this moment onwards," Stefan assured.

"I am done with this. I am leaving first thing tomorrow morning," Carlo announced, throwing his napkin on to the table.

"So am I," Harry agreed. "This has gone too far, way beyond my imagination. There is too much distrust. How can a treaty be signed under so much duress?"

"For the first time, I agree with Carlo and Harry," Leon sighed. "I was the first person to get this whole idea rolling but perhaps this isn't the right time for the Treaty. Perhaps the place isn't right. Or the name. Everything is going topsy and turvy because of the Sisi name. There are already protests happening in the town. Perhaps they are right. This is all wrong."

"Do you have any idea who could have slipped the poison into the food?" Max asked. He seemed more in control than the others.

Stefan glanced at his friend and Re inhaled deeply. He extracted the handkerchief from the plastic bag. It was dainty and edged with lace with an embroidered letter on it—A. Re held it up for all to see.

"Apparently this kerchief was found near the spot. It has an embroidered A on it. Does anyone recognise it?"

Slow gasps pervaded the room, even as all eyes turned instantly on Adria. The lady in question looked stunned for moments and then as the implication sank in, she paled. For a moment, Re thought she was going to burst into a furious denial. He saw the expression fleet across her face like an animated drawing and waited, almost breathlessly to gauge her final reaction. She had to have some explanation for how her kerchief had landed in the kitchen, right next to the sauce which contained the poison bottle. At length, she raised her head and her eyes moved boldly from one fact to the other. She was remarkably composed.

"That *is* my kerchief but I haven't been anywhere near the kitchen, not even once since I arrived," she stated, calmly.

Re admired her cool.

"But your kerchief did not walk to the kitchen on its own," Carlo drawled.

"No obviously it did not. Just the way horse hair on the cutter that cut my strap of the rein, did not walk to your room on its own, do you mean?" Sarcasm dripped from Adria's tone.

Carlo looked taken aback. "The cut horse hair in my room?" he queried.

"No need to pretend to look surprised. Officer Weiss found the damaging evidence in your room. Do you mean to say you know nothing about it?" Adria continued, her head held high in snobbish candour.

"I don't. . .I know nothing about it and I don't understand why you sound as if you are accusing me of trying to harm you. Why would I do such a horrendous thing?" Carlo faltered.

"I *am* accusing you!" Adria snapped.

"Preposterous!" Carlo turned beet red, sweeping an angry hand through his curls.

"See, this is precisely what I mean," Harry cut in, drily. "Now we are all accusing each other of doing things that we didn't do. Or at least we need the benefit of doubt. Including the fact that my secretary was stopped while he was trying to carry a parcel out of the hotel."

Stefan raised a hand. "Please, we haven't officially made any accusations."

"No, but your investigation and other implications are sure headed in that direction," Leon added. "Who knows what else is floating around which would lead to the next accusation?"

"And we still don't know how Adria's kerchief was found in the kitchen at the same time as the poison bottle was found in the food," Max added.

"That's it...I am out!" Carlo declared.

"Me too!" the others chorused.

"Wait!" Re announced. The command in his voice startled everyone into silence. Rosamonde glanced at him curiously. Stefan turned to him, a look of hope crossing his face. Re took a deep breath, as his hand automatically sought the Ganesh pendant and grasped it.

"Imagine that we are all climbing a mountain and we are close to the top and suddenly someone entangles the ropes...you could all trip or fall just when you are so close to the top. Or imagine all of you in a boat and suddenly the bottom springs a leak and then another. You don't know what caused it but you think the other person is responsible. No matter who is responsible the boat is sinking."

"What are you getting at?" Carlo frowned.

Re glanced across at Rosamonde and noticed her half smile. She understood. And he wasn't surprised.

"This whole episode is like a synchronised dance. All of you, or us, are the dancers synchronising our actions and reactions as per the music...except we are synchronised to someone else's melody, someone's script," Re finished with a flourish.

"Re—," Stefan began.

"Don't you see what's happening here? This chaos, confusion, accusations, distrust?" Re persisted. "This is exactly what Virus, as we like to call him, wants. He has played us all and especially you five. Criss-crossing messages, planting damaging evidence, creating doubt and distrust so much so that you are all pitched against each other. Dancing to his tune. That's what he wants and that's what he is achieving."

Silence ensued as each person in the room grappled with Re's theory.

"Almost killing Adria on horseback and all of us with the poison?" Harry raised an eyebrow of disbelief.

"Adria had a fall and she was lucky, I agree, but if someone wanted to really harm her, it could have been done with more finesse. As for the poison, I am beginning to wonder if it was more to frighten us then to actually poison us. We will know for sure, only after tomorrow's lab results, if at all anything is open for Christmas of course. But what I am trying to say is...consider what Virus is trying to achieve. Adria has a fall and she gets a note saying the evidence is in Carlo's room. An anonymous call tips us off saying the swans could be in Harry's parcel. And now this poison bottle, with Adria's handkerchief conveniently dropped on the floor of the kitchen to be easily found so that all of us would instantly accuse her of this crime... What does it all say? Someone is creating mischief. Creating doubt in all our minds."

"I agree. I got a strange, accusatory message on Max's letterhead and we almost came to blows." Leon interjected and Max nodded vigorously in agreement. "Luckily we sorted it out quickly and amicably."

"Exactly! That's what I am saying. This person is smart and knows exactly how to play you against each other," Re confirmed, in a triumphant tone.

"But why? Why pitch us against each other? Why create bad blood?" Max wondered.

"All this is orchestrated and leading to the last act— cancelling of the Treaty."

Henry and Adria glanced at the others. Stefan nodded at Re.

"From the beginning, Virus has not wanted the Treaty to go forward. The precious swans and the entire Treaty material stolen from the safe, making a demand to find the mysterious soul-song and sending us on a journey of Sisi's route while simultaneously creating cracks in your trust for each other. He has been very intelligent because he almost got what he wanted. He managed to get under your skin, to insert a feeling of distrust for each other and futility for the Treaty. To the point that you were all almost ready to call it quits."

Carlo shifted uneasily in his seat and Henry flashed Adria a quick glance. Rosamonde stared at the group of five by the table, gauging their reactions to this truth.

"I still don't like what's happening here," Carlo remarked.

"Neither do any of us. But this isn't the time to give in to the crooked intentions of an anonymous assailant. Or allow him to succeed in his malicious goals which could change the future of five countries," Re reminded.

The silence was tainted with the hesitation of unspoken thoughts and fear of a faceless danger. The snow was swirling and the scratching against the window panes punctuated the silence irrhythmically.

"He is right," Henry spoke up, at length. "We arrived here with a purpose and the purpose is to come together to build bridges between countries—bridges of peace, love, culture and arts and we cannot allow some evil prankster to stall those noble plans."

"I agree with you," Adria added. "Neither can we allow the future of our countries to be played around by this Virus person. We need to stand in solidarity and face this situation as a collective responsibility instead of indulging in the blame game."

Re flashed Stefan a quick triumphant smile. The worst just seemed to have been narrowly evaded and dodged.

"We are so glad that you can see this in the right light." Stefan sighed.

"I got blindsided for a moment," Leon admitted. "My sincere apologies to everyone. This whole situation made me forget what was more important here. Henry, Adria—I am with you. We will see this through."

"And no more synchronising to someone else's script," Max added, solemnly. "Right Carlo?"

All eyes were trained on the Italian diplomat. He stood against the table, his hands folded, his face devoid of expression. It was crucial that he fell in synch with the others, Re realised. It was a touch and go situation.

"Carlo?" Adria prompted.

The tall man sighed. "Well, it's just one more day. We have already written out the first draft. Tomorrow, we will sign it and then day after we will all be gone. So ya, I am in!"

A cheer of appreciation rang out. Re felt an immense pressure released off his chest and Stefan passed him a brilliant smile.

"Thank you everyone for rising to the occasion. On our part, the German and Austrian Police are here to protect you and solve this case, as soon as we possibly can. It is Christmas time and each one of you is away from home for such an important cause... It is our moral duty to ensure your safety, no matter what, from this moment onwards." Stefan's blue eyes moved from person to another, assuring them with his direct glance.

"Christmas time...for sure. I am permanently in my granddaughter's bad books now because I have missed her Christmas play." Henry chuckled.

"And my daughter is angry because I promised to look after her horse during Christmas and ride him everyday, while she travelled. She feels betrayed because I broke my promise," Adria added with a twinkle in her eye.

"It is understandable. Christmas is family time," Re murmured.

Carlo grinned. "I won't even mention my fiancée. She is livid. She wanted to introduce me to her family in Florence over a family Christmas dinner."

"That was indeed a crime," Max chuckled.

"The people of our countries would probably never know what transpired here and the sacrifices that went into the signing of the Treaty. But we do...," Rosamonde spoke for the first time, smiling warmly at everyone.

The door of the hall opened and two waiters arrived with trays of sandwiches and bowls of hot soup.

"Finally, safe food." Max rubbed his hands in glee. "I had no idea hunger could feel this special."

12

"That was quick thinking," Stefan said in a low voice. Re tucked into his sandwich. "I am just glad that the boat is steady again. And that everyone rose to the patriotic side of the situation and their nature."

"But you know it's not the end of the road."

"No. Far from it as a matter of fact. And the more I think of it, the more I realise that we are pitted against a very sharp brain. He isn't just a simple criminal stopping the Treaty from happening. This is a man who is a master at understanding human insecurities and knows how to fine-play on them. Someone who understands the deeper psychology of the human mind and knows how to use the knowledge to his advantage."

"You're right. It just gets more complicated by the minute and keeping a grasp on things is getting more and more difficult."

"The interesting bit is that Virus seems to always be one step ahead of us...it's almost as if he is leading us on a race to some pre-planned, well-orchestrated finale, holding the signposts close so that we won't be able to read them."

"And I don't like that," Stefan shook his head.

"But we won't let him win the race, Stefan. We will outrun him."

Stefan grimaced. "We would have to for the sake of the future of five countries."

"What about the food samples? Are any labs open?"

"Not in Starnberg. One of the officers has taken samples of the food and already left for Munich, since our own lab technician is on leave. It's stormy out there and everything is closed for Christmas but the police would ensure that we get the results as a special case."

"It *is* going to be a long night. The Treaty is in its final draft and the team would work late into early hours of dawn, wouldn't they?"

"Yes, I have already given instructions to keep a steady supply of coffee and one of our men is on constant guard in the kitchen. We don't want any lapses now and no repeats of the poison episode."

"I doubt if there will be," Re said. "Something tells me that that the bottle was meant to be found as well as Adria's kerchief. It was a ploy to wreak damage on people's trust and instil a sense of fear. Someone's being playing a clever Ping-Pong game of suspicion with all of us."

"That doesn't mean we eliminate suspicion from all the members," Stefan remarked.

"Not at all. Until the swans and the soul-song are found and the Treaty is signed successfully, we cannot rest and each person here is a suspect, including Rosamonde."

Stefan quirked an eyebrow and his lips twisted in a grimace again. "You like her, don't you?"

Re glanced across the dining room, where Rosamonde was talking to Leon and Max. Her back was turned to him but her silky hair swung as she leaned to mention something to Leon.

He nodded. "More than I would care to admit."

"Be careful then, be very careful, my friend," Stefan rested a hand on the investigator's shoulder.

"I will. But I do know that until I have all the answers, I won't be able to rest. Especially since something very weird happened this evening—someone leaked to the Press that Elisabeth is a reincarnation of the Empress of Austria."

"What!" Stefan looked startled.

Re told him about what had transpired during the evening and specially the hounding by the paparazzi. An amazed expression crossed the officer's face.

"Incredible," he whistled.

"Things are getting complicated enough but if there is even an iota of truth in this news, Rosamonde would forever be shrouded in mystery."

"And inaccessible," Stefan added softly, his eyes on his friend.

"I am aware of it."

"Speaking of complications, this storm and the fact that it is holiday time, has really turned things topsy and difficult for us. There are still some issues that we may need to tackle on an urgent basis," Stefan said. "For example, the swans, the main symbols of the Treaty. If we don't find them by tomorrow, we would need to find another pair as a stand-in. Also, the set of seals for the Treaty were stolen too and knowing that everything is shut for Christmas I doubt if we can get another one done in time."

"Excuse me, perhaps we can help?" Harry interrupted. "Sorry, but I just overheard you talk about the seal."

Surprised, Re and Stefan turned to face Harry and Carlo.

"You can?" Stefan confirmed.

"Carlo is a great designer and luckily I have my tools and a block of wood."

"Of course, you can!" Re exclaimed. "What a great idea."

"It is so kind of you both to offer, thank you. Do you think you could get the design and the stamp ready by tomorrow afternoon?" Stefan asked.

Carlo shrugged. "Glad to be of help. It's Christmas after all. Just the most perfect time to come together in Christmas spirit for the Treaty."

"You are absolutely right." Re smiled at the two gentlemen.

"I can begin designing right away. Do you have any drawings of the seal? It may not be an exact replica of it, but I would do my best to ensure that you have an appropriate design for a seal," Carlo said.

"And I shall carve it into a stamp in time for the signing," Harry added, with a composed smile.

"But what about the final draft? Don't you have to lock it?" Stefan asked.

"Adria, Max, and Leon have taken charge. We have already finalised the clauses and sub clauses. It's all settled."

"That sounds just incredible," Stefan said, his voice a melange of excitement and relief. "I would have the designs on my laptop. Let me show you the drawings," Stefan offered, leading the diplomats out of the hall.

Re stood by the window watching the group by the dinner table, their moods mellowed with the recent near-brush with death. Rosamonde was seated between Max and Leon; it was more than obvious that Leon was making a special effort to converse with her. Her laughter implied that she enjoyed his company and it left an unwanted taste in his mouth. Re frowned. Was he jealous of their friendship? Was he resenting Leon being attentive towards her? He probably knew her the longest in the room—and he, Re, had barely spent 12 hours in her company. That too in a professional capacity. And yet, he had felt that he had known her for a longer time. He certainly had no right to object to anything she did, leave alone how she reacted to the attentions of a rich and handsome friend. Re shook himself mentally. He had better exit this frame of mind immediately, or the case was doomed.

He deliberately poured himself another glass of wine and turning his back on the merry group and stared out at the snowflakes slashing against the window.

The tall Christmas tree in the Square was sparkling with lights. Snowflakes kissed its branches as they danced in the wind. The lanes were quiet as families cosied around fire places in their homes. Only the occasional car passed down the silky road, pausing to admire the scintillating, solitary presence of wood, snow and sparkle. Manuel took some photographs with his phone, for the local Christmas special. He had enough content for his article which would appear on 25th morning.

It was while he was double-checking the pictures on his phone that he felt a presence. A whiff of air...like someone breathing down his neck. His skin crawled. A swift movement, a rapid floating of cloth, buzzing antennae and then a burst of a loud firecracker followed by a sudden spurt of light. It all happened so quickly, that Manuel barely had a moment to suck in his breath. The next instant the entire tree had burst into flames. Manuel thrust back in force, as heat licked his face. His eyes stayed glued in shock as the beautiful tree, the silver wrapped gifts and coloured streamers and baubles turned into a charring inferno.

Doors swung open and people rushed out, exclamations and shouts turning into frightened screams over the sizzle of the crackling fire. The beautiful Christmas tree was a blazing demon against the stark snow-covered landscape, towering eerily heavenwards.

In the sky, the floating white figure was disappearing fast and merging into the dark clouds. But Manuel knew what it was. It was the Starnberg ET and it had concretised all the fears of the town, in one gruesome strike.

13

Gunter, the stable hand, stared at the three men towering over him, startled and uneasy.

"What—?" he asked, taken aback, almost rising from his chair.

"Sit down, Gunter. We need to have a word with you," Karl ordered, quietly.

The dimly lit pub was sparsely occupied with some tourists in a corner of the bar. A medium-sized Christmas tree braved more decorations than it could handle and streamers adorned pillars and the walls. The police had traced Gunter to the pub and had decided that they had to interrogate him right away. They had braved the snow and slippery roads, driving down to the Bernried Pub, by the Starnberg Lake.

Stefan and Felix drew chairs and the three men settled around the table. Gunter glanced nervously from one face to the other, his fingers curled tightly around a large glass of beer.

"I already said I don't know anything about the broken strap," Gunter said, in a tone of defence. "I am sure it was an accident; worn-out reins can snap."

"For a journalist between jobs, you seem to know a lot about horse reins and stables." Felix remarked. "What made you take up the job of a stable hand, during Christmas of all times?"

"I needed some extra cash. The hotel needed temp hands and I offered. I am between articles and jobs, extra cash is most welcome."

"What about your boat? How often do you use it?" Karl chipped in.

Gunter looked surprised. "My boat? I use it during summer, to ferry tourists across to Rose Island. But how do you know I own a boat?"

"We also know that you go out in your boat with your friend Hans, on many nights. You do, don't you?"

The journalist shifted uncomfortably in his chair. He took a long slow sip of beer from his glass, biding time.

"Really, I have no idea why you are asking me all these personal questions. Why I go out and with whom is my personal life."

"Tell me, when you last met Hans," Karl ignored his protest and continued. "Last night? Did you go out for a spin in your boat?"

"No. I haven't met Hans in the last couple of days. Why do you ask?" Gunter appeared confused.

Karl shot a quick glance at Stefan and Felix. "Hans was found dead by the pier, early this morning."

Gunter half rose again, his face registering shock. "What? How?"

"So, you don't know anything about it." Stefan cut in quietly.

"No, of course I don't! He was my friend although we didn't meet every day. What happened?"

"Someone murdered him. And we aim to find out who did it."

"Murder?" He paled. "Are you sure?"

"Yes. We are positive."

Gunter stared at the policemen for long moments, a mask of caution veiling his face.

"Do you know if Hans had any enemies? Anyone who wanted to get rid of him? Any of his projects where he may have had an issue?" Stefan enquired.

Gunter shook his head. "Hans didn't confide in me. We were more drinking buddies."

"We know that he got a call from one of his friends last night and he went out. Do you know who it could be?"

"No. I am sorry; I can't be of more help." Gunter's voice was low and resigned.

"Thank you, Gunter, but we will need to talk to you again. So please stay around and don't leave town till we give you permission," Karl ordered and all the three policemen rose.

They headed to the door of the pub and Stefan shot a quick glance at the journalist. He was staring at his glass of beer, his eyes glazed and shoulders drooping.

His legs flapped in the water, as it seemed to hold him and pull him in deeper into the lake. He gasped, struggling to breathe as the water rushed into his mouth and nose, suffocating him. He was drowning...his head was heavy, his breath cut off...he was dying... Suddenly, a hand gripped him and pulled him up, slowly dragging him through the water. He gulped in deep breaths, vaguely aware of swimming towards the shore, his legs touching ground and his body thumping against the pebbles.

"Wake up, wake up," a soft voice spoke somewhere in the distance.

His head moved and his eyes flickered open to look straight into a pair of blue eyes, her long hair wet and straggling around her. A necklace dangled from her neck. A pair of swans...

"You are safe now." She said and stood up.

"Don't go!" he shouted.

With a jerk, Re came out of his reverie. Perspiration rose on his forehead and he brushed it away as he glanced in surprise around him. Max, Leon, and Rosamonde were still chatting and dinner was being cleared away. He felt as if he had travelled lightyears and back... Time seemed relative and momentary and as if his past and present were coming together somehow simultaneously. It was his vision again but he realised now that he wasn't seeing something that would transpire but that had happened...long ago. The day he had vanished, he had almost drowned in Lake Starnberg. It was coming back in bits and pieces. It was as if his mind was playing games with him...like a film revealing the suspense scene by scene. He would have drowned if the girl hadn't saved him. But he couldn't remember how he had landed in the water in the first place. He must have either fallen in or perhaps waded in himself and had got caught by a current. Re remembered that he couldn't swim. He had been afraid of water as a child. Then how had he managed to find himself in Lake Starnberg?

"Re...," Stefan spoke behind him.

Startled, Re turned around. The expression on the Officer's face spoke volumes and Re instantly banished all thought of his vision. He needed to focus on what was important right now. And that was the Treaty.

"What's happened?"

"What I had feared for a while. The Starnberg ET has struck. The huge Christmas tree in Feldafing Square was destroyed by a fire. We have an eye witness, who says that the ET caused the fire."

"Mon Dieu! This ET means business now. But what does this 'ghost' want?"

"I don't know what it wants. But I do know what it is doing. It is creating an atmosphere of fear and panic amongst the locals. The fact that we have nothing on it, makes the ET more sinister and I am really worried with all that is going on."

Re nodded.

"But that's not my only fear. We made some headway with Hans, the murdered man. His friend Gunter owns the boat that they use some nights to go for a ride and guess who Gunter is? The temp stable hand at the hotel!"

"*Eh bien....*"

"Yes...we traced him to the local pub and interrogated him tonight. He seemed shocked to hear about his friend's murder but didn't reveal much."

"Which of course, kind of brings us closer to the conclusion that the murder is connected to the Treaty. So much happening at so many levels—incidents which seem unrelated and unfathomable but which have got to be interconnected—and such little time to solve this."

"To make matters worse, the weather is changing every minute for the worst. The event team has set up this stage and setting in the park for the play. It was supposed to be open-air but because of the weather, we together took a decision to create a long tent. An additional team from the Government has taken charge to ensure that all of it is looked after. They arrived this afternoon and are doing the needful. My fear is what if we are snowed in and cannot leave the hotel?"

"Don't worry about that. We'll manage a way out." Re assured. "Perhaps it was the wrong time of the year to celebrate the Treaty."

"It is all in celebration of Elisabeth's birthday, remember? And that's tomorrow. Anyway, it was a five-country consensus. Besides, we didn't really expect the weather to be this bad. I heard that there's been an avalanche in Austria too and everyone has been warned to stay indoors and not go skiing or hiking. Anyway, you would have to excuse me, I have to meet Mrs Weber for tomorrow's dinner party, post the Treaty signing."

"*Ah oui*, the costume dinner, I can't wait to celebrate tomorrow." Re smiled.

"And solve the mystery of the soul-song before that," Stefan reminded wryly.

"That is a given, *mom ami*. You and I, together will solve this." Re raised a defiant eyebrow and Stefan reciprocated with a thumbs-up.

"I wouldn't dare refute that, Re Parkar."

Re sat at the far end of the restaurant, close to the window, with the note from Virus spread out before him. He read and reread it and every single time, he was assured that his guess was right. Someone wanted Rosamonde involved in the search and he could see two reasons for it—the first being that since Rosamonde was making a film on Sisi, she was already in possession of a great deal of knowledge. The other was more sinister. Someone knew of her trances, had already connected the dots concluding that she was indeed a reincarnation of the Empress of Austria. In that case, she would know exactly where the soul-song was. But that narrowed down the guilty to a limited circle—Max and Leon. Re paused as he tried to visualise the two involved in criminal activities. They certainly were hiding something. And as far as his reading of the world went, he knew that power, money and youth were a tricky combo—they could lead the sanest of men astray and into wrong lanes. So, even if Rosamonde was his sister and he was obviously protective about her, there was a chance that Max was capable of crime. Leon too.

But what had that got to do with the Treaty? There had to be a connection between the soul-song and the Treaty. On an impulse, Re extracted a tissue from the box, pushed back his silver-rimmed glasses and quickly jotted down pointers. He needed a step by step, chronological order of the events. What exactly had happened in Starnberg since he arrived?

1. Letter from Virus asking for the soul-song, and involving Rosamonde in it.

   Status: Still at it.

2. The theft of the swans and the threat to the Treaty.

   Status: Still trying to figure out.

3. A group of people opposing the Treaty because it was named after Sisi.

   Status: Ask Stefan to find out.

4. The murder of the man by the Island jetty.

   Status: The man has been identified as Hans and Police are working on it.

5. Empress Elisabeth's statue covered in lingerie (although not certain that this is in anyway connected with the case).

6. Someone informing the Paparazzi that Rosamonde was the Empress reborn.

   Action required: Ask Stefan to find out from the Press Bureau who gave them this information.

7. Adria's horse trap was tampered with and she had a fall. A note implied that Carlo had done it.

Status: The stable hand Gunter questioned, cutter with horse hair found in Carlo's room by Stefan. But Hans was Gunter's friend?

8. The intercepted code message which mentioned the transfer of the treasure the next day.

Status: Nil. Still to figure out what the treasure is...

9. An anonymous call informed that the swans could be in Harry's parcel.

Status: What could the objective be? To rouse suspicion against Harry or something else?

10. The poisoned dinner, proof of the poison bottle and Adria's kerchief found in the kitchen.

Action: Find out if all the food was poisoned or just the sauce. How did Adria's hanky get there?

11. ET appearances in Starnberg and finally the burning down of the Christmas tree. What role did the ET have in the Treaty? Was it connected or an isolated incident?

Re stared at his notes, frowning slightly. On the face of it, all such disconnected and haphazard incidents, like the disrupted tracks of a train. And yet, he knew that underneath ran another smooth track and at some point, all the seemingly haphazard rungs would fall into the right places on this smooth track. A perfect plan held all the pieces of this puzzle together—and a motive that was stronger than the will of five countries put together. Who would want to oppose the Treaty and why? What could anyone gain from opposing peace, culture, and art which resulted in more opportunities for all the people concerned? If he could only find one concrete answer, the rest would fall into place.

His gaze stilled on point number 9. The anonymous call about Harry's parcel. Almost on cue, Harry's secretary Klint walked into the restaurant, looking distant and inattentive. On an impulse, Re rose and approached him.

"Has the parcel been despatched, Klint?" he asked casually.

"Yes, delivered it to a friend of mine who is travelling tomorrow back to Hungary. Just about managed, what with the ruckus outside. My car slid twice on the road. All in all, this trip is a very unusual one, for lack of a proper word to express." Klint flopped down on the sofa.

"And tomorrow is another long day," Re reflected. "I wanted to ask you something. Did anyone else know that you were going to be carrying a parcel out of the hotel today?"

"I don't know. I mean earlier in the day I had made some inquiries about courier services in Feldafing Square and was told that everything was shut for Christmas. So, anyone could have heard me speak to the receptionist."

"That's possible because someone definitely knew that you would be carrying a parcel out of here tonight. Something not quite right about it. The deliberately erroneous tip-off, I mean. In any case, if you think of anything else, or remember something—would you let me know? It is important." Re said, trying not to appear too grave.

"I will for sure. Ah, here's my coffee." The secretary smiled casually and rubbed his hands in anticipation.

Re turned to leave, then paused, a sudden sense of unease descending on him. For a few seconds, he fiddled with his pony tail, debating his stance. Then he made up his mind.

"Klint, I think you ought to be careful, just in case. Here's my card and my number. Call me if you feel like talking to me. Any time of the night."

Klint looked surprised. "You mean I should be careful because of the theft of the swans and the rest..."

Re nodded. "Yes, the rest...specially the rest..."

He knew he was being vague, but he didn't want Klint to panic. It was just a feeling...it could mean nothing.

"Ok, I will. Thank you for your concern."

The detective nodded and turned to return to his table.

A sudden movement caught his eye. A hazy figure was moving past the window. Despite the lack of clarity, Re recognised her. It was snowing steadily and was freezing cold out there. What could Rosamonde be doing out in the hotel park this late in the evening? He quickly slipped the note back into his jacket. Pulling on his beanie and gloves, he opened the door to the terrace. A deathly silence met him, taking him momentarily unawares. The wind had dropped and the snowfall had paused and an eerie silence had taken over the night. It took him a few moments to spot her a little ahead in the park. The snow was knee deep but she was slogging on relentlessly towards the far end, leaving behind a trail of deep imprints.

Without another thought, Re plunged into the deep snow. His boots sank in deep and every step was an ordeal. Only one thought rang in his head. Surely, Rosamonde knew what she was doing. Only a fool could venture out on a night like this. *Or a woman in a trance*, a small voice spoke in his head and the thought spurred him on. He reached her in a few minutes. She was standing by a marble statue of Empress Elisabeth in a chair, raised on a pedestal, surrounded by straggling ice-covered trees. Piles of snow lodged unceremoniously all over the landmark statue, piled high up to her neck, like a billowing white gown and had slid off in parts to reveal the statue's porcelain, serene face.

"Rosamonde! What are you doing here?" he rasped, catching up with her.

She continued to stare at the statue. "A beautiful statue out here in this pristine park. I came to say hello. So lonely, isn't she? Has always been. Especially after the only person who understood her died so mysteriously. June 13...I remember the poem written after his death...the pain and the longing to meet him...it was not just the death of a dear friend and cousin, it was the death of defiance, of creative instincts, of dreams and visions that dared to be born...it was the silencing of imagination which soared to dizzying heights. But more than that, it was the searing end of soul-ties..." her voice caught in a choke.

It took Re all his self-control to not step forward and envelop her in an embrace. To comfort her and tell her that it was all in the past.

"'And now, so soon thereafter, of dizzying scent,

I made a wreath of roses in full bloom,

And bore it with such care and love,

Down to your darkening tomb.

It was there that I bade you fond farewell

and in the quiet therein, I placed

A kiss, my unforgettable king

Upon your coffin's lid.' I remember this poem so well... it was like giving freedom to pain...so true..."

"Rosy!" a voice interrupted her, from across the park.

Re turned to see a figure plodding through the snow. Surprise hit him anew. Wrapped in a heavy black coat, he looked like a huge shadow in snow-reflected white light. What was Leon doing out here? Surely, he hadn't followed Rosamonde, braving the icy cold? But Re got his answer within seconds.

"Rosy, here you are. Are you okay? I have been looking everywhere for you!" Leon exclaimed.

Rosamonde nodded, looking dazed and a little uncertain.

"I have been here with her. She's fine."

"Thank you Re, that was kind of you. She gets like this sometimes...for a while now. But it passes, this 'whateveritis'. Right, honey?"

An instant frown creased Re's forehead. The sudden term of endearment and his familiar talk, as if he was laying his territory.

"You and Rosamonde..." he began.

"Oh, we are engaged. I am her fiancé," Leon explained briefly. "Let's go, honey, before you and I both freeze to death."

He latched his arm through hers and led her slowly back towards the terrace. Re stared after the couple, as they plodded their way back to the hotel. Could the chill inside his heart be any colder than the ice outside? Why hadn't he realised this before? It was the most obvious fact...Leon and Rosamonde had known each other for years. He was handsome and successful and her brother's friend. It would be the most perfect match ever! Why had he neglected realising what a handsome couple they would make? Because deep inside, somewhere, he *didn't* want to. He wanted her to be single and available, as he tried to figure out, what exactly he felt for this strange woman, whom he had met just this morning. While he figured out if their energies matched and he wove his way around a bunch of fantastic doubts and explanations, trying to make sense of the attraction he felt for a stranger while the obvious fact had slid from under his nose. Rosamonde was engaged to be married to Leon! And the thought had sparked an entirely different level of energy that hit him and spiralled through him. He didn't want to label it as jealousy, because that would make it sound petty. It was more, much more. What had she just said? A searing end of soul-ties... That was exactly how he felt.

Klint slowly walked up the stairs to his room. Something about what Re said floated in his mind, with an irritable disturbance. Scenes filtered in to his memory of their own volition. He had taken the parcel from Harry and headed downstairs. And then he had met him on the first floor. They had had a quick light exchange. He had asked Klint casually if he was heading out with the parcel. And Klint had passed a causal comment about how working on a night like this was a nightmare. That's all. A nice friendly exchange. Was it important? He glanced ahead at the low-lit corridor. It was empty. On an impulse, he whipped out the phone and the card Re had given him. He punched in Re's number. The ring went to voice message.

"You asked me to call you if I remembered something, so that's what I am doing. I am not sure it is at all important, but I think I remembered something regarding the parcel. I will share it with you during breakfast. Goodnight." Feeling a little appeased, he tucked the phone back into his pocket, inserted the key into the door lock and entered his room.

A sudden sound behind him startled Klint. But before he could turn, something hard hit him straight on the head. Blinding light and pain flooded through him, till everything went blank and he crumpled to the floor.

14

It was going to be a long night. Adria, Max, and Leon had finished their draft and headed to bed. The restaurant hall was empty. But the Christmas tree twinkled bright and inviting, spreading a glow of cosy warmth in the hall. Everyone seemed to have retired finally. It was going to be a big and long day tomorrow...or was it today? Re glanced at his watch. It was almost 2 am. He had been awake for more than 16 hours and felt no sign of fatigue or sleep. In fact, he was wide awake. Something about this whole business troubled him and couldn't figure himself out. The energies of the place were all mixed up combined with the energies of the people he had met. Leon, Max, Adria, Carlo, and Harry and of course Rosamonde. They were his prime focus. For some reason he refrained from using the word 'suspects'.

Re glanced at the banner over the cheerful Christmas tree—*Happy Birthday, Sisi!* Indeed, it was her birthday today. A lady of great elegance and intelligence but all people remembered was how unhappy she had been. Had she really been that unhappy? Lonely perhaps, misunderstood too...but surely her art had given her some solace? That was what she shared with King Ludwig II, hadn't she? Their shared love for the written and painted word?

Although the snow fell ceaselessly outside, laying blankets after blankets of pristine white, a quaint cheer pervaded inside the hotel. Suddenly, Re paused. The poem that Rosamonde had recited outside in the park. Something familiar had popped out of it at the back of his mind but

Leon's appearance had driven it away. What had it been? He whipped out his phone. Surely the poem would be available on the net?

But a detailed search yielded nothing. Feeling uncharacteristically frustrated, Re rose and strode to the night receptionist. The young boy smiled pleasantly, not at all surprised to find Re up at that hour.

"Can I help you, sir?"

"Yes. Would you have a set of translated poems by Empress Elisabeth?" Re enquired.

"We haven't really kept a collection. What exactly is it that you are looking for?"

"It's a poem that she wrote, I believe, after King Ludwig II passed away. A very intense kind of poem..."

The boy looked thoughtful. Finally, he shook his head. "Without knowing the contents, it would be difficult to find it. There are some on the net of course."

"I have checked those. The one I am looking for isn't online. Never mind. Thank you for your help," Re nodded and turned to leave.

"Please wait," the boy requested.

Re halted, a little curious. The boy opened a drawer and extracted two books.

"These two books have some poems in them. I am not sure if the one you need is in it but you could look, if you like," he offered.

Re read the tiles with interest: *Art & Pleasure of the Wittelsbachers* was a hardbound notebook with a red and black cover and *Empress Elisabeth of Austria 1837–1898* was like a coffee table book with tons of pictures in it. They would make an interesting read in any case.

"Thank you, I appreciate this. I may find something in this for sure." Re smiled. And if luck was on his side, he may even find a clue to more than the poem, he thought.

He carried the books back to the table in the restaurant. The silence and the colourful lights were like a balm to his restless energy. He knew he ought to take a bit of rest but somehow his energy was in knots and he felt a need for answers. Time seemed to be racing ahead and Re felt as if he was walking backwards, instead of jogging ahead. Was it because the past was so prominently dredging up more than he had bargained for? Like his dreams?

He secured his glasses firmly in place and scanned through the coffee table book on Elisabeth, reading bits and pieces on each glossy page. Interesting history accompanied by pictures, some of which he has seen at the Sisi Museum. Re stared closely at the Empress's pictures...why had he not noticed this before? Out of the blue, he could denote a similarity to Rosamonde. Not so much in the exact features of the face, but the tilt of the head, the expression in the eyes, the curve of the lips, the way she held her hand... Re closed his eyes momentarily. He was imagining it of course. His vision was getting coloured with the possibility of an idea of reincarnation. He couldn't allow that. He had to stare the facts in the face. No matter what. And not allow imagination to overlap and take hold of reality. He skimmed through the book, deliberately avoiding looking at Sisi's face and focussing on the search for the poem. There weren't any in the book. He closed it with a determined snap and took up the next one. It was a book of recipes and Re's interest was caught at once. His heartbeat quickened as he flicked the pages, finding interesting snippets of history accompanied by poems. Then his hand paused. 13 June...the day Ludwig II died. The recipe was outlined in detail. It was as

Rosamonde had pointed out—the same menu they were to have for dinner. With a slightly shaky hand, Re turned the page. And there it was...the poem he was looking for. The German and English versions. Had Rosamonde seen it here and recited it from this book? Or did she already know it by heart, remembering it from her past life?

He read the long poem, trying to locate the exact words that had triggered this search. What was it about this poem that had felt familiar?

'And now, so soon thereafter, of dizzying scent,

I made a wreath of roses in full bloom,

And bore it with such care and love,

Down to your darkening tomb.

It was there that I bade you fond farewell

and in the quiet therein, I placed

A kiss, my unforgettable king

Upon your coffin's lid.'

The roses in full bloom! Those were the words which had struck a chord. Re quickly extracted the threat-message from his pocket and reread Sisi's poem,

'Eagle, up there in the mountains...

The Sea Gull offers you our song in bloom.

On the path of the childhood dreams,

past the lake shrouded in gloom.

Silent we soared but deeply we understood.

the song that our souls once sang...

Now the bird guards it in its stately hood,

in the midst of the heavenly tang.'

He connected the second line with the last—*The song in bloom...in the midst of the heavenly tang... Roses?* For a second his heart raced with excitement. Could the soul-song be a rose? That Elisabeth had left for Ludwig II somewhere? Where could it be hidden? *Now the bird guards it in its stately hood... Of course...a rose protected by a stately bird!* Excitement spiralled through him as sudden light seemed to appear at the bottom of the abys.

First thing in the morning, he would discuss this with Rosamonde.

On an impulse, he extracted Rosamonde's envelope from his jacket, spreading the contents out on the table. Most of the newspaper clippings were news items and features of the many documentaries she had produced or for which she had won awards. Quite an accomplished lady, Rosamonde, he thought, with an unconscious smile of pride on his face. He skimmed through them, one after the other and then paused. It was a small write-up in a Munich paper, written by a cryptic MKR but the title of the article sent a shiver down his spine. *Who exactly is Rosamonde Hartman?* The photograph accompanying it was even more startling. A young Rosamonde, probably in her late teens, looked elegant and graceful in a long black gown, her hair drawn up high on the crown, her head angled regally. The article was vague, referring to Rosamonde's many accomplishments but hinting at her swings in moods, her poetry which resembled that of the Empress of Austria. It was an article which hinted at her uncanny resemblance to the Empress without actually saying so. Re frowned. MKR or whoever he was had taken great efforts to pin the Empress tag on to Rosamonde but had apparently failed. The article seemed to have vanished without notice, but the main point remained...that someone knew about Rosamonde's Empress obsession and had wanted to dig deeper. Had he succeeded?

Still frowning, Re picked up the last newspaper clipping. It was the news of a doctor being found dead in his clinic.

Dr Gordon practised alternate therapies, hypnosis being one of them. Mystery shrouded his death. Re wondered why the write-up had been added to Rosamonde's file, until he came to the last line of the write-up. He sucked in his breath, a little startled. The last patient to visit Dr Gordon had been Rosamonde Hartman.

Re sat back against his seat, allowing the information to register and sink in slowly. What did it all mean? Was Rosamonde really a reincarnation of Sisi? Was that why she was visiting the doctor? But there could be another more obvious reason that she had already admitted to...she had gone to the doctor to treat her depression....

Re's mind was a hive of thoughts. Could the doctor's death be connected with Rosamonde in any manner? And who was MKR? Had his article just been a one-off piece born out of curiosity or had been a deliberate attempt to prove Rosamonde's link to her regal past? Which also meant that along with Max and Leon, MKR knew about her secrets too...and most importantly, who was MKR?

On an impulse, Re searched up MKR online and to his surprise, a string of articles appeared. Apparently, he seemed to be quite a prolific writer. He scrolled through the articles, noticing that most of them were reports on the latest in science and technology. Strange then that he had deviated from his favourite topic to report on Rosamonde. What if he could ask him directly? Re wondered. Perhaps he could find an email id or a phone number. Re tapped in the key words, hoping against hope that something would turn up. For some reason, he felt an instinctive urge to do so. This was important, he felt. Re's heart beat a little faster as an email id cropped up—mkr@gmail.com. He had to assume that this would be a valid id. He drafted a quick mail, requesting a quick call in the morning and sent the mail. Within seconds an automated mail appeared.

"Hello,

I am on Christmas vacation. Will be back on the 5th Jan. Will write back on my return. Happy Holidays!

MKR"

Disappointment stabbed Re. He should have known. The whole world was on Christmas leave, so why would a Science and Technology journalist be any different? He would have to find another way to reach the guy, Re decided. Perhaps Stefan would be able to help.

The mystery around the filmmaker was getting thicker and Re's instinct told him that it was important to find MKR. But what did all of it have to do with the Treaty and the soul-song?

Re stifled a sudden yawn. Sleep was farthest from his mind but if he needed anything to be got done tomorrow, he would need to get some rest. He rose reluctantly, carrying the books under his arm.

He was in his room and preparing for bed when Re noticed the missed call on his phone. Klint sounded casual and yet there was the teeniest of an underlying tone of concern. Instant worry swamped Re. He glanced at his watch. It was almost 3 am. The first thing he would do in the morning was talk to Klint.

15

24 December, Feldafing

Re entered the dining hall early morning and instantly realised that the windows were completely blocked with snow. The restaurant hall was crowded, an eerie white-grey light filtering in through the closed windows and merging with the yellow of the indoor lighting. Re could hear shouts and sounds in the corridor.

"Merry Christmas everyone. We have a bit of an issue," Stefan announced. "Due to the heavy snowfall last night, we are completely snowed in. The snow is more than 6 feet high and has blocked all exits and even the windows."

A murmur of concern rose amidst the guests. The members of the congregation were gathered around a table, sipping coffee. Surprisingly they all looked rested and ready for the grand day of the Treaty. *Except that the swans were still missing and the soul-song was still cocooned in suspense,* Re thought. Re's restless night and vivid images had done little to appease him and he had awoken with an unusual sense of foreboding. He had never felt less prepared to face a day and a ceremony that would change the lives of the people of different countries. If only he had more time to unravel this multi-knotted, criss-crossed state of affairs.

Rosamonde walked into the hall just then and headed straight to an empty table. She appeared pre-occupied.

"How long before the snow is cleared?" Adria asked. "We have an important event near the lake."

"Has anyone seen Klint this morning?" Harry asked, a little absently.

"What would you like us to do?" Max asked. "Do you need help shovelling the snow away?"

Stefan nodded appreciatively. "Don't worry, all's good. Some of the waiters and stable hands and a couple of guests have climbed out through the higher windows. They are outside right now, shovelling us out."

"Oh, but we would like to help too." Leon rose at once. "After all, it's Christmas!"

"Absolutely. And we are famous for our Christmas spirit," Max agreed.

"Harry, you already have my design and don't need me now, do you?" Carlo rose, finishing off his coffee.

"I do and my work has already begun, so go ahead." Harry nodded.

"In that case, if you've had your breakfast, follow me." Stefan said. He shot Re a quick glance as he led a group of five into the corridor.

"Has anyone seen Klint this morning?" Harry asked again. "I have been waiting for half an hour for him."

"Oh, he'll be down soon," Adria assured.

"Have you checked in his room?" Re asked.

"No, but I did send him a message."

"When you meet him, please tell him, I would like to have a word with him."

"I will," Harry replied.

Re sat at his table, wondering whether he ought to be worried about Klint. That message he had left at night... He had called him before coming down for breakfast but Klint's phone had reported as unreachable. Well, like Harry he would give the secretary some more time to turn up. He wished his omelette would arrive soon. His stomach was rumbling with hunger and he hoped that the omelette would satiate his craving for fulfilment. Rosamonde finished her coffee, rose and turned to glance at Re. He felt his heartbeat quicken. She hesitated just for fraction of a section and then her eyes locked with his. Re could see her thinking... physically again. His lips curved in an inviting smile and a look of relief washed over her face. She walked to his table.

"You look as if you haven't slept," she said, as she slid into a chair.

Re nodded, absently touching his stubble and pushing back his silver rimmed glasses. "Good guess. I haven't. And no surprise at all. Today is the Treaty signing and there is no sign of the soul-song, swans or any answers to the case."

"True but we still have about ten hours to solve this. For Re Parkar, ten hours is like ten days!" She smiled.

"Ah, you seem to have done some reading up on me. I remember that quote from a newspaper." Re grinned.

Rosamonde laughed softly. "It was only fair to level the game."

"What do you mean?" he asked, frowning. Did she know that he had a folder full of her background stories?

"I mean you seem to know a great deal about me. I needed to know too who I was working with. And you are quite a figure to reckon with. I had no clue I was assisting a reputed investigator."

"Apparently, I don't seem to know enough about you. For example, I didn't know that you and Leon are engaged. That came as a kind of shock."

"Engaged?" Rosamonde frowned. "Who told you that?"

"Don't you remember last night? Leon came to fetch you in the park?"

Rosamonde's frown deepened for a moment, and then she nodded. "Oh that...I remember. I was staring at the statue. Felt an urge to see it and then you came and then Leon..."

"And he said that he was your fiancé," Re reminded, trying to keep an uncharacteristic bitterness out of his tone.

"You mean *ex-fiancé*," she corrected. "We broke off a while ago, except Leon is finding it a little difficult to accept and occasionally slips into the role of a protective fiancé."

A wave of relief swept over Re and he didn't pause to wonder at it.

"Oh, in that case, I have to say, he came on rather strong with the message." But he was smiling inside and suddenly the world which had a few moments seemed topsy turvy, appeared right again.

"Leon is a good guy but can sometimes be over-powering. I need breathing space, need to be on my own and do my own thing. I can't have these powerful men tailing me and judging me and ensuring that I keep on the track." She laughed.

A vision of Sisi on horseback rose before his eyes.

Re nodded. "I know what you mean. And he ought to stop introducing himself as your fiancé for sure. It can confuse people like me."

"Confuse the great Re Parkar? You who can read energies and body language and smell their fears?" Her eyes twinkled.

"Ah, *ma chérie*, you are making fun of me." Re's eyes crinkled. "If you are done, we have work to do. I had an epiphany-of-sorts last night. I think I know what the soul-song is."

"You do?" she appeared surprised.

"Yes. I think it's a rose. An expensive one studded with rubies perhaps, but I believe that it's a rose." He extracted the recipe book and shared his theory with her.

Rosamonde's eyes shone. "I think you are right. It has to be a rose. Let's read the poem again.

'Eagle, up there in the mountains...

The Sea Gull offers you our song in bloom.

On the path of the childhood dreams,

past the lake shrouded in gloom.

Silent we soared but deeply we understood.

the song that our souls once sang...

Now the bird guards it in its stately hood,

in the midst of the heavenly tang.'"

"We followed the path of the childhood dreams, *past the lake shrouded in gloom*. But then, *the song that their souls once sang, is now guarded by bird with a stately hood*... Could it be a royal bird? Does that ring a bell?"

Rosamonde looked thoughtful. "A royal bird...I don't know—"

Suddenly a loud jumble of voices and shouts interrupted the peace of the morning. Footsteps clattered down the corridor. Instinctively Re rose, shooting a glance at Harry. Their eyes met and for some reason, Re sensed an anxiety in him.

Stefan appeared in the corridor and looked straight at them. Mrs Weber stood right behind him, an anxious look on her face.

"Re, Harry, and Adria, I need your help," Stefan announced.

"What's happening?" Harry asked.

"If you could follow me to Mrs Weber's office," Stefan suggested.

Rosamonde rose too and they hastened into the manager's office. Stefan drew the curtain of the window which overlooked the street. A group of around twenty men, wrapped in thick coats, stood outside, holding up placards and shouting slogans. Their faces were flushed and determined and a certain wildness emanated from their actions.

Re frowned as their slogans carried muffled into the room. "Change the name, change the name, we want a Treaty, not a fame game!"

"Now what is all this?" Harry enquired, a deep frown on his face.

"They are protesters, shouting slogans against the title of the Treaty. Something about Sisi and her name associated with love and peace."

Harry and Adria glanced at each other.

"That is ridiculous. The Treaty is to honour the Empress and acknowledge her free and artistic spirit, bringing together the five countries she was associated with," Adria remarked.

"Exactly. But I think there are some misplaced notions that need to be clarified." Stefan remarked.

"How can we help?" Harry asked, his tone practical.

"You see that man in a blue jacket and black beanie? He is the leader of the group. I would like to call him in. I have spoken to him a couple of times and he seems like a guy who could listen to reason. Could you two please have a chat with him and explain why it is important that the Treaty be named after the Empress and how apt it is? You two are exceptional at handling such volatile situations. Would you please talk to this man?"

"Yes, of course," Adria agreed instantly.

"We would do anything to see this Treaty through. Already it has faced enough troubles. It's time to stop all of it," Harry said.

"Wonderful. There's a small conference room adjacent to the terrace. As soon as the snow from the door is cleared, which should be any minute now, I shall invite him to meet you."

"Right. And Stefan, could you please send someone to fetch Klint from his room? I have some urgent matters to discuss with him. And I would like him to be there during this meeting too."

"I will."

"I'd like to have a word with him too," Re added.

As the officer exited from the room, Harry and Adria quickly discussed in low voices their strategy for the meeting. They headed to the conference room and Re stood staring out of the window.

"You seem very tense today," Rosamonde observed.

"A lot weighing on my mind," Re admitted. "I can sense that the day is going to be a full one. Oh, Mrs Weber, can I ask you something?"

The manager had taken her seat behind her table again and appeared a little surprised at Re's sudden question.

"Yes of course, what is it?"

"Would you know any stately royal looking bird in a castle close by or anywhere else?"

"Oh, there would be many birds in King Ludwig's castles which are the epitome of beauty and glamour and glory. He spent fortunes on building these amazing gold-gilded palaces with breath-taking views and amazing decors. Swans and birds are a part of every room. It was his extravagance that is the reason why he was ultimately declared unfit and transferred to Berg." Mrs Weber explained.

"So, is there a castle nearby that would display a stately bird? Something big and which could contain something in it?" Re prompted.

"Linderhoff Palace!" the lady exclaimed suddenly. "There is a stunning peacock at Linderhoff Castle. And it sits on a huge urn."

"That's it," Re rose in his excitement. "How far from here do you think?"

"About an hour or so I guess."

"Oh, then we have to leave as soon as possible."

"Re," Rosamonde cut in. "I have an appointment at four with someone by the pier. I need to be back in time."

"Of course, we have a whole case to solve before that." Re laughed. "Thank you, Mrs Weber. As usual you have been a huge help."

The manager responded with a pleased smile. "Always glad to help."

"Let me see where Ben is and if the snow is cleared from the door. See you in 15 minutes?" Re asked his companion.

Rosamonde nodded, heading upstairs to collect her things.

Re stood in the corridor, listening to the sounds of the shovels. The door opened just then and Felix led the leader of the protestors in. They stamped their feet at the door, then proceeded to the terrace. Stefan was about to follow then, when Re stopped him.

"Can I have a word with you?" Re requested.

He ushered the officer into the empty dining hall, to a far corner.

"Rosamonde and I are tracking the soul-song to Linderhoff. We would be back in a couple of hours. Hopefully with some good news," Re said. "In the meanwhile, could you help me with something? I urgently need to speak to this journalist who calls himself MKR. Apparently, he is vacationing. But the German Police would be able to reach him, right? Find him and anything about him...his address, his whereabouts, his pictures, phone number and whatever you can find."

"Will ask Felix to get on to it." Stefan said, briefly. He seemed distracted. A group of people were still shovelling the snow away from the windows.

"Is something the matter?" Re asked, instinctively.

"The anonymous call that we got regarding the swans in Harry's parcel? That call was traced to Hans's phone."

"You mean the man you found dead by the pier yesterday?"

"Yes. So, the person who killed Hans and the person who called with the fake tip-off is one and the same person. You know what that means, don't you?"

Re nodded. "That the murder is now indisputably connected to the Treaty."

"Precisely. Now that this fact is confirmed, it also means, that this person means serious business. Murder is a whole new ball game."

"That reminds me. Klint left me a message on the phone last night. About something important that he remembered about the parcel. Did you find him in his room?"

"He wasn't in his room. Isn't he downstairs yet?" Stefan frowned.

Re's heart picked up pace. "No. Has anyone seen him at all this morning? He hasn't been answering his phone either. I am afraid, something's not right."

"Why do you say that? Klint?"

"The ease with which inside news seems to have leaked out was a little strange. Only someone who had possibly spoken to Harry or Klint, or an insider would know that Harry was sending out a parcel last night. That was why I had asked him about it. Initially, he didn't have anything worth sharing but late last night, I think he remembered something important and was to tell me this morning. What if he had remembered speaking to someone about the parcel? Only two people knew about the parcel—Harry and Klint. Yet, someone called up the police and warned them that the swans are in the parcel. Which means Klint *did* speak to someone else about it and he didn't realise that it was an important bit of information, until I prompted him..."

"Are you saying—"

The detective nodded, his expression grave. "Klint could be in danger, that is if something hasn't already happened to him. Just ask your men to look for him right away."

"This nightmare is spiralling. I am really worried. The locals fear that something bad is going to happen, especially after the Christmas tree was burnt down by this Starnberg ET. Nothing should stop the Treaty, Re, it is of the utmost importance. No protests, no thefts and not even murder."

"Stefan, we are going to solve this. I know its touch and go and we don't have much time in hand. But we are a team and we will do this." Re's tone was quiet and more confident than he felt. "How is the work going on in the park. Is the stage up? Are the actors ready with their play? Invitees confirmed?"

"Yes, all that is in control. Mrs Weber is handling the invites to the special Starnberg attendees. The actors and props are ready too. Carlo has done a fantastic design job and Harry should complete the seal by this afternoon. Those two really rose to the occasion," Stefan admitted.

"I am glad."

"And Leon is making sure that another pair of swans will stand in, as mascots, in case we don't find the original ones. I really would hate that, because that would mean the police have failed in their investigation."

"Let's rack our brains and aim for success." Re replied, on a positive note. "What about the poison in the meal? Could you get it tested?" Re asked.

"Not yet. The timing of this business is what infuriates me. Its Christmas time. People are on leave, wanting to spend time with their families. We are struggling to get people to work," Stefan moved a restive hand through his ample hair.

"And the treasure? Today is the 24th, the treasure will be transferred today at 1600 hours," Re reminded, grimly.

"We have alerted all the outgoing stations at Feldafing. There will be checks at various points. For now, we have to hope that it will work."

"I just had a thought. When and if we do find the soul-song, how do we contact Virus?" Re asked.

"I am sure he will find a way to reach out to us. I am on the sharp lookout for any more communication from him."

"Right. I'll see you soon then. I want to first have a quick word with Max before we leave. And Stefan, one thing is for sure. If something has happened to Klint, then we can be positive that Virus is very much present at the hotel and moving freely amongst us."

Stefan's blue-grey gaze locked with the investigator's deep brown. Neither of them needed to say anything more. The implication of that statement was obvious.

16

The snow had been cleared and the hardworking group had sauntered into the restaurant area, looking triumphant. Re stood by the entrance, breathing in the cool winter morning air. His pony tail flip-flopped in the wind and his spectacles fogged with the frost. He had stepped out to clear his thoughts, hoping that the biting cool wind would trigger some hazy thought process in some obscure part of his brain. The group of protestors were still shouting slogans filling the serene, snow-driven roads and park with commotion. The air was thick with vapour and the cold was piercing. Re rubbed his hands together and pulled his beanie over his ears. He saw Ben leaning against his car, ready to leave, as he removed his spectacles and wiped them with a kerchief.

Re turned around and stepped back into the warm corridor again, shutting the wooden door behind him. It was then that he caught sight of the yellow envelope resting against one of the showcases just inside the main door. It was medium sized, thick and sealed. Curious, Re picked it up and sucked in a quick breath. It was addressed to Max.

With quick strides he strode towards the restaurant, hoping to find Rosamonde's brother. He found Max outside on the terrace, smoking a cigarette, all by himself, looking reflective and cocooned in his own world of thoughts.

"A quick word with you, Max?" Re interposed.

"Yes, of course. What can I do for you?" Max turned around readily.

"Be honest with me for a change?" Re raised an eyebrow.

Max flushed. "What do you mean?" he snapped.

"Someone is blackmailing you. Isn't it?"

The young businessman paled. "What a strange question! I mean it isn't any of your business, is it?"

"It certainly is if it involves Rosamonde, *mon ami*. And before you say, that she is your sister and none of my business, let me add, that she is this moment the business of five countries and that means she is a matter of utmost interest to Stefan, me, *and* the German Police."

Max puffed on his cigarette frowning. "I am sure it doesn't concern the Treaty, if that is what you mean."

"Why don't you let me decide that?" Re suggested drily. "Let me help you, Max. Does it have anything to do with Rosamonde being here? Anything to do with her affinity for Sisi?"

Max looked taken aback. "How did you know?"

"Did someone blackmail you into bringing Rosamonde here? Was that the bargain? Who was it?" Re asked sharply.

Max nodded. "It's a long story and not at all a simple one."

"I am listening." Re folded his arms.

Max finished off his cigarette and stubbed it in the snow. He lifted two upturned chairs and plopped one before Re. They both sat down.

"Rosamonde has always been obsessed with Sisi, I told you that before. But the extent of it was quite unknown to us, until one day, she walked into a museum and just took off a dress that belonged to Sisi and wore it! There was a great deal of ruckus and Mother and I had to really pull some strings to hush the matter. We thought it was all over, till a month ago, I got an anonymous call, asking me to bring Rosamonde along for the Treaty signing. Apparently, he had clicked pictures of her in that stolen dress and he threatened to expose her trances to the media. Naturally, I didn't want her to be a brunt of unnecessary scrutiny and also, I saw no harm in bringing her here with me. Being the VP of the company, she has previously accompanied me to many official meets, so this wouldn't be any different. She was also keen on producing a film on Sisi and the timing seemed just right. I was relieved that I would be able to keep an eye on her. So, I did as he demanded but he never returned those pictures as he promised."

"Perhaps he did. I found this envelope by the door just now." Re extracted the yellow envelope from his jacket and handed it to him.

"What!" Max's eyes brightened, as he literally snatched the envelope from Re's hand and tore it open.

Coloured photographs of Rosamonde slid out of the envelope. Rosamonde dressed in a royal black gown, looking regal and composed, and staring straight out into space or at the lens. Max sighed with relief and hastily tucked them back in, but not before Re spotted a piece of paper lurking from under the pics.

"You do know that until he deletes the images form his camera or phone, these prints do not offer either security, protection or privacy," Re reminded, gently.

"I know. But he promised to erase those too and I have to believe him."

Re nodded and pushed back his spectacles. "If you don't mind, I'd like to keep one for reference," he said causally and picked up the one in which Rosamonde was looking straight at the camera.

"Tell me about Dr Gordon. Why was Rosamonde visiting him and how did he die?"

"Oh, you seem to know a lot." Max appeared surprised. "Rosamonde did not have anything to do with his death, if that's what you are implying. She wasn't even in town when he died."

"But what was she being treated for?"

Max sighed. "After the dress incident, we decided that she needed to understand what her trances were all about. A good psychiatrist would be able to diagnose her condition and treat her. She was going through depression and we were worried about her obsession for Sisi. He did some hypnosis sessions with her and made an elaborate report of her condition. We were to go meet him, but unfortunately, he died of heart attack. He was senior and frail so that didn't surprise me. Some found it suspicious but apparently, he did die naturally. However, when we looked for her records, the secretary could not find them. They had vanished."

"So, it wasn't just the photographs that you wanted from the blackmailer. It was also her report?" Re guessed shrewdly. "Can I see it?"

Max flushed again and looked abashed. "You can if you wish, but I already know what's written in it."

"A case of reincarnation?"

Max pursed his lips. "A high percentage of possibility. Dr Gordon stated that it was an unusual case and that he suspected the possibility of reincarnation. But even he couldn't say positively whether it was or not."

"The mind is a very deep and shrewd entity. It can fool others as well as yourself. Difficult to fathom what really goes on in its depths," Re murmured almost to himself. "One last question—how did this person get hold of the report if it had gone missing? Did he steal it from Dr Gordon's clinic *after* the doctor died or—"

"Good Lord! Do you mean to say—" Max appeared startled.

"The thought hadn't crossed your mind? Dr Gordon's death, the blackmail, Rosamonde's photos in his possession along with the report?" Re's eyes narrowed.

"I...I never made the connection...*Mein Gott*—does that mean Rosamonde is in danger?"

The anxiety in his tone seemed genuine and Re softened a bit towards him.

"Let's hope not," he said, casting his gaze to the floor, to avoid exposing his own deep concern.

"I will never forgive myself if anything happens to her," Max murmured under his breath.

"And you have no idea who this person is?"

"No, I've never met him and the few times I spoke to him, his voice was cleverly muffled."

"Thank you, Max, I appreciate you sharing all this with me."

"Actually, thank you. I am relieved. Glad that you are now in charge of my burden."

"Does Leon know any of this?"

Max nodded. "All of it."

"Do you trust him?"

Max looked surprised again. "Of course, I do! So does Rosamonde. Although they called off their engagement, they are still good friends. We are family."

Re nodded. "Glad to hear that."

The door of the Conference Room opened and Adria, Harry, Stefan and the leader of the protesters emerged, laughing. He shook hands with the two diplomats and murmured some assurances and departed.

Re realised that the senior team members of the congregation had taken care of the delicate situation with the finesse of their vast experience. There was no substitute for diplomacy that emerged out of experience, he thought. But Stefan still looked a little unhappy, he realised, as the officer strode towards them.

"What's up, Stefan? That meeting seemed to have gone off well."

"That is one issue certainly, intelligently resolved but another one has unfortunately cropped up," Stefan replied. "Apparently someone told the media that the Treaty isn't going through and that there would be no need for coverage. That is why almost everyone has gone off to celebrate Christmas with their families. I mean some may turn up eventually and the Government social media accounts would make the announcements but the hype will be missing. That may upset the authorities of the countries."

"Another of Virus's acts? This guy is ingenious." Re whistled.

"Good for him but a nuisance for us. What do we do now?"

"I can help," Max chipped in. "I run a media conglomerate for God's sake. What's the big deal?"

Stefan and Re exchanged glances.

"I will set everything up. With some local help and phone cameras, I will hook up everything to my TV network, Facebook pages and social media networks. My team will work form Salzburg. And don't worry about Christmas, they understand how important this is."

Stefan looked so stunned and relieved that Re suspected he would have hugged the young man.

"That is super! If you accompany me to our office, I will explain the exact schedule for the evening. Come along!"

Re watched Stefan and Max vanish indoors. He remained outside on the terrace, staring far out at the park. The snow was thick and smooth and the trees on either side of the path to the Elizabeth statue looked like thermocol cut-outs. He recalled the night before with Rosamonde near the Elisabeth statue. It was her inherent fascination for the Empress that had brought her out to the marble structure at an odd hour. Not to forget the poem she had spontaneously recited. She was so fine-tuned to the Empress's dramatic life and soul-energy that it was as if she was imagining and living it along with her own. And the possibility of the dual experience was equally thrilling and worrisome.

He was still holding her photograph and he glanced at her brooding almost haughty face, her blue-green eyes boring into his brown ones. The question formed in his mind for the umpteenth time. Was Rosamonde indeed Sisi reborn? Was her obsession justified?

17

"Any sign of Klint?" Re enquired. He glanced at his watch. It was already 10:45 am. He would need to leave soon.

"None. His luggage is still in the room and except for his phone, everything else seems to be around, including his files. We tried calling him, but there's no response. What do you suppose has happened to him?" Stefan asked.

"Two options—he may have just walked off without telling a soul. It happens sometimes, you are fed up of a job, or want a change and you take a sudden decision. The second one is what I fear. That something has happened to him. And it has to do with Virus," Re concluded, gravely.

"And that would really be terrible. We will continue to look for him till we find him." Stefan sighed. "By the way, the food reports are in. There was no poison in any food!"

"Just as I suspected. It was a scare tactic. A warning of what could transpire if the soul-song isn't found. And also to create distrust and fear amidst the congregation members, in the hope that they would retract from their duties and quit the Treaty. But he underestimated the inherent patriotism in the members. Not everyone is selfish and greedy, *n'est ce pas?*"

"You are right. They did stumble initially with doubt, but they didn't allow it to affect their duty. I am so glad that they really rose to the occasion. They were chosen by an experienced committee which did thorough background checks to ensure their best representation and the committee proved to be right."

"Which is why, we must respect the faith they have reposed in us, Stefan. They trust the German police to take care of them, find the swans and allow the signing of the Treaty to sail through without any calamities. And which is all the reason why I must leave now. I hope that I will find some answers at the Linderhof Castle."

"Well, then go. The roads are slippery and it would take you over an hour. For the evening event, everyone will be departing for the venue, from the hotel at 4:30 pm. The play begins at 5 sharp and the duration is only ten minutes, after which will be the Treaty signing. The German Police are already enforcing strict security regulations in the park, to prevent untoward incidents. Max is taking care of the live coverage so we are all set. As for the treasure, like I mentioned, we have sent wires to check-points, courier services and even train and airports to keep a sharp lookout for any special packages that would leave the country today."

"The treasure confirmed transfer. The dove will fly at 1600 hours." Re repeated the coded message. "I am worried about it. The use of the word 'dove'. Something niggling at the back of my mind."

"This has been a bizarre conspiracy from the start. We have left no stone unturned at every step of the way and yet we are being outraced. Now, it's up to you to find the soul-song and the swans."

"No pressure at all," Re said, wryly.

Stefan's lips twisted in a half smile. "I know you work best under pressure. And you will do it."

"Let's hope you are right and that the cosmic energy aligns with me," the investigator replied solemnly.

❄

Ten minutes later, Re and Rosamonde were on their way. Neither spoke. Re especially found himself trapped in his own conflicting emotions. With every passing minute, he was being privy to Rosamonde's truth…and instead of clarity, all he felt was more confusion. He felt as if he was carrying her truth like a burden now. He didn't wish her to know that he knew everything about her. Contradictorily, he had to control the urge to discuss the minutest details with her. The dilemma made him ruminate quietly.

The road was slippery and Ben drove carefully and without comment. His usual cheerful demeanour was subdued and he drove soberly.

The road stretched through clusters of quaint country houses and villages with occasional straggly trees on the side of the road, till gradually the mountains came in sight. Then the pine trees thickened, their sloping branches still gleaming green from between patches of snow. Re loved winters and specially when the sun came out to shine on the white mountain tops like golden crowns.

"I picked up this book from the reception—*Castles of Ludwig II*," Rosamonde broke the silence, showing her companion the glossy covered picture book. "Apparently Linderhof was inspired after a visit to Versailles and the castle was built in Rococco style. Is that right, Ben?"

"That's right. Linderhof was not supposed to be a show-piece castle like his other castles. It was meant to be a personal and private villa, which King Ludwig II could use for some peace and privacy. It was the only villa he saw completed and was his favourite residence. The palace is an amazing place and in summer you get to see the surrounding gardens as well. In winter, however, I am not sure even the fountains, the Venus Grotto or temple would be open. So not much of an attraction in winter. It's a fantastic tourist destination for sure but what exactly do you want to see there?"

Re and Rosamonde exchanged quick glances.

"Do you know the Castle well?"

"I have taken several tourists there of course and as a child I had a fascination for all things related to Ludwig, like many children did. You could say that I have a fair knowledge of the castles."

"Well...we are looking for a stately bird. We were told that there is grand peacock in one of the rooms."

Ben was quiet as he manoeuvred the car on the winding roads, going uphill into the mountains.

"Peacocks and swans were Ludwig's favourite birds. As far as my memory serves, there are two peacocks in the Castle. Which one are you referring to?"

"Tell us about them," Re suggested.

"The most important one is in the West Gobelin Room which is also called the Music Room. It is magnificent, the most amazing colours you can ever find. It is life-size and porcelain and gold-gilded and is supposed to be from Sevres. There is another duplicate that is kept in the Eastern Tapestry Room."

"I can't wait to see it. Is filming allowed inside?" Rosamonde asked, her voice lilting in anticipation.

"Afraid not. But seriously, the beauty of the whole experience is so dazzling, it won't ever leave your memory. You don't need a camera, believe me," the cab driver assured.

The landscape changed gradually from plain stretches of snowy land to mountain ranges on either side. The car began climbing winding roads, as snow sparkled on the slopes and the tops glowed like melting gold in the sun's rays. Half an hour later, Ben drove into the parking space.

"You would need to walk up to the castle. It's a short walk," he explained.

Re and Rosamonde climbed out of the car which was parked in front of a shopping centre for souvenirs. Immediately, a gust of cold biting wind, almost swept their beanies off. A snowy track wound up to the castle.

"Do you mind if I leave my backpack in your trunk?" Re asked.

"Please keep mine too, since we won't need the cameras," Rosamonde added.

Re walked to the back of the car and opened the trunk. A variety of stuff lay huddled in a corner—a crumpled black diver's suit, some rocks and stones and old articles along with a stack of papers and plastic.

"You are a man of many interests, Ben." Re remarked, shutting the trunk.

Ben grinned. "I told you. I am Superman. My customers like me to take them to varied spots and I like to be prepared and well-informed."

Re nodded. He and Rosamonde set off on a brisk walk up the road, barely speaking. As the path curved, the Castle came in sight and Re was surprised at the simplicity of the outside structure. Linderhof Castle appeared to be a tall, cream-coloured building, with ornate gold-gilded carved gates. What was striking were the six thick pillars which rose high above the gates, and cherubs and angels of all sizes graced the tops of the pillars. Several intricate, monotone statues adorned the upper half of the façade. Opposite the castle, the gardens stretched in terraced and layered steps.

Everywhere else, ropes warded off entry and like Ben had said, winter seemed to have dried up the entire place.

"Don't go by the outward appearance," Rosamonde warned. "Inside it's like a theatre come alive."

He was surprised at how precisely she had read his reaction. But then, he wasn't really. After all, he already knew that they were energetically aligned and like it or not, they could sense each other's emotions. Re wondered if it made her feel vulnerable. Was that why she was so quiet?

"Let's head straight to the West Gobelin Room," he suggested and Rosamonde nodded.

The moment they entered the main entrance, he realised how right she had been. If the outside façade of the Castle was simple, the inside was flamboyantly opposite. It was a splash of gold, exquisite designs, landscapes, stunning upholstery and paintings. Room after room was like a magical carpet unrolling, every room more magnificent than the other, outdoing its own glorious standard. Re could only imagine how much energy and money had gone into the lavish decor.

"And this is the West Gobelin Room," Rosamonde announced, reading from her book. "There is a rhythm, colour and contrasting succession of horseshoe and oval shapes here. It's stunning!"

Re too paused to appreciate the room's grandeur. The period furniture, colourful paintings with gilded frames that seemed like tapestries with scenes from the Rococco era, a musical instrument that resembled a piano and a harmonium...and then the peacock. Both Re and Rosamonde flashed each other quick looks. It was exquisite as it stood in all its grace and vibrant colours on a gold-gilded carved stand. They hastened to it. Re's heartbeat quickened.

The stately bird that guarded the soul-song...would they find the soul-song? Re dropped down to his knees and inserted his hand through the carved stand, feeling inside the spaces. He tapped the peacock, felt it all round, checked underneath the stand. Nothing. A few minutes later, he rose.

"It's not here. Something is not right."

"The peacock is the stately bird that could have guarded the rose, or the soul-song," Rosamonde said, slowly. Her forehead was creased in concentration.

"It seems right, but obviously isn't. We missed a turn somewhere, a clue, a phrase...."

He whipped out the poem again and they both read it in silence.

> Eagle, up there in the mountains...
>
> The Sea Gull offers you our song in bloom.
>
> On the path of the childhood dreams,
>
> past the lake shrouded in gloom.
>
> Silent we soared but deeply we understood.
>
> the song that our souls once sang...
>
> Now the bird guards it in its stately hood,
>
> in the midst of the heavenly tang.

"*In the midst of the heavenly tang!*" they both chorused at the same time.

Re looked at Rosamonde, sensing a reaction.

"If I was really Sisi reborn, I would have remembered where the soul-song was, wouldn't I? Or at least knew where *it isn't*," she said, softly.

"That makes sense," Re agreed. "But tell me honestly, does this bring you a sense of relief or a feeling of disappointment?"

"Relief of course! I don't want to parade all my life as a reincarnation of Sisi. I have an identity I am proud of—I am Rosamonde Hartman. I have a life, my own likes, dislikes, opinions, my documentaries, my passions. I don't want to be coloured in someone else's colours no matter how much I may admire or respect that person. Perhaps even obsessed as some have labelled it. I have my own dreams and I want to live for them."

"I understand what you mean. But I do believe that one of the main goals of dragging you into this charade is because of this 'obsession'. Someone is testing you. Teasing you. Even challenging you. I think it's up to you to prove who you really are. The paparazzi is a way of pushing your head in a pool of water, pressing you down so you suffocate, till you come out with the truth. Are you suffocating yet?"

"I wish I was... I wish I could stop this nonsense that has shrouded my life since childhood. The knowing and the not knowing. The guessing and soul-searching. As if I have no identity. As if there is no Rosamonde Hartman but someone constantly lurking from inside me. Like there could be two of me. One in a royal outfit and the other, marked, exposed to the harsh winds of life. And still, *I don't know.*"

Re closed the distance swiftly between them and held her hand. "You will know, soon. And this, today is an important sign. If you were Sisi, you would have known if we were on the wrong track. And you didn't. Which means you are more Rosamonde than Sisi."

"I know so." She offered a wane smile, her blue-green eyes moist.

"So, in the midst of the heavenly tang..." Re reminded, gently.

"It's the roses. You were right. We missed seeing this turn. *Now the bird guards it in its stately hood, in the midst of the heavenly tang...* When Mrs Weber mentioned the peacock as a stately bird, for a moment, I had felt that it was not right, but then nothing more appropriate came to mind. But now I know...*the heavenly tang* is the smell of the roses!"

"Which roses?"

"The roses on Rose Island, of course! That's where Sisi and King Ludwig II used to meet. On the island, away from the public, where he had planted hundreds of beautiful roses. They featured in her poems too. Why did I not think of it before?" she wondered, half to herself.

"But we need a stately bird," Re reminded gently. "Which is why we came here in the first place."

"There *is* a stately bird at Rose Island. A very prominent one."

"We have to go then," Re said, promptly. He glanced at his watch. "It's almost 1:30 pm. We don't have much time."

She nodded. "I also have an appointment by the peer at 4 pm. Leon has set it up for me. It's some guy who has more information for my Sisi film and would like to meet me. So hopefully I will be able to make it on our return from the island."

They moved to the Audience Chamber which displayed the King's writing table, framed in silk and gold embroidery and flanked by two fireplaces. They did not pause to admire the table but headed to the Bed Chamber. Both Re and Rosamonde couldn't help but pause to admire the royal bed chamber. The massive crystal candelabra dominated the room with the royal blue bed and motif, the marble sculptures and the elaborate scenes from mythology painted on the ceilings. The display of gold and blue was stunning and exquisite.

They exited by the side entrance and semi-circled around the palace. The wind had picked up but a weak sun veiled the snow-clad mountains, paths and Linderhoff gardens which were closed to the public.

They were at the head of the downhill walking path that led to the car park, when Re spotted the group of thickly clad men, in the distance, equipped and ready with their cameras and long lenses. A silent determined group, awaiting their prey, he thought. Some of the journalists were leaning against the tree, some were smoking but the quiet resolve in their stance was evident.

Re halted just as the media men spotted them and began pointing and gesturing at them. Instantly, the group began moving deliberately up the path. Beside him, Rosamonde stiffened as she saw the approaching group.

Re turned to her, with a flick of his pony tail. He pushed back his silver-rimmed glasses, tilted her head up and clasped her two hands in his.

"*Ecoute* Rosy, *ma chérie*. They are looking for a scandalous royal, reincarnation story, right? Instead, let's give them a juicy, exceptional love story—a beautiful haunting love story, something that would take their minds instantly off impossible illusions. What do you think?"

Re was aware of the approaching journalists, their cameras already trained on them. But he did not glance at them.

"Sounds intriguing! What do you have in mind, Re?" she responded, her gaze steady and inviting.

"Something heart-stopping...if you are ready."

"Yes, I am," she whispered, staring deeply into his brown eyes.

Re returned the stare, aware of the dark flecks in her blue-green gaze, feeling himself sucked into their depths. With a spontaneous swoop, he gathered her into his arms and claimed her soft lips. For an instant, Rosamonde stiffened, then her resistance melted and she merged into him. Re had known that their energies were aligned and vibrant, but he wasn't prepared for the all-engulfing lightning that would streak through him. He kissed her slow and long, savouring the moment, longing for it to go on forever. Forgotten were the hounding men, the 'soul-song', the conspiracy, the treaty... All he could feel coursing through his body was a yearning that was born lifetimes ago but he recognised as eternal... When he raised his head and glanced at her, her eyes were closed. But he sensed the joy and the fantasies behind the closed lids and felt the passion in her trembling body. And above all, he knew, without the slightest shadow of a doubt that he had found his own soul song.

The sound of the cameras clicking wildly and the whispers and laughter of the journalists intruded into his trance. He sensed the excitement spiralling in the world of paparazzi.

Rosamonde's eyes opened and she stared at him, a little disoriented but with a hint of genuine surprise in her eyes.

"That was..." She began, awkwardly.

"Time to leave, *ma chérie*," Re cut in smoothly. He did not wish to dissect one of the most beautiful moments and momentous discoveries of his life. "Walk calmly, like enraptured lovers lost in our own world, holding hands as if that touch joins us at the soul. Don't forget to pass a cool nod at them, perhaps even a composed happy wave. Like film stars do. Are you ready?" he asked gently.

She nodded, inhaling deeply and steading herself into self-composure.

He entwined his long fingers in her soft ones and she flashed him a quick smile of tacit understanding. They fell in step with each other, like a spontaneous rhythm of the bodies and began their slow progress down the slope.

"Keep talking to me, okay? We are two expert filmmakers—if we can direct, we can act too."

"We certainly can," Rosamonde agreed, under her breath.

"You are magnificent, you know that, Rosamonde? And that group of cameramen who is so interested in you, they will never know that what they just witnessed was one of the most historic moments in their journalistic career," he whispered in her ear and she laughed aloud.

The cameramen kept their distance out of sudden respect, their agitated mood and prepared questions completely diffused by the candid show of love. However, they still continued to follow the progress of the couple.

"Be ready for tomorrow's headlines, *ma chérie*—Rosamonde Hartman, the award-winning filmmaker and her handsome beau, caught kissing on the magical slopes of Linderhof Castle," Re continued, his one eye on the car.

"Or better still—Re Parkar, the famous detective, breaking a million hearts as he openly kisses his beautiful girlfriend on the stunning white slopes of Linderhof Castle!" Rosamonde laughed.

"Yes, that's a good one too."

"Re Parkar, you do know that you have offered yourself as my sacrificial guinea boyfriend, to be openly dissected by the brutal media?"

"Yes, I do, *ma chérie*, I have leapt into this sacrifice, with full possession of my senses and with an open heart." He responded with mock graveness.

"Then you really care more than I thought."

Re stopped and glanced at her, still holding her hand. "At least you deduced the truth before I did." He pursed his lips in a half smile. "We are joined at the soul, Rosamonde, caught in the magic of a snowy Christmas afternoon."

They stared at each other for long moments, the media forgotten, the long curving road with tourists forgotten. Re witnessed matching, smouldering emotion in her blue eyes.

"It is Christmas, isn't it? Merry Christmas, Re Parkar!" She raised herself on her toes and kissed him gently on the lips.

His arms went around her and the kiss deepened. Re broke off with a great difficulty.

"Merry Christmas, Rosamonde Hartman! I can see Ben standing by the car and staring at us. He knows something's not right. He has never seen us like this…" he muttered between his teeth. "And the media men are closing in. They are quiet and confused, but still determined. So, get ready to make a dash for it, if necessary."

She nodded.

Re waved at Ben, who seemed to take the hint. Just as Re and Rosamonde reached the last curve of the walking path, Ben drove towards them and halted briefly as the couple swiftly climbed into the vehicle.

As the car speeded ahead, Re and Rosamonde turned in their seats to watch the scene behind them. The cameramen were still taking shots of the retreating car.

Stefan was in Mrs Weber's office, when Felix appeared. One look at the troubled expression on his face and the officer's heart sank.

"Sir, I think you had better come. Something terrible has happened."

"What is it?" Stefan was instantly alert. He sensed erratic, depressing pressure in his chest. But he did not await a response.

Instead, with brisk long strides, he followed Felix through the hall, onto the terrace. Multiple footprints on the thick snow marred the smoothness of the landscape, heading through the park, in the direction of Empress Elisabeth's statue. With his breath coming in short gasps, Stefan hugged his jacket close and plodded through the snow after Felix, keeping all thoughts at bay and praying that he was wrong as they circled to the backside of the statue.

But he wasn't wrong. With a heavy heart, he stared at the body of the man propped up in a sitting position, at the bottom of the statue. Covered in snow, he looked like a statue himself. With snow on his blue eyelids and face, a shirt sneaking from under a slab of white, he looked like a snowman relaxing in calm mediation. Except, none of this was calm or meditative. This was evil. Murder was pure evil and there were no two ways to describe this. Because Stefan knew that Klint had not found his way here on his own. He had been murdered and planted on this spot, and allowed to freeze and harden to death. Only a devious mind could plan and execute such an evil act.

Something brown caught his eye. It was stuck in the snow above the secretary's head. Stefan carefully picked up the soaked piece of paper with his gloved hand. Half the numbers written on it were smudged and illegible and the paper was crumbling. But at least he had a clue—at this point he would even cling to a crumbling paper, he thought grimly.

18

The car raced towards Rose Island, the mountains slowly flattening into plains with trees. It was an hour's drive back and all three were deep in their own thoughts.

Re's phone rang and even before he responded to Stefan's call, he knew it was about Klint. A deep sense of helpless grief overcame him as the officer explained about finding the body in the park.

"You were right, Re. He was in danger. Poor fellow, we could do nothing to protect or save him," Stefan sounded rueful.

"Terrible news. Have you told Harry?"

"Yes. He was devastated and has demanded a full enquiry. Which we would do anyway, of course. In fact, everything that has happened from the start, has been like a one-sided show. We have been mute spectators, facing an extremely clever adversary. But for the first time, we have found a definite clue. A slip of torn paper with half a number. It may have fallen off from the murderer's coat and could be a phone number and no matter what, we will find the person with that number."

"Good luck," Re said, aware of Ben and Rosamonde listening.

He felt anger rising inside him. Anger for the mastermind who had already committed two murders and had jeopardised a world treaty for some selfish agenda. But he also experienced a stab of deep guilt for having failed Klint who had reached out to him. He ought to have contacted him immediately, even at 3 am—perhaps he would have been alive now. Re allowed the mixed feelings to surface and wreak havoc with his emotions. Then gradually the emotions abated; he knew that if he had to stay sane, the only way was to curb this disrupting and disturbing emotions and move forward. And more importantly, try to do justice. He was more than ever determined to do that now.

Thirty minutes later, Ben pulled the car into the parking lot of Rose Island Park. As Re and Rosamonde hastened through the park, walking between tall trees draped in white, Re couldn't help remembering Rosamonde by the edge of the lake, in a mysterious trance and mumbling about death. Had it only been yesterday? It felt like eons ago. Had he really known her only for 24 hours, or even less? Re felt more in awe of his situation than before. If that kiss on the Linderhof slopes was any proof of his emotion, then he had known her for lifetimes. The thought sent a strange chill down his spine.

Mercifully, the sun was out and felt warm and welcoming on their faces. As they strode towards the pier in silence, dodging slippery grounds, the huge rectangular tent came in sight. This was where the Treaty would be signed in a couple of hours. Police were swarming in and out of the tent, some others were setting up heaters at strategic spots. A stage at the far end displayed a huge hoarding with a five-country symbol and the swans as the mascot. Rolls of thick red rugs covered every inch of the ground and pretty chandeliers hung from the roof, adding a touch of glamour. A cheerful ambiance lit up the snowy grey—yellow landscape of the park. A sound system seemed to be blaring inaudible commands in German and Re inhaled deeply. The pressure of the evening suddenly weighed in on him. The soul-song, the swans, poor Klint, Rosamonde, the Treaty…was the murderer laughing? Enjoying his games and evil plans? Would all the devious planning and playing with lives, be worth it for him? Re wished he knew. He wished he could get into Virus' head and think like him to guess what his next move would be.

"In normal conditions, this would be so exciting, wouldn't it?" Rosamonde interrupted his stream of thoughts, her gaze cruising over the tent. "So would this trip to Rose Island. I can't wait to get there, you know. I have been to Rose Island as a child a couple of times. In summer a boat takes you there and back in a short while. Winter is not the right time to go of course, especially when there are no boats. It's great luck that Leon could arrange one for us. I knew he would be able to get us one."

"Quick thinking on your part to request Leon for help," Re agreed, as they headed towards the pier.

"He is a diplomat with contacts. Now is the time to use them, to save the Treaty," Rosamonde announced.

Re smiled. "No arguing that."

He sensed the excitement in her. Like a child going to Disneyland. Was the trip bringing back old memories? He wondered.

They reached the pier and their feet crunched on the slippery white board. Re couldn't help remembering Hans, the look of surprise on his cold frozen face.

A red and white striped motor boat was waiting for them. In the distance, the island looked like hazy, white-washed clump of trees in the middle of the ice-covered lake.

"Ms. Hartman? I am Druck. Welcome to my little beauty!" the boatman, a tiny, curly-haired man, with a captain's cap, beamed from ear to ear.

"Hello, Druck." Rosamonde smiled.

He offered her his hand and they stepped into the rocking boat.

"You are lucky the water isn't frozen yet. And if this hadn't been an emergency, as explained by Sir, I would have never ventured near Rose Island in winter."

"Thank you, Druck, we appreciate it."

"Wrap yourselves up, passengers. It is going to be a cold ride!"

The engine chugged and Druck steadily led the boat between pieces of semi-frozen ice into the lake. Icy wind whipped through their clothes and hair and Re and Rosamonde slipped into the tiny, single cabin for warmth. It was already freezing cold and they huddled in their jackets. Rosamonde glanced at Re with a curious look on her face.

"You are rather quiet, aren't you?" she said.

"A lot on my mind," the investigator admitted.

"We will find the soul-song, Re. I know it's on the island," she assured. "And you know what, I think I can also guess where Virus must have found this original poem by Elisabeth. The Empress and Ludwig would often leave notes for each other in a secret drawer of a writing table in the Casino on the island. I think that's where he must have found the poem. Hidden inside. And it would be so like Sisi to do something so dramatic and even romantic. It was a sweet gesture, perhaps to thank Ludwig for something he had done for her. Yes, Rose Island is the place where she would hide it and expect him to go find it. The rose, the soul-song…"

"What makes you so sure?" Re couldn't help asking.

There was a subtle excitement around Rosamonde. Her eyes were bright, the hint of a smile lay lightly in the corner of her lips. Her hands moved restlessly in her lap. He could see her teetering on the edge again. Like she was two people, pushing in and out of two worlds.

"Because once before she had done something similar. I mean almost similar. In 1881, King Ludwig had fled to the island to be alone. Sisi would often go over to meet him and this time too she did the same. She took her servant Rustimo and rowed across from Starnberg to the island to meet the king. On the way back, Ludwig accompanied her in the boat and Rustimo sang lovely folk songs on his guitar. It was a pleasant and memorable boat ride and the king was so pleased with his singing, that he gifted Rustimo his ring. Those moments were so beautiful and impressed Sisi so much, that she later wrote a poem around it, calling the King an eagle and herself as the northern sea dove. And she left the poem in the secret drawer of the castle on the island for him to find. This island was his refuge and their meeting place. It was secluded, covered by bushes and trees and it afforded them the privacy and freedom to be themselves. To talk, to recite poetry, to discuss art away from government issues...."

Re listened, the faint roar of the engine and the wind serving like background sound. As she spoke, he was transported to an era, that he could vividly imagine.

"Their friendship was special and that is why I am quite certain that this is the place where Elisabeth would hide any letter or gift for him."

"That sounds reasonable." He nodded.

"Ahoy...here we are!" Druck announced.

The boat slid into a covered landing and slowly, carefully Re and Rosamonde climbed onto the slippery, ice-laden wooden landing.

"I'll be waiting here for you," Druck said, unnecessarily.

The intricate carvings on the wooden seal, displayed a neatness of hand.

"This is simply perfect. You've added this little heart on the edge which is so apt and discreet and Harry is seriously talented," Stefan expressed warmly.

"I am glad that both of us could pull this off," Carlo shrugged.

"I am too. Where is Harry?"

"In his room, on a video call with Klint's family. What terribly sad news to deliver and receive on Christmas day." Carlo sighed. "He is naturally very disturbed and wanted to talk to Klint's family first."

"Very thoughtful of him," the officer agreed.

Stefan and Carlo were in the restaurant, even as tables and chairs were being cleared for the Ball that evening. Mrs Weber was supervising in quick fast German, and Stefan knew that the hall would be ready well ahead of time. The restaurant was closed to the public today, which made arrangements easier.

"We are running the printouts now, so I will see you later then." Carlo rose.

"Right, thank you so much again."

As the Italian strode out of the hall, Stefan replaced the seal carefully in its box. He strode to his office and locked it in the safe. He had just pocketed the key, when Inspector Karl and Felix hastened into the room.

"Headquarters has traced the number, sir," Felix announced. The expression on his face was hard.

"What is it? Who does it belong to?" Stefan asked, instinctively reading the officer's anger.

"Gunter," Karl replied.

"Well, that says it all." Stefan sensed a sudden mixed wave of relief and rage.

"Undoubtedly, he is our man." Karl concluded.

Stefan nodded. "We would need to take immediate action."

"Right away. Gunter hasn't showed up for work today, so we are going to his house. Want to join us?"

"I wouldn't miss this meeting for anything!" Stefan immediately pulled on his coat.

"Let's go."

Ten minutes later, the police car pulled up in front of a single storied house on the outskirts of Bernried. The house had no fence and the three officers strode up to the main door. Felix rang the bell and they waited for Gunter to respond. When no one did, Felix tried the door which swung open effortlessly.

Stefan glanced at the other two, frowning. Without a word, they slipped into the small sitting room. It was sparsely furnished and empty. Felix strode ahead into the next room while Stefan peeped into the untidy kitchen.

"Sir!"

Immediately Karl and Stefan rushed into the other room and stopped short. Bare essentials occupied the small room. It was on the single bed, by a window that Gunter lay, lifeless, with his eyes closed. Stefan stared at the strange sight. An empty bottle of sleeping pills had rolled near his open palm. He appeared to be sleeping, calm and reconciled.

Plastered on the wall were photographs and newspaper clippings. Almost all were of Rosamonde Hartman. Placed on top of a notebook, a note was pinned down by a paperweight. It was written in German. Inspector Karl picked it up with gloved hands and read it aloud.

"I am tired and I am ending what I started. I take full responsibility for everything that has happened including stealing the swans (which are in the cupboard) and putting the poison in the meal and killing Hans and Klint. I have loved Rosamonde and I wanted the world to know that she is no ordinary woman. She is royalty. Forgive me. Gunter." Karl glanced at his colleague and shook his head.

"Suicide note. Brief and apologetic. Looks like he tried to pull off more than he could chew. When he knew he had failed and realised that we would reach him eventually, he took his own life."

"He planned and plotted everything like an expert, but ultimately gave in to his own insecurities," Stefan commented, feeling disgusted. "I just wish he hadn't killed Hans and Klint. Two innocent lives lost for no reason at all."

Felix opened the wooden cupboard and extracted a plastic bag. Stefan's eyes lit up.

"The swans!" A wave of relief washed over him. *It was over, finally over.* "Let's get back to the hotel—we can finally enjoy some peace and joy implementing the Treaty."

He took one last look at the scene and walked out, allowing his colleagues to complete the investigation.

Their shoes crunched in the snow as Rosamonde led the way through the trees into the island.

"This was where the King's Yatch Tristram would land. In summer this whole part by the edge of the water is covered by wild rushes and weeds. Ah here is the villa, a wooden palazzo, called the Casino by the locals."

They had appeared in a clearing and right in the front, between two tall, snow-laden trees stood an ochre-coloured tall building with shuttered maroon wooden windows and balconies and a conical roof. It seemed like a mix of Pompeian villa, an Italian country house and a Bavarian Alpine house.

"I can imagine the two of them here, can you?" Rosamonde asked. "The peace, the beauty of the land, the pleasure of each other's company away from curious probing eyes, picnicking amidst the flowers or peering over the lake from the balconies. A royal romantic and exclusive retreat...."

Re was quiet. He almost didn't feel like disturbing her mood. She seemed so much at home in these wild surroundings. Or was he allowing her the time to experience the peace she needed to understand herself? They were like the only two people in the world, surrounded by the silence of the past, a strange promise of the present and a dreamy uncertainty of the future. The tranquil alpine scenery, the curving paths through the trees, the smell of the blooming wild roses...time seemed to have stood still. Almost as if the soul-song was not the key to an answer and the clock wasn't ticking ominously against the landmark signing of the Treaty. The wind lifted and an eerie sound filtered between the trees. Rosamonde seemed to be unaffected by the cold or the wind. She moved from path to path, staring out at the view of the lake, the Casino and the trees, soaking in the winter island. Her face was soft and eyes unfathomable and Re longed to know what was going through her mind this very minute. Was she moving between two worlds again? Was Sisi peeping into her inner world, tip-toeing through her memories?

"Do you think we can go inside the Casino?" he asked.

"The casino or villa would be closed for winter and anyway we don't need to go inside at all. Fortunately, *the bird that guards the soul-song in its stately hood,* is out here in the open! Follow me, please."

She walked around the villa, a spring to her feet. As if she knew every inch and corner of the island and had explored it in times gone by. Re shook his head vehemently. He shouldn't allow such thoughts to ignite his imagination. Rosamonde was *not* Elisabeth and he had better keep sharp track of the thought, for both their sakes.

Right behind the villa, some distance away, stood a tall blue and white striped column, surrounded by an oval patch of snow.

"This is supposed to be the rose garden. In summer it has hundreds of exotic flowers in different varieties. Just imagine the fragrance. And right there, that glass column, was a gift from a Prussian king as a mark of friendship. And on that column stands the girl with the parrot—the stately bird guarding the soul-song!" Rosamonde announced, her voice tapering into a whisper of awe.

She turned to stare at Re and their eyes locked. He saw the look of triumph in her blue-green eyes, a smile in her heart. She was absolutely certain and he marvelled at her certainty.

Without another word, they both hastened to the pillar. Re glanced at the tall glass column with a structure of a gold-gilded girl carrying a bird on her shoulder. There was no way he could reach the girl or the intricate carved top of the pillar she stood on.

"How could Elisabeth have ever reached the girl to hide the soul-song?" He frowned. "It's too tedious an effort. Are you sure this is the bird?"

"Positive. But you are looking at the wrong hiding place. Look at the faces of the girl and the bird." Rosamonde pointed.

"The girl is looking up at the sky and the bird is looking downwards, at the foot of the pillar. You mean..."

"Let's look!" she suggested.

A sudden surge of excitement rose in Re as he hastened to the pedestal of the glass column. He swept his hand under the ledge that covered it and stiffened. His fingers slid into a gap in the pillar and touched something hard.

"I found something," he mumbled.

Carefully, he extracted an oblong wooden box. It looked worn and weather beaten and he brushed off the layers of dirt and mud and snow gathered on it.

"Open it," Rosamonde commanded, softly.

There was a small rusted latch on the side. Inhaling deeply, Re undid the latch and lifted the lid of the box. Both gasped. Inside, the velvet bed was tattered and unravelling in the corners but the box was empty. Re experienced a stab of deep disappointment. So close and yet so far.

"Oh no!" Rosamonde exclaimed. "Someone got to it before us."

"Perhaps not. Perhaps the gift was removed from this box, ages ago." Re sighed. "Don't forget that we were just chasing a forgotten poem, written more than a century ago. It's quite likely that someone discovered this hiding place and took what was in it, leaving the box here. But you were right. The soul-song was on the island and we almost did find it."

"Unfortunately, now we will never know what the soul-song actually was," she said, her voice thick with dissatisfaction. "Was it a rose? Another poem? A statue? A vase? So *schade!*"

"Let's not dwell on it, or we will never get out of it. That's it. We need to report to Stefan. And reach out to Virus in some way and let him know of the situation," Re remarked.

He rose, dusting the snow off his trousers, trying to hide his disappointment under the guise of pragmatism.

Rosamonde was quiet as they made their way back to the landing. Re understood and shared her sentiments. He was severely and unfairly feeling let down too. He felt deflated, like facing an anti-climax. Like he had been served a raw deal. But history had a way of weaving into your life and passing out of it without comment. This was something like that. They had tried, but couldn't control the passage of time.

"Cheer up. We tried, didn't we?"

She nodded. "We did. But I was so sure..."

"And you were right. It was exactly where you felt it would be. You sure do understand Elisabeth and Ludwig and their unique friendship. It most certainly helped."

"But it wasn't enough," she concluded, in a glum tone.

Re couldn't refute that logic, so he did not respond.

Druck was relieved to see them.

"The weather can change any minute. A storm is likely to brew up. We better hurry back," he announced.

The wind had dropped, so both Re and Rosamonde stayed on board.

As the boat turned around, she glanced at her watch. "Almost four. At least I will be able to make my appointment with this film guy," she said.

Druck was in a chatty mood. "Do you know that this area around the island is a pre-historic settlement? You can find remains of dwellings and early Celtic houses from the 1st millennium BC. There are at least 111 small individual sites under this water, right now, although you can't see much with this film of ice—and they are all very well preserved. It is a UNESCO world heritage site now. Unfortunately, greedy smugglers are trying to make money out of selling the findings of these ancient sites. A pity the world is coming to this."

The boatman was cheerful and knowledgeable but Re knew that both of them were not in mood to chat with him. The snow began to fall suddenly, softening the vision around them. If Re hadn't been in a morose mood, he would have admired the show of beauty and fantasy, a play of white and grey, ice and wind and swirling flakes in the sky.

Druck manoeuvred the motorboat artfully to the pier. Through the snowfall, Re caught the blur of a tall figure standing by the pier, almost merging nondescriptly into the white landscape in his white jacket and white beanie.

"Oh, that's my resource—my 4 pm appointment. He is early," Rosamonde observed. "He has been so reserved and kind of strange. Said that what he had to share with me was very exclusive information and I would have to prove my identity with a password."

"What password?" Re asked, pushing his spectacles on the bridge of his nose.

"Wait and see," she laughed. "It's all rather mysterious. Thank you, Druck. It was very kind of you to ride us over to the Island in this cold and snow."

Re shook hands with the boatman and stepped out after Rosamonde. Druck nodded and waved at them, leading the motorboat away. Rosamonde turned to greet her guest, and Re held back, keeping a discreet distance. He did not wish to intrude into her professional meeting. Out of the blue, a sudden strong vibration hit him. Something in the air...a strong energy...

"Hello, Hank!" Elisabeth greeted the stranger. "Terrible weather, isn't it?"

"It is," Hank drawled, his accent thick. "But is the dove ready to fly?"

Rosamonde nodded. "Yes, the dove is ready to fly," she responded, slight amusement in her tone.

Re's head jerked up. *The dove ready to fly?* Like lightning, the words of the coded message flashed in his brain. *'The treasure confirmed transfer. The dove will fly at 1600 hours.'* The treasure. The treasure was supposed to be shipped at this hour. 4 pm. *Rosamonde was the treasure!*

The man was leading Rosamonde away, his hand curved around her back, speaking to her in a low voice. The world blinded for Re, as momentary indecision and anxiety clamped a fog in his brain.

"Wait!" he shouted.

Hank turned. In the falling snow which obstructed clear vision, Re saw his hand going to his jacket pocket. He sensed more than saw, the bulge of the gun. Without the slightest hesitation, Re plunged straight at him. Only one thought reverberated in his brain. *Rosamonde was in danger!* He grasped the man's hand in an iron grip, just as he withdrew the gun, thrusting it upwards and pinning it in the sky. A deafening shot rang out. Elisabeth screamed. Re pushed hard and the two men struggled for long moments, their feet skidding and slipping over the frosty boards of the wooden pier. His spectacles slid off his nose and clattered on the ice. The detective applied all his strength and they both careened dangerously on the edge of the pier, slipped and toppled into lake. The freezing water hit him hard and he gasped. He struggled to hold on to the man, but he lost his grip even as the water sucked him into its cold icy fold, freezing and numbing all thought from his brain. His last conscious thought was the memory of his fingers curling tightly around his Ganesha pendant.

"Re...Re, wake up! It's all right, you are safe!" a voice called from a distance, far away, like in a tunnel. "Re...open your eyes!"

His eyelids flickered, as the urgent insistent voice filtered into his conscious. Slowly, as if something heavy was weighing them down, he opened his eyes and stared straight into Rosamonde's anxious face.

"Re, you are safe," she repeated, softly.

Sudden images of the struggle and the gun filtered into his brain and he sat up. The blanket that was covering him, slid down. *The treasure! Rosamonde...*

"What happened? Are you okay?" his voice was hoarse.

"I am fine, thanks to you," she assured.

"And you are fine, Re, thanks to her. She saved your life," Stefan's voice cut in.

The officer looked very concerned. Re could see Ben peering anxiously from behind Stefan. His eyes met Rosamonde's as she leaned over and wrapped the blanket around him. He was shivering, his pony tail hanging limp on his shoulder. Mercifully, someone had found his spectacles and they were back in place.

"What exactly—?" He sat up, discomfort and cold making him uneasy.

Beside him Rosamonde shivered, as she hugged the blanket closer. Her eyes were downcast and Re sensed that she was in a kind of shock herself.

"She jumped into the lake and pulled you out. It was sheer madness." Stefan sounded angry. "It was lucky that we heard the shot and Ben ran forward to help us too. We managed to drag you out."

"What about that man, Hank?"

"We have taken him into custody. Actually, there were at least three more people, ready to kidnap Rosamonde."

"But who *were* they?"

"Right now, let's get the two of you out of your cold, wet clothes and into the warmth of indoors. The programme will begin in 45 minutes. We better hurry."

Stefan stepped forward and gave Re a hand, "You think you can walk? You almost froze to death. If Rosamonde hadn't pulled you out, I shudder to think what would have happened to you."

"I…I'll manage. The soul-song…," Re began.

They made their way to the parking but the investigator's mind was full of questions.

"Rosamonde told me about what happened on the island. Don't worry. We traced the half number we found near Klint's body and it led us to Gunter. Unfortunately, when we tracked him down to this room in Bernried, we found him dead. He had committed suicide but had left a confession note. He had confessed to being the mastermind behind this entire terrible charade. He confessed to stealing the swans and poisoning the food and the rest. We found ample proof in the room too, including the swans which are now safely in our custody. So, with a huge relief I can say that finally, all is well, and we can now look forward to a smooth enaction of the Treaty."

"But why did he want to involve Rosamonde in this conspiracy?"

"Apparently, he must have been following her for long. His wall was plastered with her photographs and newspaper clippings. Must be a case of obsession. His suicide note says that he loves her and that she is no ordinary woman, she is royalty."

Re was quiet as he allowed the information to sink in.

"So…it's over then?" Re's head swam. "Even without the soul-song." It was all over. He should feel relief. He would soon. He just needed to get out of the cold.

As the others walked ahead, Stefan slowed down and looked at Re.

"You did a remarkable job back there. Protecting Rosamonde. The plan was clearly to kidnap her. They were a team of Government officials. I think the message is quite clear."

"What message?"

"Re…it is obvious that the treasure is Rosamonde. But do you know why? Because officials believe that she is indeed a reincarnation of Empress Elisabeth. That can spell many things to many people and in many countries. People who mean well and those who don't. Because it can mean revelations, secrets being unearthed, unexplained stories being retold and perhaps even history being rewritten! It's a frightening thought."

Re was silent. "I understand. The rumour has taken on gargantuan proportions. Rosamonde is in perpetual danger now from all quarters."

"That's right. And what worries me the most, is that there's not much we can do about it."

Re stared at Stefan, reading a real fear in his blue eyes.

19

The guests began strolling in from the freezing cold to the warmth of the long tent. Volunteers waiting at the two entrances, received the guests and the VIPs warmly, showing them to their seats. The chandeliers were aglow, brushing the tent with an ethereal gold. Tall ceramic vases filled with flowers, placed on the red carpet brought the essence of spring in the middle of winter. On a centrepiece on the stage, carefully shielded under thick transparent glass, stood the famous mascots of the Treaty—the beautiful swans. Cameras were placed in strategic areas, ready to cover the entire event live. Max had been true to his word and had set up an entire social media and TV network linkup. Carlo had redesigned the seal and Harry had done a super job with the engraving. Adria had ensured that the draft was excellently worded and copyedited with the major agreement printed out on a large laminated sheet. Everything was in order. The play *Lohengrin*, would begin in exactly half an hour. Feldafing's who's who was present along with some diplomats from the German Government. Stefan felt an immense satisfaction at the turn out on such a cold winter afternoon. The Treaty would change the future in dramatic and happy ways and he was proud to be a part of it. He glanced at his watch. He hoped that Re would recover soon and be present to witness this glorious moment in history.

Re paced restlessly in his room. It was all over, he reminded himself, then why was he restless? Why did he feel a sense of incompletion? Was it because by choosing death, Gunter had evaded explanations? Because that's what Re needed. Explanations, answers—the whys and the hows. Without that closure, he would perhaps always experience this sense of incompletion. He opened the drawer and found the envelope with Rosamonde's details along with the points he had drawn on the tissue paper in the restaurant last night. He took a pencil, to update the list.

1. Letter from Virus asking for the soul-song, and involving Rosamonde in it.
   Status: The soul song couldn't be found.

2. The theft of the swans and the threat to the Treaty.
   Status: Confession by Gunter, swans returned.

3. A group of people opposing the Treaty because it was named after Sisi.
   Status: Matter resolved by Adria and Harry.

4. The murder of the man by the Island jetty.
   Status: The man has been identified as Hans and Police are working on it. Gunter confessed to it.

5. Empress Elisabeth's statue covered in lingerie (although not certain that this is in anyway connected with the case).
   Status: Unresolved.

6. Someone informing the Paparazzi that Rosamonde was the Empress reborn.
   Action required: Ask Stefan to find out from the Press Bureau who gave them this information.

7. Adria's horse trap was tampered with and she had a fall. A note implied that Carlo had done it.
   Status: Confession by Gunter.

8. The intercepted code message which mentioned the transfer of the treasure the next day.
   Status: ...The treasure was Rosamonde. Resolved.

9. An anonymous call informed that the swans could be in Harry's parcel.

   Status: ....

10. The poisoned dinner, proof of the poison bottle and Adria's kerchief found in the kitchen.

    Action: Food was not poisoned and confession that Gunter had done it.

11. ET appearances in Starnberg and finally the burning down of the Christmas tree.

    Status: What role did the ET have in the Treaty? Was it connected or an isolated incident?

Re paused at the 10th point. Gunter had confessed to everything but why did he have pictures of Rosamonde in his room? Why had he been following Rosamonde and dragged her into this charade? Why had he blackmailed Max and demanded that he bring her to Starnberg? Something didn't add up. Why commit suicide at all? Why give up on the soul-song, on Rosamonde? On the Treaty? So many questions unanswered yet the police were satisfied with his confession.

A sudden thought struck him. Find the soul-song or the wrath of the swans would fall on Starnberg. But what if there was no soul-song? And Virus knew that they wouldn't find one because it did not exist, in the first place? What if it was just a timer and an excuse for the wrath to befall the Treaty?

Re shook his head to clear the confusion in his head. Had the whole search for the soul-song been nothing but a farce? He wasn't convinced. Then what had it achieved? It had taken Rosamonde on a path of nostalgia...it had brought back memories of her time spent in Starnberg, renewed her obsession for Sisi and confused her about her own identity.

She had met Mrs Merwelt who had told her about her sister, Rosamonde's governess, pining for her, feeling guilty and heartbroken. And her son Conrad worked in Munich now... Re stilled. Conrad...Konrad....the K in MKR? He was a writer, working in Munich. MKR!

Virus had tried very hard to expose Rosamonde to the paparazzi, had hoped that she would lead him to the soul-song. Virus seemed to have a special connect with the paparazzi because he was a journalist, of course. *Virus was Konrad!* Not Gunter... Suddenly, the fog seemed to clear. All along he had wondered...what had Rosamonde to do the with the Treaty? And now he knew. *She didn't.* Konrad was the one who was connected to the Treaty. And suddenly he knew why and how. He knew what Klint had wanted to tell him and why he couldn't. Smart, intelligent Konrad.

Re spotted an envelope on his table. He recalled that he had asked Stefan to gather information on MKR, these were those notes. He opened the envelope and a bunch of newspaper clippings slid out—MKR's various articles—on science, travel, drones, Munich and Starnberg and Rose Island and its UNESCO dwellings and a rather bad and an old picture of MKR himself. Re sucked in his breath. *Mon Dieu...* He had to warn Stefan...the Starnberg ET was about to strike again. For the last and final time....

He whipped out his phone and punched Stefan's number, but he couldn't get through. He would have to rush to the venue. He hoped against hope that there would be a car waiting for him. He had released Ben, because official cars were to take them to the venue. He crossed the restaurant where Sisi's cake would be displayed later and the dinner party would take place. How beautifully decorated it all was. But Re didn't stop to admire it all. He headed straight out into the cold, hoping against hope that Stefan had kept a car ready for him. To his immense relief, the officer had kept his word. Just as Re stepped out into the cold evening, a uniformed man nodded and a car was at his service. Re glanced at his watch. Seven minutes to 5 pm. His heart was beginning to beat rapidly.

All the dignitaries were seated in neat rows awaiting the programme to begin. Leon Schubert, Maximillian Hartman, Carlo Pelle, Adria Gerodimos, and Harry Ramone. Other diplomats sat on either side, murmuring in low tones. Leon felt pride in the event, almost as if he had a personal stake in it. On one side of the stage, a cut-out of a boat lead by swans stood waiting. The play would soon begin and the famous Lohengrin would arrive in the swan boat to save the Princess. That was why he was the Swan King, Leon smiled. It was his favourite story. He wished that he could be Lohengrin and save Rosamonde from whatever she was going though. But he knew it was too late. He sighed. Perhaps his boat had sailed already. But where was Rosamonde?

Karl and Felix were at the entrances ensuring the comfort of the invitees and police patrolled outside, in silent vigil. Stefan moved along the aisles, a walkie-talkie in hand, as his sharp gaze took in everything. When he was satisfied, he murmured in the walkie-talkie. It was time for the play to begin. The anchor, a beautiful lady in an apt suit, came on stage to make announcements and the play began.

Re repeatedly tried Stefan's number, his heart beating erratically. Time was crucial. He had to get through to Stefan…they had to stop the final attack of the ET!

The car just turned into the parking when his call got through.

"Stefan!"

"Re, where are you?"

"Listen, Stefan. Get out of the tent and keep a sharp lookout for the Starnberg ET. And shoot it at sight," Re remarked.

"What?"

"Shoot it at sight. Do not delay even a second, do you get me? I am almost there. Shoot at sight."

The car had barely stopped when Re jumped out. He began sprinting down the path towards the venue. The sun had vanished again and a grey tone had enveloped the park. The wind had dropped ominously as if in preparation for the worst to come. Re's heart was pounding, his lips murmuring a silent prayer. Danger was looming over head, ready with its lethal strike. Lives were at stake and if anything happened to even one person, he knew he would never be able to forgive himself. He ought to have seen this coming. He ought to read the energy...thoughts burst into his head, almost blinding him. It was now or never.

He was just within sight of the event tent, when he saw it. First a speck, then a floating body emerging out of the cloudy grey sky with horns jutting out on the side...an evil presence poised to attack. Re halted, sucking in his breath. It was as if the earth had stopped rotating for infinitesimal seconds and everything had frozen. The breeze had paused, the clouds had stilled, the sky had darkened—it was the calm before the roar. Re's lips moved in a silent prayer, as the ET hovered closer to the tent. It was at that moment that a shot rang out. And another one. And the

ET burst into smithereens, pieces of metal and cloth tossed in the sky.

Relief flooded through him. For seconds Re held his palms over his eyes as tears spontaneously squeezed from the corners. He brushed them away impatiently and sprinted towards Stefan and the other cops.

"Excellent shot, Stefan! You just averted the biggest calamity and the most horrifying bonfire of the year," Re remarked, breathless.

Stefan turned to his friend. "How...what? I thought it was all over... How did you know the ET was a drone?" the officer asked, incredulously.

"I'll explain on the way. We have the mastermind to catch before he escapes," Re said, his voice grim.

"Right. Karl can come with us and Felix you better go back into the tent and control the situation," Stefan fired the instructions.

Felix nodded and headed to the tent. Re broke into a jog again in the direction of the parking and Stefan, Karl and some policemen followed suit. Finally, Re paused and took a deep breath. He knocked on the window of a car.

"Hey, Superman!"

Ben unrolled the window. "Oh, hello, did you need something?" the driver asked, surprised.

"Actually, the German Police need *you*," Re said, casually.

"What?" Momentary confusion crossed Ben's shiny bald face.

Stefan stepped forward. "You are under arrest for the murder of three innocent men, theft, hindering and disrupting international affairs and for smuggling national heritage artefacts from Rose Island. What should we call you—Ben, Konrad or MKR?"

"*Nein*! This is a mistake—" Ben began, furiously.

Karl didn't wait for his protest as the door was flung open and Ben was forced out of the car. The policeman clipped a handcuff on to Ben instantly.

"It indeed was a mistake—on our part. We trusted you but you played dirty right under our noses, pretending to help us. Murder, conspiracy, and betrayal of the worst kind," Re remarked, coldly.

"I deny all the charges," Ben declared.

"We have enough proof to convict you, Ben. You will have ample time in jail to reflect on your actions and wonder if all of it was worth it," Stefan said.

"You can prove nothing. You Re were totally useless... you couldn't even find the soul-song!" the cab driver scoffed.

"And how do you know that?"

"I know. I have been with you throughout, laughing at you. You, smitten by Rosy, hindering her path to the final realisation...her royal madness. The press was all over her, if only she had grasped the meaning of that attention, she could have lived in that glory all her life. I had made it easy for her. *To remember*... She could have found the soul-song! But she got distracted by you...it made me angry."

"What really made you angry was the fact that you felt she was responsible for your mother's heartbreak and death. Isn't that the real story?"

"Yes, she was responsible for my mother's death. My mother doted on her. She was the daughter she could never have...someone to be proud of. I was always her biggest disappointment, but Rosy? She was a princess. And I hated her! And hated her more because my dear mother pined for her all her life and was punished for something she did not do. And Rosy just walked out of her life and never looked back, as if she was just a maid or a piece of lifeless furniture." Ben's voice was cold fury.

"But that's not all. You always suspected her connection to Sisi and wanted to use her to find the soul-song but you also wanted to punish her for being who she was. Which is why you were prodding her memory in the hope that she would reveal not only the soul-song, but also expose her past to the world, thus endangering herself. And you were greedy, you didn't want the Treaty signed because you were busy collecting heritage relics from under the lake, which were fetching you pots of money, isn't that right? The Treaty would have totally encroached into your freedom. So, you clubbed it all together and matched the timing well. Personal vendetta and professional gain. Your revenge on Rosamonde, the soul-song and the Treaty...you stopped at nothing. Even murder."

"I need to meet Rosy."

"Don't mention her name ever again." Re's tone was grave, his eyes glued to Ben's. "You messed up her life unforgivably. There can be no retribution enough for your acts."

"This isn't over. I insist I need to meet Rosy, she will understand." Ben struggled against the handcuffs. His face was red and his bald head was shining.

Re turned to Stephen and Karl. "Check the trunk, please. You will find the remote for the drone, his diving suit and some relics from the UNESCO site," he said. "The relics alone would be enough to charge and retain you in police custody."

Ben burst out into German and Re was glad his German wasn't so good. He could only imagine the string of angry expletives that erupted from the cab driver's mouth.

The tent was abuzz with sizzling energy. Re stood on the side-lines, observing the well-lit, pleasantly warm tent-hall packed with eminent personalities of many nationalities. The security guards were still alert at strategic spots, their eyes cruising the venue for any untoward signs. The actors on the stage, dressed in their glittering theatrical clothes, bowed and waved in acknowledgement, as applause thundered in the pandal. Despite the commotion outside, the play *Lohengrin* was a huge hit and Re could see that Stefan appeared very pleased as he climbed up on to the stage to take the mic.

"Thank you for a truly remarkable performance," the officer appreciated. "A play befitting this very important occasion." He waited till the actors left the stage, then continued with a cheerful lilt to his voice. "Our anchor for the evening has taken ill and I have been asked to step in this evening. Now for the moment we have all been waiting for. May I call upon the stage the esteemed members of the committee, specially appointed by their countries, for Sisi's Imperial Treaty of Love and Peace." Stefan introduced the members and one by one Max, Leon, Harry, Carlo, and Adria climbed up on the stage.

They all looked resplendent in formal attires. While the men wore smart suits, Adria was suitably matched in a deep blue skirt and coat and a crisp white blouse. They exchanged warm smiles with each other, talking in friendly undertones and Re could almost detect a fondness for each other. If the Treaty had accomplished a genuine camaraderie between the congregation members, then it had already begun its work. The happy thought brought a smile to Re's lips.

As the buzz in the audience quieted down, Harry took the mic and in his neat and polished English, introduced the features of Treaty and its components. Leon stepped forward and removed the transparent hood from the swans, displaying them grandly. He explained their significance as the perfect mascot of peace and love of the Treaty and their long journey from Neuschwanstein Castle. Adria explained in detail the process they had followed and how they had mutually arrived at the cultural, social and political decisions. Carlo and Max spoke about the difference the Treaty would make to their countries and how it would benefit the rest of the world, simultaneously voicing their hopes and aspirations. The guests broke into more applause of appreciation as they understood the depth and thought that had gone into the making of the Treaty. Re relished the moment. The world would never know the pressure, the fear, the uncertainty behind the Treaty and more importantly, the cruel loss of lives. For Re, the gleam of satisfaction on the faces of the diplomats brought on a surge of gratitude.

Finally, the mic returned to Harry again.

"Before we sign this amazing Treaty, I would like to offer a tribute to my secretary Klint, who lost his life in the fight for peace and love. I will miss you, Klint." He paused and the audience-maintained a solemn silence for a whole minute.

Harry resumed his talk at the end of the minute. "Thank you. I would now like to invite one more person on stage.

Ms. Rosamonde Hartman, Vice President of Hartman Media, who has gone out of her way to ensure the safe passage of the Treaty. Rosamonde?"

The audience clapped harder and the cameras trained on Rosamonde, as she rose from the last row of the seats. A lump gathered in Re's throat, as he watched her walk gracefully down the aisle—charming, confident and yet with an invisible wall of reserve and a circle of dignity around her. His eyes remained glued to her, in fascination. And in that moment Re *knew*. The whole and complete truth. The energy of power that surrounded her, the aura of royalty, the self-assurance of a free bird....

Rosamonde climbed on to the stage and greeted the members with a shake of the hand. Then the charter was unrolled and one by one each one of the diplomats signed the document. The cameras magnified the signing on to the LED screens and all the guests spontaneously rose to honour and respect Empress Elisabeth's Imperial Treaty of Love and Peace. The audience clapped hard, with their faces beaming and the thunderous applause reverberated to each corner of the country. Outside, the whirring of a helicopter punctuated the thundering applause as it circled above the pandal, showering rose petals on the tent. A live band began playing the national anthems of the five countries and goose bumps rose on Re's arms. His heart filled with pride as he glanced at his friend Stefan standing on the stage, a little apart from the members. Their gazes locked and Stefan's smile was triumphant. An unspoken message was relayed between them. They had done it! *They had indeed done it!*

Across the world, diplomats of different countries and millions of people witnessed the heralding of the dawn of a new era, on all the social media and TV channels. It was a proud moment that would be carried forward from generations to generations, and would be retold and relived in living rooms, board rooms and schools, for a long, long time to come.

20

"It was a cruel plan, from the start to the end and completely masterminded by Ben. He used his friends who were his partners in his smuggling racket, goading them on with some lucrative carrots. But when they began to question his plan, he got rid of them. First Hans and then Gunter," Re remarked.

He was sitting with Stefan in the latter's office. There was still time for the ball and dinner and Stefan had insisted that they share notes before the grand finale.

"He was quite a genius. I still can't get over the Starnberg ET and how it slowly created this wave of fear and took a grip over entire Starnberg," Stefan remarked. "He sure succeeded in creating an aura against the Treaty, which was his goal."

"That was indeed ingenious. He was obsessed with Rosamonde and wanted to teach her a lesson, but he was also deeply caught in his smuggling activities. Stopping the Treaty from happening was his only option. It was a well thought out plan. The slow build-up of fear with the ET, creating an atmosphere of unrest in the town by manipulating and riling interested parties about the Treaty name, leaking Elisabeth's name to the press... In fact, by being our cab driver, which he manipulated with Hans's help, he ensured that he would be in the middle of things, to keep an eye and to implement his plan. Where he couldn't be, his partners could take over. Like I am sure it was Hans who operated the drone on all the occasions, until his death. Ben could easily slip in and out of the hotel, because he knew the staff, the hotel and the entire area so well. He manged to create fear, misunderstandings and drive his plan with precision."

"Smart. But what really motivated him to be so devious and how did you realise it was him?"

"I think it must have all begun when he found the poem on Rose Island. It must have immediately made him think of Rosamonde. Then there were his smuggling activities which got him in dangerously deeper than he thought. Ben had two agendas—the first being to expose Rosamonde who he felt was responsible for his mother's death. He had been following her for months, and discovered her trances, and he even went as far as to kill her psychiatrist Dr Gordon to obtain proof of her 'royal madness' as he called it. When he found Elisabeth's poem on the island, he knew that he was on the path to something fantastic. He wanted Rosamonde to find the soul-song, so that she would betray her 'royal madness' to the world and be an object of ridicule, or like we witnessed, to be in perpetual danger from interested parties."

"I am afraid he has achieved that to an extent," Stefan frowned.

"He did." Re sighed. "The second agenda was of course the Treaty. If the treaty was signed, Ben felt that he would lose complete control over his relic smuggling racket, as shared resources under the name of culture would create awareness and that would intrude into his clandestine activities and the entire area would come under a more prominent scanner. That would not only be the end of his thriving business, but would endanger his life because of the deals that he had already made with unscrupulous parties. It was when I found a diving suit in his car trunk that I first wondered about Ben. He was too suave, well-informed, and smooth. But it was when we were returning from Rose Island and Druck casually let out how people were into illegal activities, that the thought registered at the back of my head. But what clinched it were the articles on drones and Rose Island etc. that Mark had written that put him directly into focus. I saw clearly who Ben was and what he hoped to achieve."

"That was intelligent. If you hadn't contacted me when you did, I shudder to think what a nightmarish situation we would be in, with the blood of innocent people on our hands," Stefan said, quietly.

Re rested a hand on his shoulder. "I am so glad it didn't come to that. But I partly blame myself for some things too. I was so confused about the energy signals from Rosamonde, that I completely ignored the ones coming from Ben. He was so friendly, too friendly in fact but he gave no indication of his dangerous scheming, obsession and cruelty. That was my mistake and I really regret the slip on my part."

"You are human, Re. Let it go." Stefan smiled. "The Treaty was signed successfully. That's what matters in the end. It's over now."

"All is not over—just yet." Re returned the smile. "But will be, if I have my way."

"In that case, you better go freshen up for the Ball. I will see you down in twenty minutes."

Re rose, throwing his friend a fond glance. "I will be down in ten."

Ten minutes later, Re stared at his image in the mirror. A fresh white shirt over black trousers. A sash at the waist and a smaller one holding his pony tail, gave him the look of a casual bandit. But it was the glint in his brown eyes, which shone through the silver-rimmed spectacles that reflected his inner emotions. The excitement was not merely for the success of resolving a difficult case, but for the journey he hoped to embark on. He *wanted* to embark on... His mind was made and he reverently touched the Ganesha pendant. *Help me...do what you think is right...*a heartfelt prayer inadvertently appeared on his lips...*I need her....*

The snowfall was heavy and the trees were already half bent with the weight of the layers of snow and the strong wind seemed to pervade into the darkest corners of the cold night.

Inside Hotel Die Kaiserin, the contrasting atmosphere of cheer and joy was thick and evident in the chatter and laughter ringing in the air. The Christmas tree dominated the restaurant hall, highlighting the holiday fever and the success of the Treaty. Mrs Weber and the hotel staff had gone all out to decorate the hotel, befitting Sisi's 180th birthday. Drinks were being served and music played softly in the background. Hundreds of candles were lit up and the buttery glow bounced off the stained-glass pictures and the snow-reflected window panes.

The congregation members were ensconced in a corner of the hall, enjoying their private chat and drinks. Other invitees were mingling with diplomats and bureaucrats. The finery of historic costumes and the swish of glittering ball gowns lent an air of aristocracy to the entire evening. Re strayed in and out of groups, appreciating the enthusiasm of the guests despite the hostile weather.

His eyes searched for Rosamonde in the crowd but it was already half past nine and she still had not made an appearance. Should he go looking for her, he wondered, casually accepting a glass of wine from a waiter. It was then that he sensed her and he spontaneously turned around. Rosamonde was standing at the door, her gaze cruising casually over the guests, interspersed with polite smiles and nods, till it rested on him. Across the room, they both stared at each other.

Re's heart picked up an erratic pace. Rosamonde seemed to have stepped out of one era and into another. Tall, regal in an off-shoulder flowing white chiffon gown, a diamond necklace caressed her long neck and a tiara hugged the hair piled high on her head, making her appear haughty and beautiful, both at once. *My Snow Queen*, he thought, pride and love surging through him in a startling wave. She glanced across the hall at him and just as the music changed and the couples began dancing. She walked gracefully between the dancing couples, towards him. Her blue-green gaze was on him, a half almost provocative, confident smile lighting up her face. Re held out his hand and she reached out and entwined her fingers in his.

"Stunning and beautiful, *ma chérie*," he said, his eyes. "You take my breath away."

She laughed, a tinkling merry laugh. "I will always remember how charmingly French you can be sometimes."

"Along with a very strong and deep Indian energy and gravity too."

"I don't doubt it. What an amazing seamless combination, a heady mix of sensitive love and enigmatic spiritual energy."

"I am glad you approve. Do you think it is a worthy fit for your ethereal beauty and sharp intelligence?"

"I haven't the slightest doubt. We complement each other at all levels. The consequences of which would be in tomorrow's news, I believe," she added with a twinkle in her eyes.

"Ah, you mean the famous kiss on the Linderhoff slopes and the grand disclosure of our relationship," Re caught on instantly. "I can't wait to see the papers tomorrow."

"Me too!" she laughed.

A waiter offered wine and she accepted a glass. They sipped in companionable silence, watching the couples sway on the rhythm of the music.

"You are dressed as the Empress," Re observed her, over the rim of his glass.

Rosamonde smiled. "Who else would I be? The paparazzi has already labelled me as Sisi and now perhaps some countries too. I thought for once let me be and enjoy who others think I am."

"I think you are Rosamonde, beautiful and intriguing and for me that's enough."

"Are you sure? Do you not wonder, time and again if I am Rosamonde or the Empress reborn? Do you not wonder if I am lying? Or pretending?" Rosamonde looked into his eyes.

Re stared back. Her searching look, seared into his heart. He couldn't lie.

"Sometimes. But it doesn't matter. I want to explore the possibilities of finding out who the *real* you is, *with* you."

Something flickered in her eyes. She lowered her gaze and he sensed that he had said something wrong.

"Shall we dance?" she asked.

The party was on in full swing. Re saw Stefan dancing with one of the guests. Leon and Max were laughing in a corner and Harry was dancing with Adria. Other couples danced on the slow ballroom music. They placed their glasses on a table and Re led Rosamonde into the midst of the dancers. She was like a swan, elegant and graceful and he felt like he was the luckiest man in the whole world. It was a moment Re wanted to hold on to forever. It felt so right. Holding her in his arms, her energy merging with his, her dress swirling, the music spiralling an illusory magical dust around them, cocooning them in their own world. Re looked deep into her blue-green eyes. Her eyes were glistening...with an emotion and a responding love, so potent and breath-taking that Re sucked a deep breath in... Love surged inside him again and he held her tight, wanting to freeze the moment, wanting to merge her into him, into his energy. She belonged in his arms, she belonged in his life, now and forever. He knew the simple truth with the knowledge of the universe, and the sun and the moon and the deepest instinct that man had ever had about any woman. She smiled at him then and raised her lips. Re's head bent and he touched her lips with deep reverence and respect. Fire surged through him and she clung to him. It was a kiss of love so primal and soulful, that it shook him to his core. When he lifted his head, he saw tears in her eyes.

"Rosamonde...," he began concerned.

"Shh...don't say a word. It was the most beautiful kiss ever. Thank you."

He smiled. "You bring out the best in me, Rosamonde. And I want to be the one to bring out the best in you. I love you, Rosamonde Hartman. Will you marry me?"

She sucked her breath in and her eyes widened in shock. "Re..."

"Just say yes!" he urged in his ears.

"We've known each other for two days!"

"And experienced two lifetimes in it. You and I both know this is 'it'. A rare love, a love of the souls, of kindred energies. You did feel that too, didn't you?" He tilted her head and forced her to look into his eyes.

She nodded. A world of emotion in her gaze.

"Then just say yes!"

"I would if I could. You know I want to," she said, softly.

"What does that mean?" he frowned.

"Will you meet me in an hour in my room? I want to share something with you," she said.

"Let's go now. I have celebrated the Treaty enough and now I want to celebrate *us*."

She smiled, a smiled filled with the understanding of the world and which reflected the wisdom of the Universe. Wise, triumphant, satisfied and yet sad and pensive.

"Not just yet, I want to enjoy the party. We have earned it, haven't we?" she teased.

"Every minute of it. The agony of not knowing, the urgency of the chase, the discoveries..." Re agreed.

"Except we didn't find the soul-song," she reminded gently. "I let you down."

"Don't you ever say that! You did your best. Sisi removed the 'soul-song', whatever it was, from its hiding place. How could you know where she kept it? Don't go blaming yourself. That soul-song is best forgotten," Re spoke with fierce conviction.

"Still, it was disappointing."

"It was a bit, because it leaves something unfinished. But that's all it is. And no one is to blame for it, especially not you. I am convinced that Ben invented that whole thing to trap you."

"Spoken like a loyal friend."

"And I am one... Don't you doubt it ever," Re grinned. "But *you* are my *saviour*. You saved me from drowning. Those few minutes in the icy water and my vision merged with reality. My vision had always puzzled me. Was it something that had happened or was it something that would transpire in the future? It was when I was in the water, even in those few precious minutes when I struggled for breath, that I realised I had seen my future in the vision, that which was destiny. Being saved by you, was in my destiny. I can't get over the surrealist nature of it all. How the subconscious predicted the future. And that happened because the Universe connects us all through energies. And you are intrinsically connected to mine. You are my past, present and future, *ma chérie*."

Rosamonde's eyes glinted in the light.

"Thank you for those beautiful words." Her voice was filled with emotion. She blinked and added on a cheerful note, "And you, you are my knight in shining, enemy-proof energy—it was gallant the way you protected me and prevented me from being kidnapped too," she reminded. "Something that will stay with me forever."

"That was one of the most horrific experiences of my life. The thought of losing you drove me into a crazy frenzy. When I realised that you were the 'treasure', for moments I felt as if I had lost you. I didn't allow myself to think—all I knew was that I had to stop him. Thank God you are safe and here and with me." Re suddenly held her closer, a possessive streak overpowering him and making him throw caution to the wind.

Rosamonde laughed softly. "You are a tough guy, Re, you will survive anything. Even losing me."

"Thankfully, I will never have to test those of my survival skills again." He grinned. "Losing you is not an option. I am not letting you out of my sight, Ms. Rosamonde Hartman."

"You will have to let me go now though. I have some things to attend to. You will meet me in about 45 minutes in my room?" she confirmed.

"Of course, I will!"

"Goodbye, my dearest Re." She leaned forward and kissed him on the right cheek. "Always stay the way you are—honest, caring and genuine."

A violin played a melancholy tune at the back of his mind and Re caught a whiff of her energy.

"Hey, what's up? You seem sad. What's the matter, *ma chérie*?" He angled her face with a finger, scrutinising it. He blue-green eyes were moist.

She brushed away her tears. "It's nothing. Just this overwhelming feeling that this magical journey with you is over."

"It's over, yes. But another one, more exciting and fulfilling, would begin soon," he reminded, gently.

She nodded. "You are right. I have to see the brighter side of things. I'll see you in a while."

She turned to make her way through the dancing couples and he held her hand, reluctant to let her go. She wheeled around and kissed him full on the lips.

"I love you, Re!"

Before he could respond, she tugged her hand away and weaved her way through the crowd, her long white gown swishing, her train trailing. The image of the Rosamonde he had encountered the morning of his arrival, rose in his mind. When she had stood by the lake, in a deep trance and had recited a poem on death. For some reason, he wanted to wipe out that image form his mind. It created an unpleasant unease in his mind. And it was inappropriate in this happy moment—when they were celebrating the success of the Treaty, when Ben was safely in custody and Rosamonde was out of danger. The case was neatly tied and all was well that ended well. He now looked forward to focussing on his relationship with Rosamonde and the thought brought on a mood of excitement and a bubbling, happy smile of anticipation. *Oh, how much he loved her....*

The chattering, dancing and celebrations were in full swing and Re joined Stefan and the others and made small chat.

"Glad it's all over," Stefan admitted. "Thank you, my friend, for all your help."

"Don't thank me. We did it together. It was a complicated series of events that we barely managed to control and solve. But even then, three men lost their lives."

"Two were Ben's partners and the partnership went wrong. We can do nothing about that. But Klint...that was sad."

"I shall carry the guilt of his death in my heart for a long time," Re remarked.

"Me too." Stefan agreed, with a grimace.

"Thanks to you, Stefan, this case has given me more than you can imagine."

"Oh, I can imagine!" Stefan grinned but sobered at once. "I know what you mean."

❄

Re sipped his wine and his glance returned to his wrist-watch every few seconds. What did Rosamonde want to share with him? Why had she been so secretive? The time seemed to be in slow motion and Re sensed a nervous energy invading him. There were still twenty minutes for their meeting but he couldn't wait any longer. He excused himself and headed up the stairs to the first floor. He was about to knock on Rosamonde's room door when he saw the Post-it on the door.

Meet me in the Empress Room.

Re tucked the note into his pocket and headed to the second floor. For some strange reason his heart began an uneasy tattoo. What was Rosamonde up to? He opened the door of the Empress suite.

"Rosamonde?"

The light was on in the bedroom but silence met his ears.

He strode inside the room with the blue walls and stars. It was empty. Re was about to turn when he spotted the envelope on the bed. *For Re Parkar.* For moments, he stared hypnotised at the beautiful scrawl on the envelope and his heart stood still. He was suddenly aware of the low moaning of the wind outside and conscious of fear crawling under his skin. A window crashed and he was startled. Then urgency gripped him and he hastily picked up the envelope and tore it open. A note and a necklace slipped out of the envelope. Re barely glanced at the necklace, he was in such a frenzy to read the note.

His fingers trembled uncharacteristically, as he opened the single fold.

"Dearest Re,

I have to go. There is no other way. Whether I am the Empress or not makes no difference. The world thinks that I am. I am now wanted and I have to go.

But you have to do something. Open the Empress's cupboard. It has a false back. The soul-song is there. Sisi had indeed taken it from Rose Island after her cousin passed away and hidden it in her cupboard. I just remembered it later. Please take it, so we leave nothing unfinished.

I am also giving you my necklace. I have worn it all my life. It will protect you, till we meet again. If we meet again. I leave that to destiny.

Do not forget that I have loved you from the deepest crevices of my soul and will do so forever.

Only yours,

Rosamonde."

Numb with shock, Re picked up the necklace and stared at it. It was a pendant of two swans in the shape of a heart. An icy hand gripped his insides, squeezing out all warmth from his body. Images of his vision flashed across his eyes...the sinking in the cold water, the hand that reached out to grip him, tugging him to the safety of dry land, her soft voice urging him to consciousness in German, his eyes flickering open and staring into blue-green eyes of the young girl and her pendant swinging before his eyes—two swans in the shape of a heart. As if a stinging current had zapped him awake, Re jerked to the present. *Mon Dieu*... A flash of understanding illuminated the fog. It was Rosamonde—the young girl who had saved him from drowning all those years back, with whom he had sensed an instant connect, had unconsciously yearned for all his life and searched for... his lifeline, his saviour. And she had done it again. Saved him from drowning...and he had had a déjà vu but he hadn't understood what it meant...all this while. How could he not have known? How could he have not recognised Rosamonde? He slumped on the bed, pain coursing through every fibre of his existence, with excruciating intensity. *And now she was gone.*

Re broke into sobs, his head buried in his palms, his entire body shaking in agony. A spontaneous reaction to his past, present and future... At length, he took in a deep breath and rose. Elisabeth's cupboard stood rock solid all these years in the room. He opened the wooden doors, his fingers stiff. Knocking with his knuckles he explored the false back. A small panel slid open. He thrust his hand into the dark square gap and extracted a box of red velvet. Very cautiously, Re lifted the latches, opened the box and gasped. He had never seen anything more exquisite in his life before. It was a long-stemmed rose studded with rubies and emeralds. *The soul-song.* The gift that the Empress had wanted to give her cousin, soul-mate and best friend, but couldn't. The grief she must have felt then was a real thing to him now. It was almost as if the years between were a mere illusion and the passing of her grief to him was an easy journey. He felt the same. The grief of loss, of helpless, angry betrayal.

For long moments he stared at the box, disbelief clouding his thinking. The soul-song...it had been in here for more than a century and no one had known. But Rosamonde knew. How could she have known that Sisi had changed the hiding place of the gift when not a soul in the world was even aware of its existence? There was only one answer to it. *She had known it all along.* Somewhere in the deepest recesses of her mind. But had become aware of the knowledge just recently. And now that she had given the soul-song to him, *he* knew about it as well. And that was why she had left. Because she was aware that life in the limelight of a historical past and figure with interested parties chasing her for their own benefit, would have been agony.

But that was where she had been wrong. He would have helped her. He would have ensured that she was safe...

A sudden determination filled his heart. He would find her. She couldn't have gone too far. It was a wild stormy night and her progress would be slow. *He would find her.* And he would convince her that they would work it out together. They would go somewhere far where no one would find her. Yes, that's what he would do. There was no time to lose. He would find Rosamond—he would find the love of his life.

The sound of music and chatter seemed to be too loud in his present frame of mind. The cake had been cut and plates were being circulated. The 180th birthday of the Empress of Austria was being celebrated with pomp and cheer and Re couldn't help smirking bitterly at the irony of the situation.

He spotted Max downing some beers with Leon and he headed towards them.

"Max, do you know where Rosamonde is?" Re asked.

"Around somewhere, I am sure," Max drawled, toying his glass of beer. Re glanced at Leon who shrugged and shook his head.

Their casual disregard and comment, spurred Re into action. Max had no clue about his sister's plans. She hadn't told him that she was leaving. Re whipped around and headed out of the hall. He caught Stefan in the corridor and thrust the velvet box in the officer's hand.

"Take this. It's the soul-song. Rosamonde found it after all."

"She did?" Stefan looked taken aback. "How, where?"

"Details when I return. Can I borrow your car?"

"Where are you going?"

"To find her."

Stefan nodded and handed him the keys without another word. Re hugged him spontaneously and hastened to the reception counter. The boy on night duty smiled pleasantly.

"Could you tell me what is the train frequency from Feldafing to Munich? And when is the last train?"

"Every 20 and 40 minutes, alternately and the last train is at 11:51 pm, but there is one in ten minutes," the boy remarked.

"Thank you!"

The door opened with a blast of wind and snow fluttered inside like magic dust. Re hugged his jacket and made a run for the car. Within minutes, he was reversing and heading out into the cold night. The Feldafing station was a short distance away but the white road was slimy and the night seemed to be darker and denser than ever. She had better be at the station. She would head to Munich as the first leg of her journey. He was sure. It was logical and practical. He would find her if only he reached in time. The drive was excruciatingly slow and Re didn't dare risk driving any faster. He was at the end of the lane when he heard the sound of the approaching train. Instinctively, he pressed on the accelerator and the car instantly skidded, sliding dangerously off the route. Re's heart pumped, as he struggled with the wheel, veering it to avoid the bush. With a pronounced grating, the vehicle slid against the bushes and Re pressed the brake hard. The moment the vehicle halted, he flung open the door and broke into a run. His legs skidded on the road. The station is just around the corner, he reminded himself, struggling to breathe the icy wind as it stung his face. The snow clung to his hair and body, but all Re could think of was Rosamonde who would be climbing into that train any minute now. His ears spontaneously strained for any sounds of the train departing. As he turned the corner, a flash of relief engulfed him. The train was parked in the station. But he didn't allow himself to slow down. He saw Max's car parked on the side of the road. So, she was here...she had driven in her brother's car... Hope spiked in him and adrenaline rushed through his legs. He skidded dangerously and his boots plunged into deeper snow. He was almost at the station when he spotted her. She was carrying a single suitcase and was dressed in jeans and a thick blue jacket. Her back was turned to him and she stepped into the compartment slowly.

"Rosamonde!" he shouted, his voice hoarse.

His voice bounced off the air, as the wind flung it back at him. Re sprinted the last strip of the walking path and was on the platform, just as the doors closed.

"Rosamonde!"

She had found a seat and had settled by the window. She had cleared the frost from the glass and was staring out, her expression blank. He banged on the window and he saw her startled look.

"Re..." Her breath formed a white halo on the glass.

The train lurched. Re ran to the doors but they wouldn't budge.

"Rosamonde, don't leave."

He could see her tears glistening in the light of the compartment, her slight shake of the head, her gloved hand pressed against the window, her lips mouthing 'I love you'.

Re walked along with the train, keeping speed, stumbling and skidding on the piled snow, his eyes drilling into hers, willing her to change her mind. The engine caught speed and he ran along with it, till the platform reached a sudden end and the train sped ahead and gradually vanished into the dark of the snowy night.

Re stood rooted to his spot, his heavy breath creating short whiffs of mist. He stared at the empty train tracks, the snow swirling around him, enveloping him in winter dust. The icy flakes were rapidly covering him from head to toe, ttrickling into his jacket and dampening his beanie and hair but he was oblivious to the biting cold. All he could feel was the horror of seeing his life being sucked into oblivion, into a dark, never-ending night. He wished the ice would frost and freeze the unbearable pain in his heart, so that he could carve it out of his body and destroy it.

He turned around slowly, his eyes closed, his energy focussed on single thought. A thought that chugged in his mind, possessing him mind body and soul.

"I will find you, Rosamonde. I will find you..." he promised himself.

References

1. Renate Stephan, *Empress Elisabeth of Austria 1837–1898, The Fate of a Woman under the Yoke of the Imperial Court*, Glattau & Schaar Verlagsges, 1998.
2. Dorothea Baumer, *Guide to the Castles Neuschwanstein, Hohenschwangau, Linderhof, Herrenchiemsee*, Neil Moore (Translator), Huber, 2000.
3. https://en.wikipedia.org/wiki/Empress_Elisabeth_of_Austria
4. https://www.tuttobaviera.it/ludwig-sissi/
5. https://www.toursofdistinction.net/blog/poor-mad-king-ludwig-ii-of-bavaria/
6. https://sisiandaround.altervista.org/-poem-written-of-sisi.html
7. http://www.kulturpfad-ludwig2.de/roseninsel/
8. https://www.authorapiperburgi.com/2019/09/empress-elisabeth-of-austria-animal.html
9. www.kaiserin-elisabeth-museum-ev.de.
10. http://www.princemichaelschronicles.com/elisabeth-and-ludwig-or-the-cursed-cousins-part-iii/
11. https://sisiandaround.altervista.org/the-beloved-cousine-ludwig-ii-of-bavaria.html
12. https://uh.edu/engines/epi2473.htm
13. https://www.mygermancity.com/neuschwanstein-castle
14. https://www.thelocal.de/20171004/10-surprising-facts-about-neuschwanstein-castle
15. https://www.neuschwanstein.de/englisch/idea/schwan.htm
16. https://en.wikipedia.org/wiki/Neuschwanstein_Castle
17. https://en.wikipedia.org/wiki/Knight_of_the_Swan
18. https://www.guide-to-bavaria.com/en/the-sisi-road.html
19. http://www.sisi-strasse.info/en/lake-starnberg.htmlor
20. https://folkestonejack.wordpress.com/tag/lake-starnberg/
21. https://www.ancient-origins.net/history-famous-people/ludwig-ii-bavaria-suicide-or-murder-how-did-swan-king-meet-his-end-006599
22. Christoph Prinz von Bayern, Art & Pleasure of the Wittelsbachers, With Original Recipes from her Stays in Feldafing at Lake Starnberg and Poems by Kaiserin Elisabeth Von Osterreich.

Acknowledgements

I am a vagabond at heart, a traveller and a seeker. Which is probably why I write destination thrillers. But also probably why Sisi and her character appealed to me at a very basic, core level. I am grateful to the spirit of Empress Elisabeth of Austria for inspiring me to write this tale of love, longing and intrigue. I have tried to do justice to her free spirit and have responded to an intuitive sense of guidance.

As also with King Ludwig II—the opulence of his palaces, his epic vision as well as his sad end, inspired the base plot of this novel. And for that I am ever grateful to him.

However, I would have never written this novel if it hadn't been for Pauline Jansen van Rensburg and her generous invitation to host me during the Christmas holidays and for sharing wonderful family time with me. So, a heart full of gratitude to my dear friend Pauline and her family for introducing me to Sisi's Starnberg, instilling in me a deep interest in Elisabeth and King Ludwig II and basically driving me through amazing, romantic landscapes. Pauline was also gracious and kind enough to translate the main poem in the book to German—Adler, dort oben in den Bergen—adding that touch of authenticity to the work.

My destination thriller series was born with *The Trail of Four* in Salzburg and *Legend of the Snow Queen* is now the third book. Salzburg Global Seminar has staunchly supported this series right from the beginning and I cannot thank them enough for their unconditional encouragement. So, a heartfelt thank you to Thomas Biebl, Daniel Szelényi and Clare Shine for believing in me as a writer, and offering me comfortable time at the stunning Schloss Leopoldskron, to write my novels in peace.

I am grateful to Dr Shashi Tharoor for endorsing this series and launching the books. His support has made me strive harder to write better and smarter novels.

Dipankar Mukherjee and Readomania need a special acknowledgement. As usual he rises to every creative challenge with enthusiasm and stands staunchly by me with every book. So thank you Dipankar. Also thank you to Indrani Ganguly for her meticulous editing and Sourish Mitra for the beautiful cover.

Grateful to my family, their love and wisdom—they make every effort of mine worthwhile.

And a huge cheer and hats-off to my readers who give meaning to my life as an author and help me continue proudly on my author journey.

The internet is a rich source of information and I would like to acknowledge all the sources I have used to build my plotline including the many books I consulted.

Above all, thank you to God, the Universe and the powers that shine on me and open doors when I am looking for windows.

MANJIRI PRABHU
Pune, 2022

About the Author

Dr Manjiri Prabhu holds a Doctorate in Communication Science and is a short-film-maker, an award-winning international author and also the Founder/ Director of two Festivals. She has directed over 200 children's TV programmes, more than 50 short fiction and travel films and has authored 19 books.

Prabhu is the first female mystery author to be published outside India and has been labelled as the 'Indian Agatha Christie'. And much recently, Prabhu has been acknowledged to be a 'match for Dan Brown' by Dr Shashi Tharoor.

She has been invited to reputed International Literature Festivals like Bouchercon, Cheltenham Litfest, the International Agatha Christie Festival, UK and International Women Fiction Writers, Matera, Italy.

Her novel *The Cosmic Clues* was selected as a Killer Book, by Independent Mystery Booksellers of America and *The Astral Alibi* was honoured as a 'Notable Book' in the Kiriyama Prize.

As the Founder/Director of Pune International Literary Festival, Prabhu has brought Pune city on the International map of Literature and Arts festivals. Recently she also founded the International Festival of Spiritual India (For Humanity and Wisdom).

Winner of multiple awards, Manjiri is also an animal welfare activist promoting caring and adoption of stray dogs for more than 35 years.

eadomania exists to nurture, curate, and bring to you content you love. We are a publishing house that takes pride in encouraging talent, new or old, and provides a wonderful platform for awesome stories.

We make this possible in multiple ways.

The first as an independent publishing house. Readomania boasts of multiple imprints across various categories— fiction, nonfiction, children, to name a few. An eclectic mix of content for its readers, when you read a Readomania title, you enter a world that's yours, supported by unique and quality narratives.

The second, as an online publishing platform for writers— a place to share stories, poems, opinions, travelogues, a way to explore your creative talent. Available as premium, as well as free-to-read content across multiple genres, the reader is spoilt for choice.

Join us in this journey, as we explore, develop, and present stories to our readers and audiences. Welcome to the world of Readomania, get ready to craft stories that enrich lives.

You can visit us at: www.readomania.com